the pas de Deux

A CLASSICAL BALLET ROMANCE

ERIN BOMBOY

Published by Curtain Call Press

Publisher's Note: This is a work of fiction. Names, characters, places, and incidents are a product of the author's imagination. Locales and public names are sometimes used for atmospheric purposes.

The Pas de Deux/ Erin Bomboy. -- 1st ed.

Print ISBN: 978-0-9984830-2-3

Ebook ISBN: 978-0-9984830-5-4

For Mom and Dad, who let me spend the '80s dancing, reading, and dreaming.

"Put a man and a girl on stage and there is already a story."

George Balanchine

ENTRÉE

The beginning of a *grand pas de deux* in which the danseuse and danseur make their entrance.

Tombé

(FALLING)

IT FELT as if the world was consuming itself. Yesterday, an earthquake had struck Mexico City, swallowing thousands into its rubbly mouth while AIDS had become such a scourge that the movie-star-turned-president had mentioned it three days earlier.

Peridot "Peri" Jones slammed her car door, swung her dance bag over her shoulder, and looked up at the Hollywood sign wavering through the film of smog. Its silvery promise of dreams coming true seemed a mirage that only the most naïve could believe in.

A wave of fatigue crashed over her, like curtains closing at a performance's end, as she walked toward the studio. Her stomach was wobbling. This wobble was recent, but omnipresent, as her life—once predictable, mostly pleasant—threatened to crumble into a heap of useless shards that she, no matter her desire or effort, would be helpless to reconstruct.

She inhaled, a futile attempt to prevent the truth from splattering against her guts. Bob, her dance partner for and best friend of fourteen years, was dying, his wasted body fighting to take him somewhere far away. Hell, if you believed a man loving another man was a sin. Heaven, if you knew Bob and his kindness.

Peri herself was dying, but it was a different death—the death of a dancer. What once was easy was now hard, and what once was hard was now impossible. Maintaining the illusion of brilliance was chewing at her.

She yanked open the door to the studio, willing herself to survive the next hour, so she could go home and dive into bed where, under the black-silk canopy of night, she could ignore the question chiming in her head: *What next?*

She entered the studio where artistic director Levon Dektember was leaning against the mirror, his hand pressed hard into his cane.

"Peri-jan," he said, turning her name into an Armenian expression of affection. "Thank you for coming."

Although Mr. D spoke stiff, formal English, his accent smoked the words with the scent of far-off lands.

Peri tossed off the jacket and jeans she'd thrown over her pink leotard and tights. She pawed through her bag for a hair tie and bobby pins. Her hand closed over an ancient rubber band that was gnarly with bits of hair twisted around it.

She groaned. She'd left her new hair supplies on the kitchen counter, too depleted to remember minutiae like that. Shrugging, she bunched up her hair into the approximation of a bun and wrapped the rubber band around it. This would have to do.

Mr. D frowned as he smoothed an imaginary wrinkle from his white suit. He'd called her in to run a *pas de deux* after receiving word about a promising male dancer. Mr. D wanted to see how this potential hire would look with her.

The door opened, and someone jogged into the studio, panting a little. Peri didn't look up, too busy tying the ribbons of her pointe shoes: criss then cross, a double wrap into a knot, which she balled under the silk banding her ankle.

Her pulse slowed to an adagio. How many more times would she do this? She was twenty-nine, but her body was an inventory of aches and pains on par with a ninety-nine-year-old grandma.

Peri stroked her left calf, the map of veins threading across it visible beneath her tights. "Don't fail me," she whispered and then sighed, resigned to the truth. She couldn't will her body into behaving.

She forced her lips into a welcoming curve as she walked to where the man who'd entered seconds before was shuffling his feet. He jerked his head backward, knocking a swoop of maple syrup-colored hair out of his eyes.

"This is Mark Maroulis, Jr.," Mr. D said. "He is auditioning." "Nice to meet you," she said, the words colorless, perfunctory.

This was a waste of time. For Peri. For Mark Maroulis, Jr. For Mr. D who seemed to think he could replace Bob. Nobody could replace Bob.

She looked again at the recruit and blinked. This wasn't a man; this was a freckle-faced teenager.

"Mark, this is Peridot Jones."

His alert blue eyes met hers warily. "I know," he said, his voice a bright tenor.

Peri cocked her head at him.

"Five years ago, you and Bob, uh, Robert Winslow, danced at my school." He laughed, an awkward *haha*. "It's why I'm here today."

She smiled, touched by his earnestness. "Call me Peri."

Mr. D clapped his hands. "Let us start." He turned toward Peri and told her what they'd be dancing. "Mark knows the choreography," he added.

Peri touched her stomach. The wobble had increased to full-blown shaking. This wasn't one of Mr. D's hardest pieces. It was conceivably something two people who'd never danced together could get through without decapitating each other, but still, it required stamina, focus, and precision, qualities she was lacking these days.

The last time she'd danced it had been four years ago when she was on top of the world, able to tick off the endless balances, multiple pirouettes, and six-o'clock extensions with effortless glee. Four years before everything began sliding toward atrophy and irrelevance.

Mr. D inclined his head toward the accompanist. "An easy pace." He wiggled his cane at Peri and Mark. "Do what you can. It is your first time dancing together."

Peri stationed herself at the edge of the floor. She placed the tip of her right pointe shoe on the ground and pushed her arch over before repeating the action with her left. She ran her tongue around her lips and patted her haphazard bun. She performed this ritual every time before she danced in a small, hopeless gesture to ward off misfortune.

Five, six, seven, eight, she recited to herself as she pointed her foot forward. The entrance began with walks toward center, the deliberate pacing misdirection before the fireworks erupted.

Right, then left, a half dozen more steps until she reached center where Mark was waiting, his arm outstretched. She placed her hand in his; sprung into *sus-sous*, her toes the roots from which her body grew; and unfolded her right leg into a *developpé*. Mark raised their clasped hands to lead her into a slow pirouette. She ended with her leg in attitude, a hook of one knee juxtaposed against the rod of the other.

Mark walked around her, his grip steadier, warmer, more comforting than she'd expected. He led her into another pirouette to end facing him. With his hands on her waist, she arced into a deep backbend before he guided her up. Mark wrinkled his forehead as the freckles spilling across his nose and cheeks paled.

He didn't remember what came next.

She whispered the steps. His eyes brightened as he whirled her back and forth, her arms sweeping like curlicues.

A boy, she thought as they executed a *pas de bourrée*, a graceful grapevine of a step.

They turned toward each other, their arms lifted like garlands. Mark's jaw clenched as he split his legs into a *grand jeté*, his body a flesh-and-bone asterisk imprinting the blank air.

He's an acutely nervous boy who thinks this means something, she thought. *That ballet means something. But it doesn't. It really, really doesn't.*

It wouldn't stop Bob from dying or any of the rest who'd died or the more who would die because AIDS was a plague. And even if humanity survived and ballet continued, it didn't mean anything because this boy, even with his talent, would end up like her—old and broken, with no plan for the future beyond staying in the present.

Peri's eyes felt gummy, but she shook off her dark thoughts as they continued, not dancing well but not poorly either for their first time. Mark was a good height for her, and he was a much better dancer than his ordinary looks suggested.

Then, one of the last moves—a *penchée* where her body would seesaw forward until one of her legs pricked the sky. Anxious to get it over, she pitched forward, not waiting for Mark to initiate. He grabbed her waist, but it was too late. She threw her hands on the floor to prevent herself from falling.

Mr. D held his hand up for the accompanist to stop. "Peri-jan, show him where to put his hands."

Mark plucked at the neckline of his white T-shirt. It had a pinkish cast, as if he'd thrown it in with everything else he owned, not knowing whites needed to be separated and washed with a splash of bleach.

Where was his mother? Father? Big sister? Anybody?

He seemed young to be here, all alone, auditioning for the company, without an adult watching through the window to offer encouragement and/or sympathy depending on the outcome.

Mark coughed. "They were too high." He paused. "My hands, I mean."

Peri took his hands and placed them on her hipbones. "Here."

He nodded. His eyes, bright blue like forget-me-nots, had gone flat with worry.

She patted his shoulder, hoping to ease his nerves. In spite of her bleak mood, she liked him.

"Again," Mr. D said as he glanced at the clock on the wall.

Peri followed his gaze. Only a few minutes until Mr. D crushed this sweet boy's dreams. Why was Mr. D even trying? No one could replace Bob.

Mark initiated the *penchée* correctly, and they flew through the finger turns and promenades where he walked around her as she struck pretty pictures with her legs.

Finally, they got to their last move—a romantic lift. She rocketed toward the sky, her hands on Mark's shoulders to give her a boost, him catching her legs. As he hoisted her above him, the tatty rubber band split and her blonde hair fluttered around them. Behind that gossamer curtain, they stayed immobile, gazing into each other's eyes, communing, telling secrets, their hearts tapping out a rhythm for everyone to hear, as the outside world became smudgy and then nonexistent.

Slam. The accompanist hit the final chord.

Peri gasped as she flung her arms upward into the last pose. The accompanist's emphasis made it clear. They'd missed it the first time around.

"That is enough, children," Mr. D said.

Mark slid her down the warm wire of his body until she landed on firm ground. She sipped in some air, so she could say something, anything, to escape the claustrophobia of her confusion.

She'd missed the ending. She'd never done that.

Peri bit her lip and turned to Mark, who was gaping at her.

She stepped away, looking at Mr. D. The corners of his lips were curling upward as his eyes glittered like black glass.

Mr. D knew.

Peri touched a finger to her lips. But there was nothing to know. Nothing had happened beyond her getting caught up in the dancing and, for once, forgetting about the rot overtaking her life.

Mr. D inclined his head toward her. Peri dipped into a curtsey before grabbing her bag and zipping to the exit.

"Mark, the variation," Mr. D said.

Peri closed the door, her hand dewing the handle.

Not a boy, she thought and then shivered.

2

Soubresaut

(SUDDEN SPRING OR BOUND)

MARK WAS DOUBLED OVER, panting from trying to scrape the ceiling with his leaps.

It wasn't perfect, he said to himself. *But it was better than good.*

He'd landed heavily on his cabrioles because he'd lingered too long in the air, and his last pirouette could have been cleaner, but he'd hit everything else to the best of his ability.

He let out a breath that whistled with worry. The last hour had been full of embarrassment and fear. That it wouldn't work out. That all the steps he'd taken to get here would add up to nothing.

Mark turned to Mr. D to get it over with.

"I would like to offer you a contract," Mr. D said.

Mark grinned. He pushed his arms against his body to keep himself from punching the air. He was in a ballet studio, after all. This white box with a mirror on one wall and a metal barre around the other three didn't look much like the palaces where ballet had started four centuries earlier, but still. Good manners ruled, then and now.

"Will you accept?" Mr. D asked. "Where do I sign?"

"Can you sign?" Mr. D rubbed the weird green stone that was on top of his cane. "Your teacher said you were seventeen."

"I'm emancipated."

"I am not familiar with the term."

"It means I'm legally an adult. I don't need a parent to sign for me."

Mr. D raised an eyebrow.

"It's a long story." Mark swiped at the sweat dotting his upper lip.

He didn't want to explain how one foul baseball had resulted in him standing here in tights praying for a job.

Mr. D smiled. His teeth were white and strong against his skin, which was beige and wrinkly like an old lunch bag. "Go to the office. Trish will take care of you."

In the hall, Mark gave into his joy and relief. As he raised his arms in a victory salute, his gaze snagged on a black-and-white picture of Peri and Bob. Peri had one leg wrapped around Bob's waist as his uplifted arm framed her.

Mark froze.

Were the rumors true?

Was this why Mark had gotten the job?

He pushed his hair out of his eyes, his excitement icing over. He could never be Bob. Nobody could be Bob. No matter how high Mark jumped, no matter how many turns his pirouettes had, he'd never be like Bob. Bob had been a real-life Prince Charming who even bored audience members in the nosebleed section liked.

Mark was a freckle-faced guy with a crazy talent for ballet. Nothing more, nothing less. Even the best teacher in the world couldn't make him good looking or suave.

The door to the studio creaked.

Mark cursed. He didn't want Mr. D to find him here, mooning over a photo of Bob and Peri, so he double-timed it to the office.

"You're the new hire?" Trish asked.

Mark was too busy gawking at Trish to answer. She was wearing so much mascara that her lashes clumped together like an army of ants. Mark averted his eyes although Trish didn't seem to notice his staring.

"Is your mother around? She's going to need to sign." "I'm emancipated."

Trish opened her mouth, but he cut her off. "The state considers me a legal adult."

He lifted his eyes upward. This was going to get old quick.

She gestured toward a ratty club chair. "Might as well get comfortable. I have to redo the contract."

Mark slouched in the chair and tapped his hands against the cracked leather armrests in time to Trish's typing. *Hurry up*, he wanted to say.

He longed to get out of here, so he could call his ballet teacher and tell her the good news. If he timed it right, he could catch her in between classes. Maybe she could figure out a way to let his mom know everything had worked out without too many details.

He gazed out the window. Peri was walking across the parking lot toward a shiny beige hatchback. She wore slim jeans and a white blazer with big, structured shoulders as if she were a model in a fashion magazine.

His stomach wiggled.

Peri opened the trunk, tossed in her dance bag, and slammed the hatch shut. She pushed her baby-fine blonde hair over a shoulder as she headed toward the five and dime at the end of the strip mall. The palm trees lining the parking lot cast long, thin shadows, so Peri looked like she was walking through a jail cell.

An idea wrapped itself around his brain and squeezed tight.

"Do you have a piece of paper and a pencil I could borrow?" Mark asked. "I want to remember something Mr. D told me." He tilted his head low, so his hair would hide the lie burning in his eyes.

Trish looked up, a flake of mascara stuck to the bridge of her nose. "Sure." She ripped off the top sheet from a pad of paper and selected a nub of a pencil from a bunch crammed into a coffee mug. She pushed both toward him before turning to her typewriter.

"I'll be right back," Mark said. "I have to dance it to remember it." Trish kept her focus on the typewriter. "I'll be here."

He jogged to the men's room, gagging as he entered. It stunk of piss and unshed tears. A balled-up paper towel rested on the sink. He nudged it into the trash and placed the paper on the edge of the sink.

Written in a swirly script at the top:

Morning, Noon & Night Locksmith 24-hour service

At the bottom lay a number to call and a fancy drawing of a door under a moon and some stars.

Mark tried to figure out what to say. But there were so many things, all pushing and pulling at each other, that he had to wait until one rose above the others.

Thank you, he wrote.

He looked it over. The big, messy words tilted downward, like something a little kid would write. He started to crumple the paper but changed his mind. He'd have to ask Trish for another piece, and he didn't want to deal with her questions.

Thank you

Words said so many times they meant nothing. He frowned, hoping for something better. In his head, he completed the phrase.

Thank you for helping me remember the steps and for showing me where to put my hands during the penchée.

That wasn't going to work. It was too many words for the small sheet of paper. Plus, he didn't know how to spell *penchée*.

Mark groaned.

Should he add a period? An exclamation point?

A period felt weird, like there was something final about the note even though it was a beginning rather than an end. As for an exclamation point, that seemed girly.

Mark shrugged. No punctuation then. He couldn't go wrong with nothing.

He gazed at the two clumsy words. His handwriting was bad, not unreadable, but not neat and definitely not sophisticated.

Should he at least rewrite it?

He rubbed the end of the stubby pencil. Instead of an eraser, the pad of his finger plugged up a metal hole.

Mark sighed. This would have to work.

After changing into his jeans and sneakers, he left the bathroom, glancing over his shoulder to make sure he was alone. He snuck out the front door, fingers crossed that no one would see him in the blaring white sun, and made a beeline for Peri's car. He placed the note under her windshield wiper, message facing in.

Heart thumping, he turned to run inside, but a couple of girls were blocking his way as they got into the car next to Peri's.

"Oh. My. God," one said as she opened the door. She had to bend extra low so her bangs, a row of shellacked curls, could clear the door. "That clerk needed to bag her face."

"Totally," the other girl said. "I've seen, like, better-looking dogs."

Mark lifted his eyes heavenward. Kids his age with their stupid slang make him feel old.

The girls rolled down their windows as the engine rumbled to life. "I, like, love this song," one said. "Turn it up." A pop song poured from the car's open windows.

Mark struggled to catch the words as the girls sang in a tone that brought to mind cats getting their tails tied in knots. Through their yowling, he heard something about wanting to know what love is. Wanting to be shown what love is.

Mark glanced at the note on Peri's windshield. Tingles spread from the back of his neck to his face. As the car streaked out of the parking lot, the girls' voices fading, he shook himself and turned to head back inside. He still needed to sign his contract.

"All done?" he asked Trish.

She shoved the contract and a pen toward him. "Autograph here and here and here." Trish pointed to a few lines on the document.

He started to skim the contract but got jumbled up by all the legal terms. So, shrugging, he took the pen and scribbled his name. "Is that all?"

"You start on Monday. Company class is at ten."

He pushed open the office door and walked toward the exit but then went rigid, his breath all stopped up. Peri was strolling to her car, a bag dangling off her arm. She reached into it, pulled out a butterscotch candy, unwrapped it, and then popped the golden disk in her mouth. As she carefully folded the cellophane in quarters, her eyes widened.

His mouth went dry. She'd seen his note.

Peri snatched the square of paper and read it, one cheek bulging as she sucked on the butterscotch.

It's from me, he wanted to yell.

He didn't because she knew. She had to. Her forehead creasing, she tossed the note into her purse and got into her car.

Mark slumped across the door, his body hot and itchy like he had a sunburn.

She thinks I'm a kid, he thought. *A really weird one.*

ADAGIO

The opening section of the classical *pas de deux*, in which the ballerina, assisted by her male partner, performs slow movements and *enlèvements* in which the danseur lifts, stabilizes, or carries the danseuse. The danseuse, thus supported, exhibits her grace, line, and balance.

3

Renversé

(UPSET, REVERSED)

"MARK STARTS TOMORROW."

Peri's palms moistened. She stopped the pathway of her wineglass, which was halfway to her parted lips. Carefully, so as not to disturb the sloshing Bordeaux, she replaced the glass onto the circular indentation it'd created on the tablecloth. "He can't replace Bob."

"No one can replace Bob."

"Then why . . ." Peri's voice drifted off. She rubbed her damp hands on the napkin in her lap.

Mr. D took a sip of wine, his eyes never leaving her face. Peri crossed her legs and then uncrossed them. Mr. D's expression was benign, but his lips were twisting as if he knew something she didn't.

"I hired Mark for himself. He is a once-in-a-generation talent. Even if he does not understand the magnitude of his gifts, I do," he said.

The waiter materialized, his pen poised to scribble their order.

"Cassoulet for the lady," Mr. D said as Peri handed the waiter her unopened menu. There'd been no point in perusing the options. Mr. D always ordered for her.

She sighed internally. She didn't like cassoulet, but it could have been worse. The menu contained plenty of dishes more heavily creamed or sauced than this.

Mr. D loved French food, something to do with the years he spent as a young man in Paris, the city where he'd discovered ballet. If it weren't this restaurant, it'd be another one with a leather-bound menu, a mustachioed career waiter, and velour high-backed chairs.

She'd been to them all a thousand times. This one was her least favorite. Although the food was palatable enough, the restaurant never seemed clean with its splotchy silverware and plates filmed with cheap dish soap. A few times, she'd recoiled at finding lip prints on her wineglass.

Peri touched the tablecloth, which should have been snowy white but was a dull gray, as if it had been washed without bleach.

An image of Mark in his pinkish T-shirt popped into her head.

So she'd see him tomorrow. And every tomorrow after that. The wobble in her stomach expanded through her until even her heart was wavering precariously.

She ran her fingers through her hair, remembering the moment he'd lifted her high above him, his warm hands on her waist, his blue eyes meeting hers, how the whole world had receded until it was just them.

She flinched, disgusted at herself. Mark was what? Seventeen?

I'm mixed up on the inside, she told herself. *Because of Bob.*

"Eat," Mr. D said, pointing to the dish of cassoulet the waiter had slid in front of her.

Peri forced thoughts of Mark from her mind. Obediently, she picked up her fork and pushed the tongs into a bean. She chewed and swallowed, forcing the oil-slimed mush past her boredom and revulsion.

Would she ever be free of these lunches? They'd been going on for fourteen years.

When she was fifteen, Mr. D had plucked her from the classroom of a top ballet school in New York. She moved to Los Angeles, blinded by the bleached-out sunshine and the golden opportunity. There'd been a whirlwind of classes, rehearsals, a new ballet Mr. D was making with her as the lead, an uncomfortable doctor's appointment where a nurse had pressed a plastic clamshell into her hands. Upon opening, there'd been twenty-eight pills arranged in a horseshoe. "One a day," she instructed Peri. "Don't forget or else."

Or else what? Peri had thought as she swallowed the first pill. She found out a few weeks later.

Mr. D took her out for lunch to celebrate her first month in California. She'd done her hair three times, changed at least half-a-dozen more, practiced making adult conversation in the mirror, and borrowed an etiquette book from the library because she'd never been to a fancy restaurant.

After plying her with *boeuf bourguignon*, which she'd barely touched, and pouring her glass after glass of wine, Mr. D took her to his home that was cluttered with bejeweled knickknacks and paintings of colorful squiggles. He guided her to his bedroom where her heart hammered at the bed hung with burgundy velvet.

She'd been too tipsy and terrified to protest as he peeled off her dress and then took her virginity as the silver cross dangling from his neck jabbed at the hollow of her throat. When he finally completed his choreography of pokes and grunts and a wet mouth that went everywhere, she wanted to curl up in a ball and cry at the foulness of the experience. Mr. D, though, handed her a tiny wineglass filled with Armenian brandy.

He clinked his glass against hers and said, "I will make beautiful ballets for you."

She thought about running away, but where would she go? Back to her hometown of Pittsburgh where nothing awaited beyond marriage to the first man who asked and a house full of screaming babies? Back to the school in New York where everyone would wonder why she'd given up the chance to dance for the famous Mr. D?

So she stayed put and drank the brandy.

Now, every Sunday, after he went to an Armenian church that Peri had never set foot in, they met for lunch. He used to take her to his home afterward, but that had lessened over time and now had become so rare she couldn't remember the last time it'd happened. She didn't miss sex with Mr. D although she longed to be touched by someone she desired, to have that someone desire her, to find out if sex could be more than an obligation.

Peri pushed a bean around the dish. Her stomach quivered; the few bites of food she'd forced down were threatening to come up.

"Mark's parents agreed?" she asked. "Shouldn't he be in school?"

"He is emancipated. The state allows him to make his own decisions."

Peri's thoughts fuzzed over. "Did he say why?"

Mr. D gazed at her with eyes that betrayed nothing. "It is not my place to ask."

Emancipated? That was a serious step, to divest himself of his parents. What had gone wrong? Again, she wondered, *Where was his mother? Father? Big sister? Anybody?*

Mr. D guessed her thoughts. "It's not your place to ask either," he said.

She ducked her head to keep Mr. D from seeing her eyes narrow in annoyance. She wanted to retort, *Who are you to tell me what to do?*

17

But even if she could, she wouldn't. He was her boss. Telling her what to do was his job. Doing it was hers.

Mr. D dabbed his lips with his napkin. He placed it on the table and leaned forward. "I am making a new ballet."

"You are?" Peri fumbled with her thoughts. "That's great?" Her voice swung high at the end.

Mr. D hadn't made a new ballet in a while. The last few years, the company had been cycling through his previous works, which had a lot to do with their falling fortunes. People wanted new. People wanted interesting. People did not want to see the same thing they'd already seen.

It'd taken Mr. D years to put together enough seed money to fund his company. He spent his youth and then his middle age traveling to wherever someone would pay him to choreograph: backwater regional companies, large civic troupes, the occasional plum gig for a musical theater show.

His style was specific, distinct. He liked splashy, over-the-top pieces with extravagant technical feats and excessive emotion. He made short pieces, so even people who were wary of ballet might come. He used music that was easy to enjoy.

"People work too hard. Let me give them an hour or two of pleasure and then send them on their way," he always said. "A dance performance should not last longer than a nice lunch."

It'd worked for years until Mr. D's creative well had dried up.

Which might be Peri's fault. She'd inspired him for ten years, and then everything went wrong. A dull ache in her calf that she'd chalked up to overdoing it in a long rehearsal left her howling in pain days later. She could barely hobble from the bedroom to the bathroom, after which, she'd crawl back to bed where she'd pull the sheet over her head and pretend what was happening was not happening.

Dancing was out of the question.

She went to doctor after doctor, all of whom grunted in frustration when they couldn't find anything wrong. At the studio, she lay crumpled on the sidelines, gently kneading the meaty knob of her muscle, praying for it to heal. Because if it didn't, then she was out of a job with a broken body to boot.

As for Mr. D, he was still signing her paychecks through the end of the season, but he'd shifted his attention to a sprightly brunette with impeccable batterie, her slender legs switching back and forth like a chef's knife as she skimmed through the air.

Lightness and brightness were what he wanted. Peri only had anxiety and discontent to offer, neither in which he was interested.

Finally, a visit with a new physician identified an overstretched nerve in her back. The pain had manifested itself in her calf, which was why no other doctor had been able to diagnose it.

"What do I do? For how long?" she'd asked, ready to do anything and everything to get back to classes, rehearsals, and performances. Maybe before that brunette stole all her roles.

"You rest," the doctor said. "For six months. Maybe a year, so the nerve can heal."

So she sat out the rest of the season and the summer break, her stomach sloshing with fear that she'd never dance again. Or walk without pain.

Healing was nonlinear. Her calf would feel better, and then a trip to the grocery store where she waited in a longer line than normal would send her to bed for three days.

She finally improved enough to return to the studio at the start of the next season. Bob suggested they skip company class, and he'd teach them their own slowed-down version. Together, they broke down big movements into small ones, which Bob refined into smaller ones. He stopped often to make sure she didn't push herself.

Her progress was glacial until it wasn't, and she was back on top thanks to a couple of cortisone shots in her back and the departure of the brunette who'd gotten a job with a better company in New York.

But she wasn't really back on top. The months she'd spent away from the barre had done a number on her technical aptitude. To get it back, she needed to take risks. Push for the extra revolution in her pirouettes. Take the chance of losing her balance by lifting her leg higher. Maybe stumble on the landing after a soaring jump.

To reach the heavens, she needed to gamble falling to the earth.

Yet she couldn't. The door had slammed shut on her youthful conviction that she could fly, and the best she could do now was maintain what was left.

From time to time, her calf would flare up, but Bob always guessed and he'd pull them out of company class to work slowly and methodically. His heartfelt positivity helped dry the cold sweat pouring down her back.

A few months after she'd returned to the stage, Mr. D suffered a minor stroke. He returned using a cane, his ability to choreograph new ballets depleted. Peri felt too overburdened with her physical strain and emotional pain to rejuvenate him.

Then, the men started dying: first, a new company member who'd been healthy one day and gone a week later, his body found in a dip-dye of his feces; next, Bob's friends; and now, Bob.

Each setback had chipped away at her self-confidence and self-motivation until her spirit hung at half-mast permanently.

Peri rolled the hem of her napkin between her fingers. Mr. D was making a new piece? Her shoulders sagged at the pressure of the months ahead of her, rehearsing *The Nutcracker* as Mr. D choreographed his new work.

Hours upon hours of trying to force her body to do what it wouldn't—it couldn't—do anymore. Each of those hours laced with fear that the nerve would give out and her calf would melt into a puddle of pain. And, no matter how hard she tried, even if she could find the energy to try and that trying didn't repay her by injuring her, she was never going to dance the way she had.

Will, when confronted with age, had no power.

She exited her thoughts and returned to Mr. D's news. "What's the new piece about?"

He blew on his cup of tea. "It is one I have wanted to make for a long time." He gazed into the distance. "*The Maiden and the Mountain*. It is an Armenian folktale. For the first time, I will return home for inspiration."

Peri raised her eyebrows. Home? Mr. D had been the United States for something like five decades.

He rarely spoke about his childhood in Armenia. He'd never visited, never hosted family or friends from there, didn't even have a picture up of a church or scenic vista. It was one of those things she considered to be true, but not important, about him.

"Three principal roles." He looked at Peri. "You, obviously. A princess who has lived a long time under the thumb of her lord protector."

She nodded, forcing a smile.

"Mark. A young prince, whose six brothers have perished trying to defeat your kingdom."

Mr. D brushed a piece of lint from his finely tailored white suit.

"White like canvas," he told her when she asked why he never wore any other color. "A pure background that reflects, but does not absorb, the colors of life."

She hadn't understood what he meant by that. Maybe something about artistic inspiration? Mr. D was fond of grand sentiments that, once unpacked, didn't make much sense.

He stared at her, silent, building tension by doing nothing, just like in a dance. "And me. Your lord protector."

Peri swallowed. This sounded like a joke, not a ballet.

Mr. D was going to dance? He could barely walk. He didn't even teach company class anymore, preferring to pass it off to Stick and Stone, the two rehearsal mistresses who were nicknamed for their figures. When he needed to demonstrate something, he used his hands and his words as he sat or sometimes stood, his back pressed against the mirror, his hand heavy on his cane.

"We will have exquisite sets and costumes," Mr. D said. "A backdrop of a magnificent mountain. A crown of pearls for you. An elaborate tableau for the wedding scene." Mr. D drained his teacup. "We are in Hollywood, after all. They want beauty, richness, magnificence. Let them enjoy minimalism and formalism and coldness in New York with that Georgian upstart."

Mr. D hated George Balanchine, feeling that Balanchine had stolen the thunder of critical acclaim that should have rightly sounded for Mr. D.

Mr. D closed his eyes. "God has given me one last opportunity to make a ballet so beautiful that it can stand the test of time. One that will be performed over and over, like *Giselle* or *Swan Lake*."

Peri's head jerked back. A ballet to stand the test of time? Mr. D was deluding himself. Even his best-known works were minor additions to the canon. What made him think this one—particularly one he'd be making with a wet-behind-the-ears guy, a washed-up ballerina, and an old man past his artistic prime—would be anything more than a blip on the radar?

"We begin tomorrow."

Peri ground her teeth together, already anticipating and resenting the demands he'd make of her. Her job never ended after rehearsal. He'd want her to accompany him to the costume shop, show her the mockups for the sets, play for her the music from the composer.

It wasn't because Mr. D cared about her opinion. He wanted her to be the ballerina on top of a music box, twirling around and around, reassuring him that everything he touched would turn to gold.

She was tired of it, even more tired of him.

The show had to end. She couldn't go on much longer, playing a role she'd long outgrown.

Peri tucked back a lock of hair and her resentment. She had something important to discuss with Mr. D.

"Have you seen Bob?" she asked.

21

He shook his head. "I do not go to hospitals. I cannot tolerate the odor of death."

"Why?"

He waved a hand. "It makes me remember what I wish to forget."

"Bob's out of the hospital." She hesitated. "For now." It wouldn't be long before he'd be back in, maybe for the last time.

"Has he received my flowers?"

Peri bolded her words with acrimony. "He has."

Mr. D sent large, colorful bouquets every week, as if their gaudy presence would excuse the lack of his.

"He'd rather see you," she said. "He asks every time I go."

Last year, Bob had been the picture of health, his tan skin glowing as he tossed off cabrioles, his legs beating against each other as he pierced the sky. Now he was a scaffold of fragile bones, barely able to mutter a few words through his raspy breaths. When he did get something intelligible out, it was to implore Peri to ask people to visit: Mr. D, his mother, friends who were in the throes of their own battles with AIDS.

She didn't know what to say to Bob. Mr. D wouldn't come; his friends couldn't come. As for his mother, Peri had the number in her purse. She was going to call tomorrow, beg her to visit. She would come, wouldn't she? No mother could abandon her dying child's wish for a few minutes of togetherness. She shivered, feeling like a coffin lid was about to slide over her.

Peri looked at Mr. D, her eyes teary with fear. "He's dying, Levon. He doesn't have much time left. Please see him. Just for a few minutes."

Mr. D shook his head. "I cannot take the risk."

"You can't catch it from visiting," Peri said in a snarl. "Bob danced for you for fourteen years. He wants to say goodbye. To thank you. Let him do that."

Mr. D raised his hand for the check. "You are overwrought, Peri-jan."

Peri grabbed her purse. "Bob is dying, and you won't see him. If I'm overwrought, then I've got a good reason."

She darted out of the restaurant, ignoring the hostess' startled look. Once outside, she collapsed against the stucco wall of a store that rented movies. She gave into the tears that were beating against the back of her eyes. As the deluge increased, she reached into her purse, hoping for a tissue. Instead, her hand closed around the note that Mark had written.

Thank you

Two words often spoken yet rarely meant. But Mark meant them. Enough so that he'd written them down and made sure she saw them.

It was sweet. Because he was sweet with his enthusiasm and sincerity and inability to punctuate two words.

She pressed the paper against her cheeks, its edges rough against her damp, tender skin. She felt hopeless, like everything that had come before this hadn't mattered at all.

Finally, the storm slowed to a drizzle. She wiped her nose with the note. She pulled the tear-sodden, snot-streaked paper away. The words were faded and blurry, but she could still make them out.

Thank you

Words Mr. D had never said to her.

She'd talked back to Mr. D. once. She'd been eighteen and upset about him paying attention to another dancer in class. He put her in her place.

"I make ballets for you." He stroked her cheek with the tip of his fingernail. "What more could you want?"

Peri wanted more now. She wanted him to see Bob. She wanted him not to make a new ballet that would tax her to the point of extinction. She wanted him to tell her what she already knew—that she should retire. Instead, he seemed to think a new piece was the panacea the world needed.

She looked at the posters hanging in the window of the movie-rental store: *Sixteen Candles, The Breakfast Club, Fast Times at Ridgemont High, The Last American Virgin.*

Movies about teenagers for teenagers detailing their common experiences of high school dances, football games, detentions, and writing dedications in a yearbook.

Things she'd never experienced. She rubbed the note between her fingers. Things Mark had chosen not to experience. Because ballet was a jealous god that didn't allow the time nor the space for normal coming-of-age rituals.

Peri placed the note back in her purse and walked to her car. Tomorrow was Monday. She didn't know what else to do beyond go home and prepare for the inevitable.

4

Pirouette

(WHIRL OR SPIN)

MARK SETTLED himself on the floor among the loose ring of dancers. A few had spread their limbs into a wide *V* while others sat with their heels touching, noses pressed to their ankles.

He fumbled with the tab of his soda. He tipped his head back and then drained the entire thing, enjoying the bubbles stinging the back of his throat.

He sat up taller as he parked the empty can next to him. The rush of sugar and caffeine had lifted him from his post-class daze. Some gray moment always grabbed him at the end of grand allegro, when he'd landed from heaven to earth, like ballet, which had felt like everything, now felt like nothing.

Mark checked out the other company members. More women than men, most young, a few older ones who weren't good at dancing anymore but who were good at remembering choreography and staging. He'd been too busy trying to prove himself during class to watch a lot, but from what he'd seen, nobody was that special.

The company had been great once, back in the '70s, when Mr. D's choreography was seen as bold and exciting. But its reputation had slid and was on the way to vanishing. Mr. D had stopped making dances a few years ago, and now one of its two stars lay dying. Nobody would even call the company good these days.

Mark gazed again at the dancers surrounding him. Most of them were here for a season or two. Use this job to *grand jeté* on to greener marley.

He laughed internally at his joke as he scratched the dirt-speckled plastic that covered the sprung wooden floor.

Mark could have aimed higher. Gone to New York or even Europe where the hotshot choreographers were. He imagined himself walking the cobblestone streets of a grand old European city, but then he sighed. Everything had happened so fast that moving from Los Angeles to a new city, let alone a new country, would make what was going to be hard almost impossible.

Plus dancing for Mr. D had been his dream since he was twelve. And now it was his reality. A grin split across his face, which he quickly flattened. He didn't want to look uncool.

Maybe some of these people would be his friends. They weren't that much older than him. The guy sitting to his right looked nice with reddish hair and a roundish face. A cowlick stuck up like a feather from the crown of his head. Mark was pretty sure his name was Glenn.

Mark had seen him before class, zooming into the parking lot on a motorcycle that rumbled like a jackhammer. Glenn looked to be twenty-one, twenty-two tops. That wasn't a huge difference, considering they'd be coming to the same place and doing the same thing every day.

Glenn turned in his direction. Mark threw him a shy half-smile. Glenn's eyes, hard with dislike, met his, before Glenn's nostrils flared as he looked away.

Mark groaned. Maybe he and Glenn weren't going to be friends. And it wasn't because Mark was young. It was because he was good.

In ballet, working hard only worked if a dancer had something to work with. Mark had a lot to work with. It didn't mean he worked any less hard than other dancers did. It just meant his work paid off in ways theirs never could.

That was ballet. Hard work helped talent, but it couldn't invent it. Yet that didn't stop people like Glenn from hating him even though all he did was show up and work hard.

He shrugged, accepting the loneliness that lay in his future. He'd chosen this, fought for it, after all. If he wanted friends, he would have stayed away from the dance studio.

Mark sniffed. The air smelled like the color pink: strawberry ice cream, roses, heart-shaped candies. It was Peri, slipping into a spot in front of him.

Mark's chin dipped as he remembered lifting her high above his head, him looking up at her as her hair drifted around them like rays of sunshine. Then, her sliding down him to end under his chin, her hair clinging to his hot cheeks, his damp chest.

He swallowed hard. He'd read something into that moment.

Something that was one-sided. His-sided.

But it'd just been one of those things that happened when two people danced together. The intense motion created fake emotion.

Peri reached back to adjust the strap of her lavender leotard. Her eyes, strange brownish gold things, met his. Mark rubbed the back of his neck.

"Hi," she said.

"Hey." He flinched at the sound of his voice—soprano with a hint of tremble. He searched for something, anything, to say, so he could prove himself with a more manly tenor.

She smiled at him. "Congratulations."

He gazed at her blankly. "For what?" Then, the clouds cleared. He laughed. "Thanks. It feels like old news." He glanced down. His white T-shirt had a yellowish tinge as if it hadn't been washed although he did just that yesterday.

Laundry. Something he needed to figure out. Among other things.

He jerked his head back to sweep back the hair dangling in his eyes and peeked up. Peri was still staring at him. She opened her mouth to say something, but Mr. D hobbled in, his hand gripping his cane, the other clutching a book with a pen-and-ink drawing of fairies on the cover.

Everyone straightened their backs, tucked their hair behind their ears, and arranged their faces into smiles. Mr. D's best days might be in the past, but he was still the king who could make or break dreams. Mr. D eased himself into a chair and peered out. Mark shivered.

Mr. D had eyes like a bug—so black it was impossible to tell where the pupil started or ended.

"Children." He lifted the corners of his lips. "I have two pieces of news." He gestured toward Mark. "Likely, you have already guessed the first. This is Mark Maroulis, Jr., our newest company member. I hope you will extend a warm welcome to him."

Reluctant applause greeted Mr. D's words. Mark wiped away the sweat drizzling his upper lip and offered a lame smile. He felt like a moron.

Mr. D cleared his throat. "As for the second, I am canceling the current March program."

Eyebrows shot up. Jaws dropped. Programs were set months in advance.

"Is this a subtle way of telling us we're all unemployed?" someone whispered.

A few giggled quietly.

"I bet it has something to do with that kid he hired."

"Let's hope not," another person replied. "We've been sweating it out here while he was playing in the sandbox."

A couple of dancers cackled.

I'm not a kid, he wanted to yell. *I'm in charge of myself, just like you.*

Mr. D smiled. "I am making a new piece."

Gasps echoed through the studio. This was big news.

"*The Maiden and the Mountain*. It is an Armenian fairy tale. I have wanted to make it for years, and now is the time." Mr. D opened the book and began to read.

The kingdom was almost perfect. A sparkling ocean lapped its sandy shores. Further inland, a forest, green and cool, contained enough game to keep the king's people fed and happy.

But the kingdom was not complete. At its center rested a mountain that did not belong to the king. It was an embarrassment, a visible one. For years, the king was too busy with royal matters to give it the attention it needed. On his deathbed, he gathered his seven sons around him.

"Unite the mountain with the glade, the stone with the sea," said the king.

The first son saddled his horse and set off for the mountain, confident he would return victorious. Days, weeks, then months passed with no word. The next brother saddled his horse and set off to find his brother, so he could reunite the mountain with the glade, the stone with the sea. But he, too, did not return, so the next son set off.

So it went until only the seventh son was left. He was young, barely a man, and the king's people begged him to stay. For if he did not return, there would be no king. The seventh son listened to their counsel but saddled his horse and set off, nonetheless. He would reunite the mountain with the glade, the stone with the sea.

The seventh son took his finest men to the mountain and left them at the bottom with instructions to do nothing and say nothing until he returned. He roamed across the mountain, hearing the rustle of footsteps, seeing the flash of color, though neither man nor beast presented himself to the seventh son.

He returned to the bottom to find his men dead or dying, clutching their stomachs and pointing to tables laden with flasks of wine and platters of sweets. The men had ignored his instructions and been poisoned. By whom or what the seventh son could not tell. So he tied his horse alongside the others and climbed a walnut tree to hide and wait.

28

"I will avenge my men," vowed he.

Night fell. When the moon was high in the sky, a slender warrior walked amongst the bodies, counting them. The warrior called for his servants to take the horses of the dead men away.

"Stop," cried the warrior. There's an extra horse that is unaccounted for. To whom does it belong?

The seventh son leapt down from the tree and brandished his sword. "It is my horse, and I command you to tell me why you have slain my men."

"They were trespassers," said the warrior.

"I will avenge my men," said the seventh son.

"Then, we must fight," said the warrior. "Tomorrow, when the sun is high above the mountain, meet me at the bottom of the stream."

The warrior threw off his helmet. The seventh son gasped. This was no hardened warrior. This was a beautiful maiden with flowing blonde hair.

"Do not be late," she called over her shoulder as she sped off on a magnificent white steed.

The seventh son mounted his horse and took off in pursuit of her. He had to concede. A man could not fight a maiden. The night was dark and his horse lost the scent and the seventh son grew colder and colder. Finally, he stumbled upon a cottage. A good fairy bade him to enter.

After hearing his tale, the good fairy said, "It is not the maiden you seek to vanquish, but her lord protector. He bids her to kill any man who enters."

"But why?" cried the seventh son.

"Because the kingdom will rightly be the maiden's when she marries."

The fairy handed the seventh son a mirror. "The lord protector looks over the mountain at sunrise to see what men have entered the kingdom. Hide in the cave on the western side of the mountain. Use the mirror to reflect the sun and direct it to the lord protector's eyes to blind him."

The seventh son followed the fairy's instructions, and lo-and-behold, the uncle fell to his knees, his hands thrown over his eyes.

The seventh son took his sword and drove it through the lord protector's heart. He snatched the crown off the lord protector's head and rode to the meeting place of his duel with the maiden. He approached the maiden, knelt, and offered her the crown.

She placed the crown atop her head and extended her hand to the seventh son. "You are the first man worthy of me. Let us marry," said she. "And no more men will die."

They did, and the seventh son reunited the mountain to the glade, the stone with the sea.

Mr. D looked up to gauge their reactions. Mark tried to drum up some excitement, but he wasn't that impressed. *The Maiden and the*

Mountain didn't sound that different from every other folktale with all the mumbo-jumbo about a seventh son, a good fairy, and a virgin princess who was controlled by some evil dude.

The important question was who got to play the leads. Peri would be the maiden, obviously. Who would be the seventh son, the lord protector?

"I will be choreographing *The Maiden and the Mountain* as we rehearse and perform *The Nutcracker*. It will be busy. Stay sharp. Stay healthy." He paused. "As for the principal roles, Peridot Jones will be our maiden."

"Naturally," someone said under her breath.

Mark guessed Peri had heard by the way her shoulder blades tightened.

Mr. D continued. "I will play the lord protector." Although no one moved, the disbelief was clear. *Whatever*, Mark thought.

It wasn't like Mr. D was going to be doing any heavy duty dancing. He'd mime a few things and then die dramatically.

Mr. D eyeballed him. Mark sat up tall, his heart racing. "And Mark will play the seventh son."

Yes, he screamed to himself.

Then, he looked to his right and met Glenn's gaze. Glenn's face was stony although his eyes looked wet. A girl with black hair poked Glenn's side, and Glenn bent his head to her. Mark didn't catch what Glenn said, but it must have been mean because the girl widened her eyes as she giggled reluctantly.

His shoulders slumped. He and Glenn were officially not becoming friends.

What else was new?

It could be worse. At least he was here, cast as a lead in a new ballet. And his dad couldn't do anything about it. His throat felt scratchy, and he swallowed, hard. To take his mind off his dad, he looked at Peri, his new dance partner. The strap of her lavender leotard had rolled inside out. His fingers itched to flip it right side.

Weirdo, he scolded himself.

He rubbed his hands, his gaze still fixed on Peri. Was she okay dancing with him?

They'd be spending a lot of time together. It would be awful if she hated him, thought she was too good for him.

Mark scooted to his left, so he could get a better look at her face.

Her forehead was creased, her lips pursed.

She was scared. But of what? The new ballet? Mr. D? Him?

Feeling his stare, she turned. For a moment, their eyes met through the hate and gossip that was swirling around them. She looked away, her cheeks two red roses.

It was Mark. Probably thought he couldn't match Bob, which was true. But he could bring something else, be someone else.

I can do it, he wanted to tell her. *I will do it.*

5

Temps Lié
(TIME LINKED)

PERI RUBBED the quarter between her thumb and index finger.

Maybe three times would be the charm.

She'd tried before class, after class, and was going to try again now, on her lunch break. The first two times there'd been no answer and no machine to leave a message on. Her only hope was to keep calling and keep hoping somebody picked up.

Peri dropped the quarter down the slot and dialed the number Bob had croaked out.

One ring, another, another, then, at the end of the line, a voice that sounded like it'd been cooking in a deep fryer.

Bob had grown up in Arkansas where his father was a pastor. His family had relocated to Los Angeles after his father had an affair with a parishioner. His mother had kicked Bob out when he was sixteen for kissing another man. Bob got a job at a restaurant next door to a ballet studio. He took classes between shifts, and when Mr. D held auditions for his new company, Bob had been first in line, hoping his talent and good looks would get him a job. They had, and then Peri joined the company, and they'd become best friends and dance partners. Although Bob hadn't reconciled with his mother, he'd never stopped trying, sending her flowers on Mother's Day and calling her on her birthday.

"Hello," Peri said. "Is this Mrs. Winslow?"

"Who wants to know?"

"I . . . I do. My name is Peridot Jones. I was your son's dance partner."

"I don't have a son any—"

Peri rushed to correct her. "Bob isn't dead. Yet." She stuck her finger through the plastic coils of the cord. "He doesn't have much time left, and he's asking for you. Will you come to see him? Just for a few minutes?"

"Bobby is a homosexual, and God is punishing him for his sins." Mrs. Winslow spat the words.

Peri pressed her lips together, stopping her outrage in its tracks. In a careful, measured tone, she said, "You're his mother. He needs you." Mrs. Winslow didn't say anything. Peri felt an opening. "Please." She yanked the phone cord. "You can't get it from visiting. Come. It would mean the world to Bob." She held her breath, hoping Bob's mother would come around. "I . . ."

Please, please, please, Peri recited in her head.

Mrs. Winslow's voice hardened. "I'm not going anywhere near that filth."

"Even to say goodbye?"

"I said goodbye when he decided to fool around with boys."

"Bob was a wonderful dancer, and one of the finest people I've ever met." Peri's register had dropped to a growl.

"Bobby can take that up with Jesus." Slam and then a dial tone.

Peri hung up, her mouth slack with disbelief.

She made her way inside, her thoughts fraught and frantic, until she got to the nook by the soda machine. She pressed her back against its cool surface and slid down until she was sitting, her tears about to froth over. She drew up her knees, placed her cheeks on them, and gave into her grief and terror.

I hope no one sees me, she thought. *I'm not up for pretending everything is okay.*

She was probably safe. A *Nutcracker* rehearsal for "Waltz of the Flowers" was going on in one studio while Mr. D worked with the six brothers in *The Maiden and the Mountain* in another.

Peri lifted her head heavenward. *Are you really punishing Bob?* she asked God. *And all the rest?*

She waited, hoping for wisdom, but God didn't answer, so she tried again, dredging up memories of her mother praying, something she'd done every day, every hour. Maybe if Peri got the choreography right, then God would reply.

Peri interlaced her fingers and bowed her head. *Dear Holy Father,* she prayed. *Help me understand. So I can help other people understand. Did you really create AIDS to kill gay people?*

She waited, but God still didn't respond. Inside her and out lay nothing but the blankness of confusion.

She held back the scream that wanted to breach her closed lips. What was she going to tell Bob? That his own mother wouldn't see him? That she considered him already dead?

Like a geyser, her anger spurted up and over at Bob's mother's callousness. She turned and punched the soda machine. "You bitch," she yelled, wishing Bob's mother could hear her. Her heated fist thumped off the cold plastic as the machine rattled halfheartedly.

She cradled her sore hand. Her anger had boomeranged back to herself.

"Are you okay?"

Cursing her bad luck, Peri looked up. Mark was standing in front of her, scuffing a foot against the floor.

She tried to say something, but her heart was too big and raw for her to push any words past it.

"Can I, uh, do something?" he asked.

"I'm fine," she said and then hiccuped.

Mark jerked a hand through his hair as his mouth opened and closed wordlessly.

He wants to do something, she thought. *How sweet.*

She sagged against the soda machine, feeling its motor whir against her back.

Mark's face brightened. "Be right back." He jogged out of sight and returned a minute later with a handful of paper towels. Then, he fumbled with some change in his hand before tossing it into the machine. "Tab, right?"

Peri nodded. "How did you know?" She blew her nose, wincing at the snotty snort that, thankfully, was covered by the thunk of a can hitting the plastic cradle.

He opened the soda and handed it to her. "You're a ballet dancer. It didn't take a rocket scientist to figure out you'd want the one without sugar."

She took a sip. "Thank you."

He shifted from foot to foot as if making his mind up about something. Then, he plopped down beside her and stretched out his legs. "Is it Bob?"

"He wants to see his mother, so I called her." Peri couldn't say anything for a moment. "But she won't," she said, in a reedy voice. "She won't come see her dying son." Her whole body was trembling.

She took a few shaky breaths to muster enough oxygen to continue. "She said God is punishing him for being gay."

Mark looped an arm around her and gave her a quick, tight squeeze. For a moment, she couldn't breathe, her lungs knocked askew by the warmth and kindness of his gesture.

"Why do people base their love on stuff like that?" he asked. "I mean, being gay. It doesn't have anything to do with whether someone's a good person." He stopped as a storm cloud passed over his face. "I'm not gay, but my dad thinks I am."

"Why does he think that?" she asked through her wheezing.

"Because I like ballet."

Peri dabbed at the sticky crust on her cheeks with a paper towel. "Where are your parents? Mr. D told me you're emancipated." She ripped off a corner of the sodden paper towel and rolled it between her fingers. "It's not my place to ask," she said, remembering Mr. D's words.

Mark gazed at the grime-streaked wall. "They're around, but I won't see my dad and I can't see my mom because I don't want my dad to find out where I am and take it out on her." He sighed. "Do you really want to know?"

"I do," Peri said. "It's a big responsibility, being on your own and dancing the lead in a new ballet. It's not something most seventeen-year-old guys are capable of."

He flicked his head to remove the hair that was flopping in his eyes. "I'm not like most seventeen-year-old guys." He laughed ruefully. "I couldn't be like most seventeen-year-old guys if I wanted to dance. No going to the mall after school or to football games on Friday or watching TV all weekend. I went to the studio. Every day."

Peri patted his leg, just above his knee. Her fingers caught on a snag that would turn into a run soon. "You said you were inspired by a show Bob and I did at your school."

"The story starts earlier." Mark folded his hands in his lap. "My dad was a baseball player. A good one. He played in New York before moving us out here. One day, when I was ten, he was standing in the dugout with the rest of the team, and this foul ball comes out of nowhere and hits him in the head."

"That's awful."

"It messed him up, and he had to quit. He'd always had a temper, but after that, it got out of control. He threw fits every single day about every single thing. If the chicken my mom made was rubbery. If his beer wasn't cold enough. If traffic was bad."

Peri patted his knee.

"He began drinking. All the time. First thing in the morning, he'd pop the top off a beer and then sit in his easy chair popping more tops off more beers." Mark placed the tip of his ballet slipper against the wall. One of the elastics was pulling loose from its clumsy stitches.

"I started acting out. At school, I mean. Not at home because my dad would take a belt to me," he said as he traced a circle with his toe on the wall. "I stopped paying attention in class, wouldn't do my homework. I teased kids and pulled pranks on my teachers. I was pretty much headed to juvie."

He inhaled. "To be honest, juvie sounded good. I wouldn't have to listen to my dad yell and my mom cry."

"Why didn't your mom leave?" Peri cringed. "Sorry. That's a personal question."

He shrugged. "She's Catholic. Married until death." Mark didn't say anything for a moment. "Anyway, my mom didn't know what to do with me. Then, you and Bob did a demonstration at my school."

"Bob loved doing them," Peri said, over the fat knot in her throat. "He thought it was important to reach the younger generation."

"He reached me." Mark gazed at her. "So did you." Her stomach fluttered. "I'm glad."

"I thought it was stupid when you two began to dance. I was sitting in the back with the other bad kids, and there was so much to make fun of. The tights. The tinkly music. How stiff and formal it was. But then, I don't know. I got into it. It was beautiful. It was athletic. It was like a fairy tale come true."

"Mr. D says seeing ballet for the first time is like meeting God."

Mark laughed. "That's about right. But if seeing ballet is like meeting God, then trying ballet is when God leaves the room."

Peri giggled. "That's a good one."

"Bob taught a class afterward. I'd played baseball until my dad's injury, so I had basic coordination. But there, I was always moving in response to the ball. Throwing it, hitting it, running after it. In ballet, it was about me trying to be better than me." He paused. "Bob taught a *pas de chat*."

She conjured up an image of Bob in her head, handsome like a matinée idol, eager to touch the new generation with the elegance of ballet but playing it cool because nothing turned off an almost teenager like enthusiasm. Peri squeezed back her tears as she said, "He thought a *pas de chat* was a relatable step. Everyone knows cats. Fun name, easy to picture, but hard to do."

"I got it on the first try." He rapped his fingers against the linoleum in the one-then-the-other-leg skip of a *pas de chat*. "But I didn't know how to point my feet, and my shoulders were up to my ears." Mark bounded to his feet and demonstrated.

"So you were a scaredy cat?" She tugged on her left earlobe, surprised by her joke.

Laughing, he dropped beside her. Peri swallowed some of her Tab and looked down. Mark's slim, warm body and easy humor were attractive in ways that she, a twenty-nine-year-old woman, should not find them to be so.

Mark leaned against the soda machine. "Anyway, Bob came over and gave me a couple of tips. He did it in a low-key way, nothing that would draw attention. I did it a few more times, and each time I got better." His face lit up. "It was the coolest thing to feel the improvement."

"That's what got me hooked," she said. "Small, measurable progress."

Peri thought of her dancing these days, its creep toward decay, and twisted her hands. What was she going to do when she couldn't dance?

Mark grinned, as if remembering the moment. "My teacher saw me. She called my mom and said I might enjoy a ballet class. My mom doubted that, but she figured it couldn't hurt to drop me off for an hour at the local studio. So she did. I wouldn't leave after the class. I kept practicing, trying to remember all the steps I'd learned." Mark's eyes danced. "My mom saw an opportunity. She promised I could come back if I started behaving and got my grades up. I did, and so I went back. A few months later, I transferred to a good school an hour away. My mom had to drive me until I got my license, but she didn't mind. We kept it hidden from my dad. For five years."

"How'd you do that?"

"I had a double life, like a spy. There were my home and school lives where nobody knew I danced. Because I couldn't tell my dad, and I wouldn't tell anyone at school—"

"Even your friends?"

"I didn't have too many of those. I didn't want to get beat up if anybody found out."

She opened her mouth to say something sympathetic. He jumped in. "I had lots of friends at the studio."

Peri frowned. Guys had it so hard in ballet, everyone thinking they were sissies because they wore tights even though ballet attire didn't look that much different from a football uniform.

"And your dad never suspected?" she asked.

"He never went anywhere, and he never talked to anyone. My mom told him I was taking karate. He didn't care because it was quiet when I wasn't around. Every once in a while, he'd ask me to show him some moves. I'd do a *grand battement* with my leg turned in or a *grand rond de jambe* with a flexed foot." Mark widened his eyes in amazement. "He actually bought it."

"How did he find out?" She ran a finger along the strap of her leotard. "He did find out, right?"

"He went for a beer run one day, totally wasted. A cop pulled him over, and long story short, he went to a place to dry out. When he came back, he started paying attention. For the first time in years." Mark yanked at the snag on his tights, which caused a run to sprint down his leg. "But he was still mean."

For the third time, she patted his knee, her finger grazing the top of the run.

"He saw that I was standing up straight, walking like a duck with turned-out feet and a puffed-up chest. He heard me humming classical music. He got the feeling I wasn't studying karate. So he followed me to the studio one day. I was driving by myself, had the radio turned up to a metal station—"

"Metal?"

"It's harder than hard rock." He fiddled with his collar. "Outside the studio, I like listening to stuff that doesn't sound like ballet music."

She nodded. "It's loud, right?"

"So loud it hurts. But with a glam edge, like David Bowie if he were singing on a factory floor."

"So you were driving to the studio listening to the radio and . . ."

"I wasn't paying attention. Didn't even think to pay attention. I was singing along at the top of my lungs, and at the stop lights, I thrashed my arms like I was playing the guitar."

Peri rubbed her hands together as she anticipated where Mark's story was going.

"My dad came in at the end of pliés." Mark's face paled as Peri swallowed, trying to force her heart back down her throat.

"Did he have a fit?" she asked.

He closed his eyes. "A huge one. He threatened my ballet teacher and smashed the mirror. He threw a chair at me, saying 'I will beat the faggot out of you.' The receptionist called the police, and they hauled him away. He went to jail, but it was only temporary. When my mom went to see him, he told her he was going to send me to military school to toughen me up. My mom was beside herself. She thought he was serious." His shoulders drooped. "So did I. He was ashamed of me. Baseball players' sons don't become ballet dancers."

"I'm sorry." Peri groped for words. "When did this happen?" "Right before school let out for the summer." Mark shook his head.

"Not that it mattered. He would have found a school that was year round and then told them to take me and throw away the key. I don't even want to think about what that would have been like." Mark paused. "Plus there was the other thing."

"What's that?"

"I still had two years left of school." "Two? I thought you were—"

He shook his head. "My birthday is in early November, so I started late. Then, I failed fifth grade. It was the year my dad got injured, and the year before I saw you and Bob dance. My mom refused to support anything unless I graduated." He groaned. "I hated school. All that sitting still and taking notes and filling in bubbles for tests. Plus, it was boring and useless. I was going to dance."

"I never graduated," Peri said. "I tried to finish my degree through correspondence classes when I moved to Los Angeles."

"You can do that?"

"You can. But it's tough, way more than going to a regular school. After a year, I'd completed two classes. The next year, only one. So I dropped out at seventeen when the state would let me." She stared at her feet, counting the neat stitches that connected her elastics to her ballet slippers. "I regret it now."

Boy did she regret it. What was she going to do in a year or two when she found herself out of a job? Bag groceries? Ring a register at a cheap clothing store?

"That's what my mom was worried about, that I'd need it at some point. My ballet teacher's husband was a lawyer, and he suggested I take the GED and emancipate myself, so I could dance without my dad having the power to stop me." He pushed his hair out of his face.

"I took his advice. After I got my GED, my ballet teacher called Mr. D and set up the audition." He looked at her. "And now I'm here, about to dance with you."

She looped an arm around him and pulled him close for a short hug. Her heart stuttered at his smell—fresh and honest like a new bar of soap. "I'm glad I get to dance with you." She hesitated and then finished in the bright rush of a comet's tail. "Bob would be too."

6

Relevé

(RAISED)

THE CRAZIEST THING HAPPENED: Mark had made a friend—Peri.

He stood behind her at barre. She had a good memory for combinations, something he did not have. He followed her on the right side, and by the time they'd turned to the left, he was up to speed. After class, they did their cool-down stretches in companionable silence. He would warm up with her, but he pressed snooze so many times on his alarm that he ran into the studio right as class was beginning.

Lunch was the best. They claimed the spot by the soda machine where they stretched out to eat—four bologna sandwiches for him, a small bowl of tuna salad with six wheat crackers for her.

Cooking. Something he needed to figure out. He was surviving on hunks of meat shoved between slices of white bread and bowls of cereal. For dinner, he ordered eggs and bacon at a cheap diner that served breakfast all day. He couldn't afford anything else on the menu.

Mark was proud of himself for hitting the high notes of adulthood: working, paying his bills, staying fed, keeping himself and his things clean. But there was plenty of room for improvement.

Brushing the crumbs from his T-shirt, he turned toward Peri, who was neatly placing her fork and Tupperware container in a brown paper bag. She blotted her lips with a napkin, balled it up, and then tossed it into the trashcan that lay a few feet away.

Mark grinned at her. "Nice shot."

She returned his smile, which made him twitch with happiness.

Peri, although she tried to speak cheerfully, always seemed sad, with drooping lips and slumped shoulders. She was sad about Bob, but it went deeper than that. He couldn't put his finger on it. So he tried to make her smile.

"Ballerina by day, basketball player at night," she said as she reached into her dance bag for a butterscotch. She unwrapped it and tossed it into her mouth.

"You really like those," Mark said.

She half-smiled, the candy clacking against her teeth. "It's how I keep life sweet."

He cocked his head.

Peri extended her legs. "Dance is hard." She placed one cheek on her legs, her eyes still connected to his. "Life is hard." She sucked on the butterscotch for a moment. "There's so much uncertainty. It's nice to know that, no matter what, one of these . . ." She waved the wrapper. "Guarantees me five minutes of happiness." She sat up. "Plus, they're low in calories compared to chocolate or cookies."

"Why butterscotch?" Mark didn't have much of a sweet tooth, but if he did, he would go for something bright and fruity, like those little lollipops doctors gave out at the end of appointments.

"They're sweet and savory." She reached into her bag, pulled out one, and pushed it toward him. "Try it."

He popped it in his mouth and then gagged at the taste of rotten honey. Quickly, he crunched it and swallowed, grimacing as the fragments scratched his throat.

"Did you like it?" Peri's eyes were sparkling.

"Uh . . ." He threw her an apologetic smile. "Not really."

She giggled. "I would have been surprised if you did. Old ladies and I are single-handedly responsible for the butterscotch consumption in the United States."

I like you, he thought, the words catching him by surprise, like a car cutting across traffic. The tips of his ears burned, and he ducked his head, worried Peri would read his mind.

Fortunately, she took a sip of her Tab, giving Mark a second to think of something to say.

"What a class." He pushed his hair out of his eyes. He needed a haircut. One more thing to add to the list. "Why does Stone insist on such long combinations?" He jumped up and extended his leg in a *tendu*. He closed and opened it a bunch of times, slowly and then quickly.

"And now," he said in a passable imitation of Stone's British accent. "We continue with another 128 counts of *tendus* in an impossible-to-remember sequence."

Stone, whose real name was Margaret Haywood, was one of the rehearsal mistresses. She taught company class on Tuesdays and Thursdays. She'd been a well-respected ballet dancer back in the '50s although no one on the streets would guess that now. She'd grown enormously fat over the years with a heavy bosom and legs so stout that Mark couldn't believe she could still cross them toe to heel in fifth position.

"It's so she runs out of time," Peri said. "Why would she want to do that?" "What's the one thing we never do?"

Mark thought for a moment and then slapped the side of the soda machine, laughing. "She's too fat to demonstrate the jumps in grand allegro."

Peri giggled. "She used to when I started. But it's been at least ten years."

Mark chewed on a hangnail as, beside him, Peri stiffened.

And there it was—the awkwardness that edged their conversations. Peri was eleven years older than him. Technically, it was eleven years and a few months because he hadn't turned eighteen yet. Their friendship was weird.

But I'm weird, Mark thought. *Peri is too. Anyway, I'd rather have a friend, even if she's older, than no friends.*

Peri perked up her tone. "We make up for it when Stick teaches."

Tara Rabinowitz, called Stick behind her back, was the other rehearsal mistress. She was the opposite of Stone—skin like leather and bones so brittle that it looked like she would crumble into a heap of sand if someone poked her. And if Stone gave long combinations, then Stick gave hard ones that, although she was in her late forties, she still demonstrated full out. Not always well, but still. It was impressive.

"How'd you end up here?" Mark asked.

"Mr. D was looking for dancers. He came to the school I was studying at in New York, watched class, and then offered me a contract at the end of it."

"How old were you when you moved to Los Angeles?" "Fifteen."

He whistled. "That's young."

"It was before kids started appearing on milk cartons. Nobody knew to be afraid for me."

"Was it hard being away from your family?"

Peri shrugged. "Not really. I'm one of seven children—"

"Seven! I'm an only child. What's that's like?" Mark tried to picture growing up in a houseful of kids. When he was younger, he used to beg his mom and dad for a little brother, but he never got one. After that foul ball hit his dad, Mark had become grateful he didn't have to protect someone from his dad's temper.

"It was loud. It was messy. There was never enough of anything—time, money, affection—to go around." Her face wilted. "I was in the middle, and I had a bunch of wild brothers on either side, so my parents left me alone."

"That sounds rough." He patted her knee, which was covered in pristine pink tights. She'd done the same thing to him, so he hoped it was okay for him to do to her.

"It was and it wasn't. I learned to take care of myself from an early age." Peri hesitated. "I went home a few years ago for my dad's funeral, and it felt like my family was someone else's family. I didn't have anything to say to them, and they didn't have anything to say to me."

"Do you see them anymore?"

She shook her head. "We grew apart a long time ago. After the funeral, we stopped pretending we hadn't."

Mark reached out to pat her knee, but pulled his hand back. He'd just done that, and he didn't want it to be weird. He searched for something to say. "How'd you start dancing?"

"When I was eight, a new family moved on the block." "You're from . . ."

"Pittsburgh," Peri said. "My dad worked at a steel mill." She fell quiet, her forehead creasing.

Mark winced as the silence stretched on. His bad. "So the new family . . ."

She shook herself. "They had a girl my age—Antoinette. She was odd. She wore beautiful clothes and had the prettiest dolls, but she never made eye contact, and she barely talked. Any type of loud noise would cause her to have a fit."

Peri stopped to tuck a wisp of yellow hair behind her ear as Mark stared at her, forgetting to be cool.

Because Peri was beautiful. But in the strangest way. She looked like a pixie, with her big eyes and pointed chin and upside-down mouth where the top lip was larger.

Embarrassed, he fiddled with the sleeve of his T-shirt, which, in the fluorescent light, looked greenish, like cough syrup. *Laundry*, he reminded himself as he gaped again at Peri, who, thankfully, didn't notice.

I can't help but stare, he explained to himself. *I like pretty girls, and Peri is really pretty.*

She continued. "I didn't mind Antoinette. Her mom made the best snacks. Deviled eggs or crackers with cheese melted on them. I could play with her dolls. It was quiet, and her parents said hello to me and asked me how my day was."

Mark nodded, wanting her to tell him more.

"They were happy Antoinette had a friend and I was happy to have a place to go after school and Antoinette didn't seem to care one way or another," Peri said. "They enrolled her in ballet classes and signed me up too. When I was twelve, a woman from New York came to our school. She was scouting for one of the top academies. After class, she offered me a full scholarship for the next year."

Mark's voice rose. "So at twelve, you moved to New York?"

"Thirteen. My birthday is in August. It's why I'm named Peridot." Mark rubbed his chin. What did August have to do with peridots?

To be honest, he wasn't sure what a peridot was.

She winked at him. "Every month has a gemstone associated with it. August is peridot, which is light green."

"Got it." He stopped for a minute. "Why do you go by Peri if your real name is a jewel?"

"Because Peridot ends with a t, most people think they should pronounce it instead of leaving it silent. So I decided to go by Peri. It was easier than correcting people all the time."

Mark nodded. He snuck another look at Peri, her cheekbones high and proud. *She couldn't have been named any better*, he thought and then flushed.

"When I moved to New York, I lived with a retired couple who were supporters of the school." Peri's smile flattened into a frown. "When I came home for the Christmas break, Antoinette's family had moved away. I never heard from her again." Her eyes took on a faraway look. "What happened to Antoinette?"

Mark thought fast. He wanted to say something big and bright that would raise her spirits. "I bet she's out there, following your career.

She's probably come to a show or two, but she's too scared to come backstage and talk to you."

"I hope so."

"I know so," Mark said. He looked at her to see if it'd worked. She was staring down at her hands, the corners of her lips sagging.

Still blue. Frowning, he zigzagged around his brain, desperate to find something to say.

"How's Bob?"

"He's back in the hospital," Peri said in a dead voice. "It's not looking good."

He sat up straight. "Are you going to see him after rehearsal?" She nodded. "I'm one of the only ones who can come."

"His friends . . ."

"Dead or dying or at funerals."

Mark cursed. "I didn't realize it was that bad." "It's a plague, and nobody cares."

An idea sparked. He'd planned on going home to watch game six of the World Series between the Kansas City Royals and the St. Louis Cardinals. Mark had his fingers crossed that the Cardinals, who'd already won three games, would win since a couple of his dad's old buddies were on the team.

Although Mark hadn't played baseball since he started ballet, he still enjoyed the games, especially the playoffs. After his dad's injury, it'd been the one nice thing Mark could do with his dad—watch baseball. From his easy chair, his dad would yell at the umpires and groan at the coaches' decisions and cheer for the players he used to know.

But his dad wasn't around anymore, and Peri was. Plus, if she agreed, then he could spend more time with her, which made his stomach flicker with excitement.

"Can I come with you to the hospital?" He pulled at the neckline of his T-shirt. "I want to tell Bob about seeing him dance. How it helped me. How it got me here today."

"I don't know." She tugged on her left earlobe. "He's in bad shape. He doesn't look like Bob anymore." "I can handle it."

She tipped her head back and forth as if she was deciding. Finally, she said, "Okay. We'll go together after rehearsal."

7

Fondu

(SINKING DOWN)

"START THERE." Mr. D pointed to a spot upstage. "Tentative steps in a circle. You are nervous, a maiden about to face hand-to-hand combat with a young warrior. If you fail, at worst you die. At best, your lord protector will punish you."

They were rehearsing the second major scene of *The Maiden and the Mountain* between Mark and Peri. In the scene just before, Mark had killed the lord protector, played by Mr. D.

Mr. D's big return to the stage wasn't much more than a handful of frenzied gesticulations and a dramatic crumple to the floor. Even still, he could turn on the pathos, and Peri's heart went rat-a-tat when Mark blinded Mr. D, who'd clutched his eyes with his thin beige fingers, his face flaccid with shock, his spine bent with resignation. Mark, his mouth open with surprise, had been late reaching for his sword, too caught up in Mr. D's performance.

Maybe this will be good after all, Peri thought as she orbited with small, uncertain steps.

Mr. D shook his head. "More unsure. Rub your hands. Touch the hilt of your sword." He paused. "You do not know the seventh son has slain your uncle." He gestured toward Mark. "You do not know he is coming to pledge his troth."

Her heart blinked on as Mark flushed.

Mr. D swung his gaze to her, his eyes impenetrable. "You are only thinking about death."

A pall fell over the studio at the mention of death.

What would it be like? she asked herself. *To feel the fingers of death wrap around my throat, know they would tighten and choke all the air out of me.*

Peri paced again in the circle, her fingers winding around each other, then pawing at the imaginary sword at her waist.

"Better." Mr. D pointed to Mark. "Step out from the wing. Stop, stare, acknowledge your future bride."

Mark flicked his hair out his eyes as he followed Mr. D's instructions, a circlet of pearls hanging from one of his hands. The crown for the performance would be more ornate, but this would do for rehearsal.

Mr. D held up his hand. "Drink her in. She is beautiful, she is brave, and she is about to be yours. Your feelings must elevate these actions into transcendence."

Mark squared his shoulders and tried it again. "Yes." Mr. D's voice was a silky caress.

Curious, Peri peeked over her left shoulder. Mark was gazing at her with eyes that shone true-blue with love.

Her breath caught in the back of her throat. Mark was a good actor. Better than she was.

"Make your way to her. Extend the crown." Mr. D turned to her. "Your hand touches his as you reach for the crown. Look at him. A moment where neither of you moves, yet you say everything." He issued a few more instructions and then waved for them to try it.

Mark extended the circlet of pearls to her. She placed her hand over his. Maybe it was the warmth of his skin or maybe it was Mark's good acting or maybe it was just her, who was desperate for the touch of another human, but Peri's muscles went fuzzy as her memory filmed over. Mr. D had told her what to do, but she couldn't remember for the life of her what that was.

"Dance, children. Do not think," Mr. D called. So that's what they did.

Weakly, she lifted her eyes to Mark's. They were soft, inviting, and Peri pitched herself forward into their blue depths. Indulging herself in the moment, she placed the pearl crown on her head, keeping her gaze on Mark. He reached for her hand and pressed a kiss against it as goose bumps tiptoed up her arm.

The logical part of her sounded an alarm, but she'd fallen so far into their communion that it barely registered. Mark wrapped his arms around her and pulled her close. Peri laid her head on his chest, her body yielding to his. Then, following intuition rather than instruction, she rose onto her toes and lifted her leg into an attitude.

Mark walked around her as she arced into a backbend, her surrender to his seduction made manifest.

Slowly, he brought her up until they were eye to eye. He lifted his arm, and they—

Mr. D clapped his hands. "That is enough, children."

Peri almost choked. That hadn't been Mr. D's choreography. They'd made it up, using their feelings—their fake feelings, she corrected herself—to guide them.

Her cheeks blazed hot and ashamed as if they'd been slapped. Peri gulped. Mark still had a hand on her waist. She stepped aside, arranging her features into bland disinterest, as Mark said sorry under his breath.

Why is he apologizing? she thought. *That was all me.*

Mr. D jerked his eyes from Mark to her several times. His lips were upturned in a pleased way. "You do my work for me," he said in a soft, knowing voice.

The tension was unbearable as Mr. D continued to eyeball them. Beside Peri, Mark shifted from foot to foot as he fingered the neckline of his T-shirt. Peri latched her arms around herself, feeling like her skin had turned inside out.

Mr. D knew. That she was responding to Mark in a way she never had to Bob, to Mr. D, to anyone.

Finally, Mr. D called for a five-minute break, and Peri dashed to the bathroom, eager to get away from whatever that was in the studio. She splashed water on her heated skin, hoping it, by osmosis, would cool her emotions. She patted her face dry with a paper towel and confronted her appearance in the mirror. High color tinted her cheekbones, and her lips looked as pink and plump as a freshly picked piece of fruit.

What had gotten into her? Mark was her dance partner. He wasn't her . . . He would never be her . . . Because he was . . .

Peri pressed her forehead against the mirror.

She was acting like a man, allowing herself to be aroused by youth and vibrancy. Men, though, were allowed to do that with younger women. And nobody cared; in fact, it was expected.

Women were supposed to like an older man who had money, power, a strong personality that he'd use to beguile her and bend her to suit his will.

But she'd had that with Mr. D. Her stomach contracted.

She still had that with Mr. D.

Peri lifted her head. With brisk, practical strokes, she washed her hands.

I'm responding because I'm scared and lonely and eager for anyone to make me forget about what's happening to Bob, she thought. *If it weren't Mark, it'd be whoever was in his place.*

She didn't believe herself, but it was the best she could come up with.

"This is embarrassing," she said to her reflection in the mirror. "You are embarrassing. Pull yourself together."

Peri threw the dirt of her self-reproach over her heart. Shoulders squared, she headed toward the studio, determined to spin her focus to her technique, which needed all the attention it could get these days.

8

À Terre

(ON THE GROUND)

MARK FOLLOWED PERI to her car, smoothing down his hair, wishing he'd worn something other than blue jeans and a T-shirt the color of a traffic cone. He looked like a bum next to Peri, who had on a light purple off-the-shoulder sweater and stretchy black pants with stirrups. He sprawled in the front seat and squeezed his hands together, which were empty.

Should he have brought something? Flowers? A balloon that said *Get Well*?

What did you bring to someone who was dying?

He peeked at Peri, her pixie features pinched with sadness and worry. He wanted to pat her knee, tell her it was going to be okay even though it wasn't.

She cleared her throat. "I want to prepare you. Bob is thin, very weak. He might not know you're there," she said. "He doesn't always remember who I am." She hesitated. "He's not in control of his bowels. It can be . . . unpleasant."

The four bologna sandwiches he'd scarfed for lunch made a beeline up his throat. He swallowed them back down. If Peri could do it every day, then he could do it for one. "I'm glad to see him no matter what."

Peri turned into the hospital's parking lot and pulled into a spot close to the entrance. As they headed toward the sliding doors, Mark became more and more aware of himself. His arms were swinging like a gorilla's, and his hair hung in his eyes.

He blew his hair out of the way as Peri led him through the sliding doors and then down the hall. She stopped outside a room numbered 1130 and turned toward him.

"This is such a nice thing to do." She reached for his hand. "Thank you."

His heart lurched at the feel of her small, soft hand in his big, hot one. Peri pulled him into the room and guided him toward a chair into which he plunked himself.

Mark almost barfed when Bob came into focus. If this pale scarecrow could be called Bob. Peri walked over to Bob and placed her hand on his cheek, which was polka-dotted with purple.

Don't do that, he yelled in his head. *What if you catch it?*

He wanted to grab Peri, throw her over his shoulder caveman-style, and flee from this tiny cube of hell where the bleach couldn't cover the stink of death and diarrhea. Mark threaded his fingers around the arms of the chair and grounded his feet into the floor to force himself to stay. He turned his eyes away from Peri toward the window where the palm trees waved in the golden haze of the late afternoon sun.

On the windowsill stood a card of Jesus, his hands clasped in prayer. Mark tilted his head to read the message.

Dear Bobby,

I hope by now you understand the error of your ways. Homosexuality is a sin, and God is punishing you. You have no one to blame but yourself. I hope that you will repent in time, so we may meet again in heaven.

Sincerely,
Your Mother

Mark's jaw crashed open. *What kind of mom writes that?* he thought. Her son was dying, and all she could offer was judgment and cruelty. He shook his head, feeling sorry for Bob.

"Bob," Peri whispered. "I've brought someone to see you." Bob's eyes fluttered and then opened hopefully.

Peri didn't give Bob a chance to be disappointed. "Mark is here. Do you remember how I told you about him? You taught a class at his elementary school. Now he's about to be the lead in Mr. D's new piece."

She tipped her head in his direction.

Mark inhaled, a shaky, shallow one. It wasn't enough air to push him through what he wanted to say, but it would have to do. "Hey," he said. "I wanted to come and say thank you."

He told Bob the story as best he could. He forgot to mention the *pas de chat*, so he went back to add it, but then he forgot where he was before that and repeated a few parts. So he hopscotched through the memory, hoping it was clear although he wasn't sure it mattered because Bob kept nodding off. Peri stayed close to Bob, patting his shoulder and holding his hand.

"So, uh, now I'm a professional ballet dancer," Mark finished up lamely. "Thanks to you. I mean, thank you."

He winced as he repeated the words in his head. He sounded like a moron.

Bob's eyelids flicked open. With effort, he turned his head toward Mark. Bob opened his mouth, but no sound came out. Then, with what looked like a big effort, Bob rasped, "Outlast him."

Mark did a double take at Bob. *Outlast who?* Mark thought. He peeked at Peri, who shook her head, her eyes pained. Mark shrugged it off. She'd said that Bob didn't always know what was going on these days.

Peri stood and kissed Bob's forehead. "We're leaving, but I'll be back tomorrow."

She extended her hand to Mark, which he grabbed. He couldn't wait to get out of there.

Squeak.

They turned to the door at the same time on the same foot, like it was choreography.

Mr. D was struggling through the door, trying to manage his cane and a massive bouquet of purple flowers.

Peri jumped in. "It's Mr. D, Bob. He's here to see you," she said, her joy jarring with the gloom in the room. She turned toward Mr. D. "Thank you for coming."

"You were very persuasive, Peri-jan," Mr. D said. He inclined his head toward Mark, his lips tight. "How kind of you to accompany Miss Jones."

"Mark wanted to tell Bob thank you. Since he's why Mark's dancing."

Mr. D's gaze drifted to their clasped hands, and his eyes glinted. "Have a good evening, children."

Mark's heart dropped.

Mr. D knew. That Mark liked Peri more than just as a friend. A lot more.

He scuffed a toe, embarrassed his skin was too flimsy to keep his feelings hidden.

Mark thought about Peri all the time. A funny thing she'd said at lunch. How her blonde hair glinted almost white in the sun. The way her laugh sounded like a flute. It would have been annoying if it weren't so nice.

But nothing's going to happen, he thought. *She's out of my league, way too pretty and mature to be interested in a guy like me.*

Besides, he'd picked up from the studio gossip that Peri was Mr. D's girl. She'd never told him this, and they rarely talked about Mr. D. But still. It wasn't like Mark could ask Peri out.

He would have to be satisfied with being friends.

9

Chassé
(CHASED)

FOR THE FIRST time in a long time, her spirits, so long underwater, had risen. She placed a hand on her stomach. The wobble was there, but its effect had diminished. Only one thing had changed—Mark.

It still seemed unbelievable. They'd become friends. The age difference, which should have been vast and unconquerable, had receded until she rarely noticed it. Fortunately, there'd been no repeat of what had happened in that *M+M* rehearsal (*The Maiden and the Mountain* proved too clunky for everyday usage and had been shortened by the dancers). Not that Peri would let it happen again. She considered herself to be Mark's older sister.

Peri shook her head. She didn't feel like Mark's older sister. She felt like his . . .

She didn't know what she felt like except that she looked forward to seeing him every day, bounding in behind Stick or Stone, making class by a few ticks of the clock as he mouthed "thank you" to her for saving him a spot at the barre.

Most of their friendship had to do with Mark himself, who gave her so much—jokes, joy, hope—and didn't seem to want anything in return. Maybe it was because he was so young, didn't know how to be anybody other than himself, but he was equal parts ambition and good humor, all of which rubbed off on her.

Her energy and verve would never return to her pre-injured self, but Mark kept the doldrums from coming for her. Even her calf was holding up, much to her gratitude.

Mark was also kinder and braver than plenty of people twice his age. Take visiting Bob. Mark's face had collapsed when he'd seen the living corpse that Bob was. Yet he stayed, told Bob his story. Bob couldn't say much, but Peri was pretty sure he understood, had known all those classes he'd taught hadn't gone to waste.

She looked at Mark, who was sitting beside her in the studio, drinking a soda and writing down the phrases from their earlier rehearsal in the little leather-bound journal she'd bought him for his birthday.

A couple of weeks ago, Mark had turned eighteen. Peri didn't have much time or money, but she'd bought the journal for him after seeing him struggle to remember choreography. It wasn't a problem she had, her body able to hang on to sequences of steps years after she no longer needed them, but other dancers did. A few of them made it a practice to write down what they learned after rehearsal and then studied it, as if for a test.

She took Mark to one of those all-you-can-eat buffets, betting that quantity was more important than quality to him. It was, and Mark ate plate after plate heaped with fried chicken drizzled with gravy and rosy circles of ham and buttery mounds of mashed potatoes. She'd sipped a Tab and picked at a hunk of overcooked fish, pleased she'd gotten it right. At the end, she handed him the journal, embarrassed it wasn't anything bigger or better, but she wanted him to have a present. Eighteen was an important milestone.

After she'd explained the purpose, his face lit up before it fell.

"I don't know how to spell the names of any of the steps," he said.

"It's not a spelling test. It's a remember-the-dance test." She smiled at him. "Write down whatever you need to jog your memory."

He gave her a quick hug. "Thank you." He turned the journal over in his hands. "For this." He sliced his hand through the air of the restaurant. "And this."

"Is it okay?" she asked. "This isn't how most eighteen-year-olds spend their birthday."

He shrugged. "I'm having more fun here than I would at a kegger." His eyes brightened as he stood with his plate. "And it'd be even more fun if I had another helping of apple crisp."

He'd started using the journal soon after. Peri peeked to see what he'd written down today.

Fiee, assamblay, sisown ouverr

She blinked and swallowed her giggle. He hadn't been lying about not being able to spell any of the step names.

Failli, assemblé, sissonne ouverte, she mentally corrected.

Mr. D walked in the studio. His hand was still pressing into his cane, but his step had a spring in it. Even he appeared energized by Mark's presence. The rehearsals for *M+M* were going better than anyone had expected. Mr. D had unearthed the creativity and chutzpah that had defined his work in the '70s, and the ballet held the promise of being memorable. Maybe even brilliant.

Mr. D settled into his chair, smoothing down his white suit pants. "Today, we start the *grand pas de deux*. Act One was devoted to the dramatic, the emotional, the sensual. Act Two will be a display of classical perfection."

Like obedient children, Peri and Mark nodded.

"There are five parts to a *pas de deux*: entrée, adagio, male variation, female variation, and coda. And, although not technically part of the dancing, the curtain call." Mr. D smiled. "A greeting, a conversation, two monologues, a goodbye, and then accolades. In ten minutes, using shape and sound, we convince the audience of your happily ever after."

Peri and Mark nodded again.

"You will begin from opposite sides of the stage—"

Trish stuck her head in the door, dabbing at her eyes. Her mascara had driven down her cheeks like tire tracks. "The hospital called. Bob died."

The call had been expected for weeks, but still, Peri gasped. The tremble in her stomach radiated through her trunk to her limbs until she was vibrating back and forth like a soprano's high C.

"Dismissed," Mr. D said as he hobbled out of the studio.

"Are you okay?" Mark asked, his forehead wrinkled with worry She tried to respond but couldn't. Tears were coursing down her

cheeks as she wheezed. She dropped to the floor, her bones and muscles unable to support the hurricane surging through her: rain, wind, structural collapse.

Mark creased his brow. "I'll drive you home." He gazed around the studio that glowed amber in the early evening sun. "I bet we're done for the day."

He gathered his bag and headed to the door. "I'll pull around, so you don't have to worry about changing," he said. "One minute, tops."

Mark jogged out of the studio as she tried to find a puff of air to lift her to her feet, but all her breath had left. Convulsing, she looped her fingers around the barre and yanked herself to standing. She took tiny, halting steps until she got outside where she stayed doubled over.

Bob's gone, she thought as she buried her face in her hands.

Although he'd been stuck in the going to be gone for a while, she'd never fully grasped that he'd really be gone. Forever. Her life would now be defined by this moment that sliced it in half from the presence of Bob to the absence of him.

Mark drove up in a gunmetal gray boat from the '70s. He dashed to her, guided her to the car, and settled her in the front seat. He fumbled with the buckle as he tried to avoid touching her body with his, but he ended up brushing his chest against hers.

"Sorry," he muttered.

Peri should have tried to help, but her sadness was too all-consuming for that. Mark ran around to the driver's side, got in, and released the handbrake.

"One question, then I won't say anything else," Mark said. "Where do you live?"

As he navigated the few blocks from the studio to her apartment, she crimped her body into the fetal position and gave herself over to her grief.

Bob had died alone, a hollowed-out, broken-hearted version of his former self. He'd died not knowing who he was or where he was, abandoned voluntarily by his family and involuntarily by his friends.

If I'd known it was going to be today, I would have gone and held your hand, so you wouldn't have to go alone, she wailed to Bob, who was on a journey to a place far away from here.

Just last year, he'd been the picture of health, tan and corded with muscles, making plans about going to Hawaii for vacation. Now he was dead.

She could die. And who would care? Probably not many more than nobody. She'd spent all her time at the studio except when she was at home, the landing pad from which she prepared for or recovered from dancing, and she'd built no life outside of those places beyond what Bob had shown her.

She hadn't just lost Bob; she'd lost the acquaintances she'd made through Bob—sharply dressed, sharply witted men—and the future acquaintances she would have made if Bob had lived. His friends had cooed over her and made her laugh and cheered for her, onstage and off.

She was twenty-nine, and these men whom she only knew indirectly had done more for her than she'd done for anyone. People might point to her dancing, say it was inspiring and memorable, but for real. The curtain came down and people forgot and time moved forward in its inevitable march toward oblivion.

Existing in the present tense, using the invisible ink of movement, dance was the cruelest of arts. She'd sacrificed everything for it, yet dance would allow her nothing to leave behind. The best she could hope for was a video cassette moldering on a library shelf that no one would watch and maybe a sentence or two in Mr. D's encyclopedia entry.

Mark pulled into her apartment complex, a stucco building painted a polite ecru, which roused her from her bleak thoughts. He shut off the engine and cleared his throat. "Here we are."

Peri had fallen so far down the shaft of despair that she couldn't respond with anything sensible. Instead, she honked a few times.

Mark reached past her to open the glove box. A pack of tissues lay inside. He yanked out a few and passed them to Peri. "This car used to be my mom's. She was prepared for everything."

She was crying too loudly to say thank you.

For at least an hour, they sat in the car while the sun set, the world shading from orange to black, as Peri sobbed. Mark didn't say anything, just sat there with her and patted her knee when the velocity of her yowls threatened to crack the windows.

Why? she asked God. *Bob was kind. He never said a mean word about anyone. He showed up every day and tried to be the best version of himself.*

She choked on a sob. *Bob believed in you,* she said to God. *He tried to make you proud, to follow your teachings, your Son's teachings as best he could. Yes, he was gay, but that didn't end up hurting anybody but himself.*

In her head, the volume of her thoughts increased until she was yelling at God. *There are so many awful people you could have taken instead: murderers, rapists, dictators, pedophiles, kidnappers. Why take Bob? Do you really hate homosexuality that much? More than every other sin? Because I need to know why I lost my best friend.*

She paused, willing her thoughts calm, so God could fill them with the wisdom that would make her feel better. God, though, didn't respond, which just made her cry harder.

Finally, the tears receded, leaving her gutted and broken. She sat slumped in the seat, knees pulled to her chest, rolling a damp tissue between her thumbs.

"Do you want me to walk you to your door?" Mark asked.

Her heart thrashed at the idea of going into her apartment, which was small, dark, and empty like a crypt. She didn't want to be alone with her thoughts, her feelings. She didn't want to think or feel, period.

Peri shook her head. "I want to go somewhere so loud I can't hear myself think or feel."

"How loud?"

"So loud my ears hurt worse than my heart."

"I know a place," Mark said. "But you have to change. Nothing nice though."

Peri looked down. She was still wearing her powder-blue leotard and pink tights from earlier. Even her pointe shoes were on. She ran her fingers over her skin, which was clammy from spent emotion.

"Do I have time for a shower?"

"You've got plenty of time. Things start late." "Do you want to come up?" she asked.

~

Peri followed Mark toward the club, touching her hair self-consciously. In a moment of inspiration, she'd aimed a can of hair spray at the wisps around her forehead and spritzed until they arced up and over like a comma. She'd wriggled into blue jeans that were so tight they looked painted on and a cropped black T-shirt. Then, she'd outlined her eyes with kohl and daubed a bow of hot pink over her lips. It wasn't her normal look, but the last thing she wanted now was to be her normal self.

"Are they going to let you in?" she asked as they joined the line outside. She leaned down to pick up a flier that was fluttering in the tepid November breeze. Underneath a crude drawing of two guns twined with red roses was a picture of five men, their hair like balls of yarn after being attacked by a kitten. In the photo, they held plates of spaghetti as they leered at the camera.

ADDICTED . . . Only *The Strong Survive* captioned the picture. "One of my roommates works as a bar-back. He'll get me in."

Peri pointed at the paneled façade of the venue where *The Troubadour* was written in vaguely gothic script above the door. "You've been here before?"

He nodded. "When I need to blow off some steam, and I don't want to sit around watching TV."

"Where do you live?"

"I share a house with three guys between here and the studio." He laughed. "It's a pigsty."

Peri wrinkled her nose as they inched closer to the door.

"It's loud too. One of the guys is in a metal band, and they practice at the house."

"Are they any good?"

Mark shook his head. "They do it to score girls and booze." He pretended to clutch a microphone, and in an off-key shriek, he sang. His volume was pitched so loudly that Peri only got a few words, something about home sweet home.

"Mötley Crüe," Mark said. "The actual song sounds better."

"I believe it." She winked. "You didn't set the bar awfully high." He grinned amiably.

"It sounds like you live in a frat house," Peri said.

"I don't care." He shrugged. "I'm not there that much."

When they reached the door, Mark asked for his roommate, a rat-like guy with a skinny ponytail. He waved them through after giving Peri an up-and-down look.

"Bodacious," he whispered to Mark, who flushed.

Peri recoiled when they entered the club, the noise assaulting her like a thick, meaty fist. Onstage, a group of men with puffy hair pranced and posed as a skinny blond guy with a big nose screamed into a microphone. Peri couldn't make out what he was saying, but she seemed to be the only one. People were nodding their heads and mouthing the lyrics as, next to her, someone mimed playing a guitar.

Mark tapped her shoulder and, with exaggerated gestures, told her he'd be back in a minute. Peri rubbed her arms, feeling alone and out of place. She gazed around the club, a seedy wooden box with a balcony ringed by a bulbous, old-fashioned railing.

Through the crowd of bobbing heads and writhing bodies, Mark made his way to her, clutching two bottles of beer. He got to her side, pushed one into her hands, and clinked his against hers.

She took a sip of the beer, bitter and frothy like tears. She only drank on Sundays, at lunch with Mr. D, and then, it was always wine.

Mark leaned toward her. "Loud enough?" he yelled. She nodded.

"The good band will start soon." "When?"

"10:30, but really whenever they're drunk enough."

Peri swallowed more beer. The alcohol zipped through her, warming her up from the inside out. She'd nibbled at a slice of pizza earlier, but once she'd seen Mark eying it hungrily, she'd pushed it toward him.

Mark stood next to her, and he smelled like life, all sweat and optimism. At that moment, Peri's muscles sagged with age and disillusionment, like the only thing life had in store for her was more loss and frustration.

Onstage, the band was exiting as the energy in the crowd picked up. Someone pushed against Peri, slamming her into Mark. His beer splattered across her shirt. He dabbed at it as she mouthed that she didn't care. Mark pulled her in front of him and turned her to face him.

Drink up, he mimed.

She didn't want the rest, so she passed the half-filled bottle to him. He tossed it in a trashcan as the headliner band took the stage. The audience exploded into uproarious cheers. To Peri's left, a girl with black hair blown out like a fright wig was listing back and forth as if she were about to faint.

Peri knew nothing about popular music, but even she could tell this band was special. They were rude, lewd, almost feral in their devil-may-care attitude. They burst into a song she'd never heard before, something about leading a reckless life. The beats smashed around her like a sledgehammer.

The lead singer, a redhead in leather chaps, sang as if he were a wounded animal, screechy and insistent. Although Peri had lived a careful life, the urgent lyrics, the singer's volatile sincerity, and the intense throb of the lashing guitars and relentless drumming seduced her. She wanted nothing more than to prove them right, to lead a reckless life as her only vice.

The crowd pressed tighter and tighter against Mark and her as everyone squirmed and flailed and twisted. During a cover of "Jumpin' Jack Flash," a song she actually knew, she gave into their appeal and wiggled her body.

She was awkward—too much classical training to ever be sexy—but she reveled in moving without worrying if it was good or right or pretty. She threw herself into dancing, hips circling and shoulders rolling, while the music battered her thoughts and feelings into oblivion.

The band segued into a new song, a loud, brazen one about seduction, as the crowd thundered their approval. Her body was glued to Mark's because there wasn't a spare inch to move. She turned to say something to him, like, "Thank you, I needed this," but someone jostled her and her open mouth connected to his.

It was unplanned, not appropriate, but Peri was a body now, operating only on instinct and ardor. Who knew who turned the accidental bump of lips into a kiss—possibly, probably, most definitely her—but she didn't care.

Mark was the second person whose lips she'd pressed hers against, but his soft and searching kiss was so much better than Mr. D's thrusting, pointy-tongued ones that it felt as if she were being kissed for the first time.

Peri melted her body into Mark's as he wrapped his arms around her. Rational thought made a feeble stand—*STOP!*— but she batted it away. Instead, she let the crowd crush her into Mark until she couldn't tell where she ended and he began.

As the kiss deepened, became something that couldn't be laughed aside as an accident, Peri acknowledged the shadowy side of her desire. She was going to do something she should never do, ask Mark for something he may not be ready to give (only a hunch, but a strong one).

She needed, though, to hold and to be held, to do something, anything, this one thing that would make her feel like she could outrun death until she did something meaningful with her life. But she needed someone to do it with.

She didn't need someone. She needed Mark.

Onstage, the lead guitarist caught her eye, his springy black curls barely contained under a gray hat. He hinged almost horizontally to the floor while he stroked his guitar furiously. This song had lurid lyrics about sex, about how anything goes tonight.

Anything was going to go tonight.

She pulled away from Mark, not because she wanted to, but because she needed to. She had to ask, to make sure he was okay with this horrible, wonderful thing they might do.

"Do you want to?" Peri asked. She hadn't spoken loudly, and she didn't know if Mark had understood.

He had.

He grabbed her hand, and they fought their way out of the wall of bodies. Everyone was singing about green grass and pretty girls in a paradise city.

10

Piqué

(PRICKED, PRICKING)

YES, Mark shouted to himself as he shadowboxed the air. *I'm a man. In every way.*

In Peri's bathroom, the water was running. He'd driven them here although his place was closer. But if she saw the dump he lived in, she might change her mind. That was the last thing he wanted.

So they'd come here, and then it'd happened, and now Mark was buzzing as if he'd hit a home run when the bases were loaded and the team was down—a cliché come true.

Mark thought back through it. There'd been kissing so good that if it'd stopped there, he would have been happy. Then touching and a fumble to remove their clothes. The embarrassing moment when he'd shown her his pale, gangly body. The starry one when Peri had shown him her pale, perfect one. A few pokes by him in the wrong direction. Bliss when he'd gotten in.

In the bathroom, the water stopped. Mark's skin chilled. Had it been okay?

It'd been quicker than he would have liked, but Peri hadn't seemed displeased. He pushed a hand through his hair. She hadn't seemed pleased either.

He groaned. He'd forgotten to ask about—

The door opened, and Peri stepped out wearing a frilly robe. A braid dangled over her shoulder.

Mark blinked at his good luck. If someone had been around, he would have pointed at Peri. *Look at her,* he'd say. *She's beautiful.*

She walked to the bed and climbed in, pulling the satiny peach coverlet up to her waist. "You can stay over." She looked down. "If you want."

Mark wanted to do something, say anything to bridge the awkwardness between them, so he flung an arm around the tiny, white-clad figure curled on peach sheets beside him. She looked like a shell on the beach.

He rubbed the back of his neck with his free hand. He can't tell her that.

Instead, he asked her a question, his voice halting and embarrassed. "I forgot to ask. Should I have used . . ."

She kissed his shoulder. "I'm on the pill."

He exhaled and prepared himself to ask a harder question. "Was it . . . okay?"

She rubbed her cheek against his upper arm. "I think so." Mark's spine stiffened. "What do you mean?"

She shrank into her nightgown. "I . . . I've only been with Mr. D, so I don't . . ." Her voice faded. "Know," she whispered.

"Are you still . . ."

"I have lunch with him every Sunday. We haven't in a while." "Why?" Mark asked.

"I don't think he can anymore." "When did it start?"

"When I was fifteen."

"Fifteen?" His jaw dropped. "Did you want to?" The corners of her mouth wilted. "Not really."

"What happened?" He was being rude, but he wanted the story. "He took me out to lunch a few weeks after I moved to LA," she said in a flat tone. "I was so excited that I couldn't sit still. He ordered all this fancy food, kept pouring me wine. It was magical until he took me to his home." She hesitated. "To his bedroom," Peri whispered, her eyes big and tortured. "How was I supposed to say no to Mr. D?" Peri's hands were clasped to her breastbone, and she'd fixed her blank gaze on the opposite wall.

"Peri," he asked, his voice thin and high. She made a noise in the back of her throat.

"I want to, I mean, how do I . . ." His whole body was red and itchy like a rash "Help you have . . ." Mark forced the words past his humiliation. "What I had?"

She placed her hand over his and guided it to her. She positioned it over a soft, damp nub of skin.

A button, he thought. *Who knew?*

Peri steered his finger over and around the button in a dance of pressure and release. Her moaning turned into shrill cries as Mark repeated the choreography, concentrating hard so he wouldn't miss a move. Then, she pulsed against him, and he flopped on his back. He wanted to throw his fist in the air, but instead, he licked his finger, savoring the taste of Peri.

In a move he wasn't expecting, Peri rolled on top of him and pressed her body to his. Mark looped his arms around her as her braid tickled his neck.

And then again, too soon, it was over.

She laid her head against his chest. "Goodnight." "Goodnight," he said automatically.

She fell asleep immediately, but Mark was wide-awake. He stroked the tip of her braid and sniffed it. Pink. Like a watermelon.

Moonlight tumbled through the open curtain, and he used it to get a good look at Peri's body. A bellybutton like a thimble. Two moles on her right shoulder blade, one on her left breast. A bruise smudging her knee. A chest that rose and fell in an even rhythm. Whiffling that was too cute to be called snoring. Her right hand rested on his heart, and he patted each of her nails with the pad of his index finger.

I'm glad it was you, he said silently to her.

Gently, he slid her off his bladder. He had to pee, but he'd die before he bothered Peri by getting in and out of bed.

As he drifted off to sleep, he said a quick prayer. *Please don't let it make things weird between us.*

Things didn't get weird. They got wonderful. Wordlessly, they'd started dating. Secretly dating.

"You can't tell anyone," Peri said, her face white with worry. "Promise?"

"I promise." He shrugged, not really caring. Who'd he have to tell? One incredible week later minus the black hours of Bob's funeral,

he was spending all his time at Peri's. They drove to the studio separately and he slept in later than she did—"The last possible second," he told her when she asked him what time she should get him up—but, otherwise, they'd become a couple.

Mark kept waiting for her to get bored of him, realize he had nothing to offer her beyond himself, but she didn't. In some twist he couldn't wrap his head around, she seemed to like him more and more as they spent more and more time together. And she liked the actual Mark, who was goofy and opinionated and excitable, so he kept being himself and kept enjoying being liked for himself.

Knowing Peri wasn't much more experienced than he was gave him confidence in the bedroom to try things. Like when he used his mouth instead of his finger on her button. She'd almost knocked his head off when she rumbled beneath him.

That had been fun. So much fun, he did it again the next night.

She held out her arms to him eagerly, and when they were too tired for anything else, she curled herself around him like a cat and went to sleep as he shook his head in wonder.

That's my girl, he wanted to shout to the world.

It wasn't just the sex—although that was great. It was everything else. Mark had gone with a girl last year, dated some, and crushed plenty before, but nobody and nothing was like this.

Peri was different from any girl he'd met. She was girly. She wore pretty clothes, smelled good, had soft skin. But she didn't act like a girl. She didn't play games, run hot or cold, nag, or get her feelings hurt over stupid things. She answered Mark's questions honestly whether it was a small one about what she wanted for dinner or if it was a big one about her past. If she wanted him to do something, she asked nicely and then he did it.

Girls, as he was discovering, were picky about where things were kept, so he placed his dance bag in the hall closet and arranged his clothes in the drawers she'd cleared out and put his toothbrush and razor in the mug she'd set out. She asked him to take his sneakers off as soon he walked in the door, so he did. After a couple of days, it became second nature to walk around in his bare feet, and a few days after that, he started to look down on anyone who wore shoes indoors. Because it was gross, tracking dirt everywhere.

Mark kept waiting for their age difference to make problems, for him to do something idiotic that would remind her he was eleven years younger than her. He kept not noticing it, though, until one day he figured out why he kept not noticing it.

He'd shown up a few minutes earlier than usual for class. He stepped into the studio but stopped, his heart drumming against his chest. Peri was lounging in a stripe of sunlight, bandaging her feet before she put on her pointe shoes. Her fingers moved like hummingbird wings as she snipped bits of tape and yanked apart cotton balls that she wrapped around her toes. He'd seen her do this a bunch of times, but something about the way the sun hit her today made his breath catch.

He wasn't the only one.

At the opposite end of the studio, Mr. D was peering at Peri through the open door, his hand heavy on his cane. Its green tip sparked through his gnarled fingers. Mark's mouth went sour in understanding. The gem was a peridot.

Yuck.

He glanced at Peri who was wrapping a length of tape around her big toe. He'd bet a week's worth of groceries that she hated that cane.

One of the female company members scooted toward Peri, probably to ask for some tape or to borrow her scissors, but stopped because Mr. D was shaking his head at her. Her mouth open, she scuttled away from Peri, who hadn't noticed anything.

His heart slowed as he put it together.

That's why I don't notice the age difference, he thought. *Because on the inside, we're about the same. Mr. D hasn't let her do anything, which makes her younger, and I've had to do so many things, which makes me older.*

A cloud passed over the sun, pitching Peri into darkness, and Mr. D turned from the door, which was good, because Peri was waving at Mark, her face lighting up like a struck match. She pointed to the spot beside her where she'd placed a soda, so no one else would stand there.

That night, he brought the conversation around to a question he'd thought of after seeing exactly how alone Mr. D kept her.

"What do you do for fun? I mean, outside of dance."

"It's easier if I show you." She gestured for him to follow her to the bedroom. She opened her closet, which was bulging with clothes. "I made them all." She pointed to a little table topped with a fabric-covered hump. "When I'm not dancing, I'm sewing." She smiled shyly. "I'm pretty good."

He rubbed the sleeve of a purple silk blouse between his fingers. "Wow," he said.

He didn't know what type of answer he was expecting, but now that she'd told him, it made sense. She always dressed well, and the quick, fluttery movements she used when she taped her toes reminded him of the up-and-down motion of a needle.

"I started when I was a kid. I wanted pretty clothes, but my family didn't have the money. One day, I threw a fit. I absolutely had to have a new dress for the first day of school, one that hadn't been worn by my sister five years earlier, one that was in a color I picked out. So my mother pointed to the sewing machine and told me to make my own."

Mark nodded.

"I hated it in the beginning. But I got into it after I started dancing. I spend so much time doing what I'm told at the studio that I like

71

making up things outside the studio." She smiled. "A couple yards of fabric, a spool of thread, a handful of pins, my imagination." She twirled her hands like a magician. "And voila. I've made something pretty."

"Wow," he said again.

"I've gotten so fast that I make outfits in a couple of sizes and then donate them."

"Where?"

"Thrift stores. Most of the clothing at those places is horrible. Out-of-date styles, ugly colors, missing buttons, or dodgy zippers." Peri shrugged. "Every woman deserves something beautiful."

With each word, Mark's heart pumped up like a bicycle tire being inflated. He wanted to take an advertisement out in the paper, so he could tell Los Angeles how incredible she was. Instead, trying to be casual, he said, "That's really cool."

He hated sewing, his hands big and clumsy, his stitches more so. But he had to do it often because he had ballet slippers that needed elastics attached and holes in tights that needed to be closed and dropped hems in T-shirts that needed to be reconnected.

"Let me," she said one night, extending her hand for his ballet slipper, the needle and thread dangling from it.

He'd stopped sewing because he'd pricked his thumb. He'd pushed the needle too hard through the leather of the shoe where it landed in the soft pad of his finger. It was the second time he'd done that.

He licked a drop of blood from his thumb. "Really?"

"Really. There are things worth bleeding for. This isn't one of them."

Mark passed her his shoes, relieved but also feeling weird. His mom had done his sewing before, but she was his mom. He didn't like Peri doing it if he wasn't doing something for her. He looked around the living room, searching for something he could do.

There was nothing.

Everything was clean and organized, no dust to be wiped away, no dish he could wash, even the bowl of butterscotch candies Peri kept on the coffee table was brimming. This was the opposite of the house he shared with the guys, which reeked of week-old garbage and food-crusted plates.

Mark looked again. There was one thing. Today's newspaper was sticking out of the magazine rack, its front page ruffled. Peri had it delivered every day, but she'd never done more than skim the cover stories before putting it away.

"Hey," he said, reaching for the paper. "How come you never read this?"

She glanced at the paper spilling out of his hands. "It's too depressing to start the day with, and I'm too tired at night."

An idea flickered. "I'll read a story out loud while you sew." "You don't want to watch TV?"

"Not if you can't."

"You're sweet," she said. "Something positive. Nothing political."

Mark opened the paper to hunt for something cheerful. It was harder than he thought. The articles were either boring or scary, stuff about a tax reform bill, stock prices shooting up, Great Britain performing a nuclear test. He kept turning the pages until he found one that might work.

"Here's a good one," he said.

The article was about the lesson plans recently submitted by the teacher who would be the first civilian in space. She was going to broadcast live from the Space Shuttle Challenger to tell students about the equipment and introduce them to the other astronauts. Peri giggled when Mark read about the experiments she'd do in space like seeing if an Alka-Seltzer tablet would fizz in zero gravity.

"Plop, plop. Fizzle, fizzle," she said, tugging her left earlobe. She'd interrupted Mark, who didn't care and laughed at the joke. *She's good with words*, he thought.

Mark wasn't as good with words, but he made it through the article, definitely mispronouncing the teacher's name and probably a few other words as well, but he read with a big, enthusiastic voice, which Peri liked.

"How lucky," she said. "To see the stars up close. To brush up against the moon."

"It would be cool."

"What would it be like to dance without gravity?"

"To jump up and never come down?" Mark scrunched his brow as he pictured himself in the never-ending leap of a *grand jeté*. "Awesome."

She passed him his ballet slippers. "That was fun."

He ran his fingers over the tight, tiny stitches. "Thank you."

It became routine that when Peri sewed, he read an article or two from the paper. He searched for fun, interesting stories. They read about

Phoenix, Arizona, getting three inches of snow and the first woman receiving an artificial heart and the establishment of the position of the poet laureate. It expanded their world beyond ballet, and Mark reached happily for the paper when Peri pulled out her sewing basket.

They came up with other routines that Mark liked. Peri had been on her own for a while and was set in her ways. It took a few days before she figured out her ways were not going to work as their ways.

Take dinner. For years, she came home and heated up a can of vegetable soup. After a couple of nights of vegetable soup, Mark couldn't manage another bite. It tasted like erasers and looked like barf.

I need meat, potatoes, a square meal to fill me up after a day of dancing, he thought as he pushed a lima bean around his plate. *Not diet food.*

Mark looked up. Peri was staring at him, chewing her lip. Then, she laughed apologetically.

"Get your keys," she said. "We're going out." "Where?"

"To get you a burger. Then, we're going to buy a cookbook." She chucked his soup into the trashcan and tipped hers in after. "We both need to learn how to cook real food."

They bought a cookbook that had hearty, heart-healthy recipes. There were more than a few disasters—chewy pork chops, gluey mashed potatoes—but successes as well: chicken shish kebobs, chili, a splurge on a rack of lamb where Mark sucked the bones dry. Peri only took a small portion, which left plenty for him.

This is fun, he thought as Peri sliced green peppers and onions while he rubbed salt and pepper over a wedge of flank steak that had been discounted. *It's the simplest thing in the world, two people making a meal together, yet there's nowhere else I'd rather be, nothing else I'd rather be doing, and definitely no one else I'd rather be with.*

He gawked at Peri, his emotions warm, sweet, and homey, like apple pie.

She felt his gaze on her and turned. "Everything okay?"

He slammed his mouth shut. "Great!" he said. The back of his neck heated up at the obvious excitement in the word. He wanted Peri to think he was cool, not some chump in his first real relationship, which was pretty much what he was.

She leaned over and kissed the tip of his nose as he beamed at her. "You can throw in the steaks," she said.

He finally solved his laundry problem. Since he was practically living at Peri's, he went with her one night to her complex's laundry room. He was about to dump all his clothes into one machine, sprinkle powder on top, and toss quarters in the slot when she placed a hand on his arm.

"Have you ever wondered why your white T-shirts aren't white anymore?"

He scuffed his foot against the linoleum. "Maybe," he said, feeling moronic.

"You have to separate by colors. Whites should be washed alone with a little bleach."

"But I only have enough quarters for one load."

"Let's share. I've got a couple of small loads, and you've got one big load." She pinched the toe of a sock that had flopped out of the machine. "One really big load."

After that, he took over laundry. He did it on Sunday when Peri was at lunch with Mr. D. He sorted by colors and textures, his fingers lingering over her underwear, small, soft scraps with lacy edges and perky ribbons. After starting the machines, he settled into one of the hard plastic chairs to watch sports on the black-and-white television bolted to the wall.

"Yes!" he said under his breath the first time he pulled out a tangle of T-shirts that were as white as a full moon.

Peri brought him her leftovers from the fancy French restaurants Mr. D took her to. He plowed through the *boeuf bourguignon* and *coq au vin* while ignoring who'd paid for it and why he'd paid for it.

Mr. D was the shadow that loomed over Mark's happiness. Although they kept their relationship under wraps, he caught Mr. D nodding at him in rehearsals, his lips curled.

Mr. D knew. Not all, but plenty of it.

He and Peri kept things light and friendly at the studio, but Mark couldn't keep feelings this huge hidden. His outlet was *M+M* where he gave his heart a place to run free.

Mr. D was big on filling every movement with emotion. "People come to the ballet to feel what they do not allow themselves to feel in their everyday life."

This meant that Mr. D began his choreography with what the dancers should be feeling. Mark had never taken an acting class before, so he had to trust his instincts. Sometimes, he overdid it, making stupid faces and hammy gestures, which Mr. D said was better than no emotion, but still. Mark didn't want to look like an idiot.

During his scenes with Peri, Mark didn't have to pretend. He just let himself feel. Peri did the same thing, and their dancing was on fire.

Once the music stopped, they went back to acting like they were nothing more than friends.

Their chemistry during rehearsals had drawn curious company members to the windows to watch. Even though no one said anything to him, he picked up on the gossip, which Glenn was the ringleader of.

Glenn had taken it personally that Mark, who was four years younger, had snagged the lead in *M+M*. Glenn ignored Mark except when he talked about Mark behind his back. It bothered Mark—he hadn't done anything to Glenn beyond dance well—but there wasn't much Mark could do. Mark wasn't going to suddenly become a worse dancer, so he could have a friend.

Mark pretended he didn't hear the whispers about Peri and him even though no one could shut up about them.

"She's dancing better than she has in years. Must be the thrill of dancing with someone who could actually do her. Bob couldn't, and Mr. D can't." This was what the girls of the company said about Peri.

As for him, Glenn kept it short and unsweet. "Puppy love," he said under his breath when he walked by Mark and Peri eating lunch together.

Mark pretended not to hear him, but in his head, he yelled, *It's not puppy love. I know Peri. I've smelled her breath in the morning, I've seen her have a snotty cry, and I've listened to her snore. We make dinner together every night. I do our laundry, and she irons it. We are equals.*

Mr. D didn't see it them as equals. He was always asking Peri to help Mark out with this lift or fix that grip.

"Show the boy how to hold your hand," Mr. D would say to Peri as Mark ground his teeth together to keep something stupid from leaving his mouth. He needed this job after all.

I'm sorry, she mouthed to him when Mr. D couldn't see them. Mark told her with eyes that it was okay. And it was. She was just doing what she was told to do.

Mr. D did it to remind her how young Mark was. And so Mark didn't forget how much older Peri was.

The whole thing made Mark uncomfortable but not as uncomfortable as Peri's story about Mr. D. It sounded wrong. Peri had been fifteen, alone, dependent on Mr. D for her paycheck. Mr. D hadn't even asked, just took what he thought was his, and then told her he'd make ballets for her.

Mr. D placed Peri on a pedestal except when he took her down, so he could treat her like his slave. For all the compliments he showered on her, for all the demands he made of her, Mr. D didn't respect her.

Peri treated Mark with respect, which he was grateful for. It was one thing for society to call him an adult. It was another thing to be treated as one by another adult.

Thank you, he telegraphed to her.

En Cloche

(LIKE A BELL)

PERI HADN'T CARED about Christmas in years. Every year, it was the same canned music, the same overflowing shops, the same corny decorations, the same rote sentiments. It was a performance for the public by the public, who only cared that everything was the same this year as it had been all the years before this year.

Maybe if she hadn't been a dancer, Christmas wouldn't bother her so much. But because she was, Christmas meant one thing—*The Nutcracker*. For years, she'd danced the role of Frau Silberhaus, Clara's mother, in the party scene and the Sugar Plum Fairy in Act II. Bob had always played Clara's father and the Sugar Plum Fairy's cavalier.

In the beginning, she'd loved it, basked in the dream coming true. A few years in, she felt like falling asleep every time she heard the overture. She was tired of the noisy children, both onstage and off; the lavender tutu that left a rash under her right breast; the endless performances marching across the December calendar like a line of toy soldiers. After the last show, she retired to her apartment and spent the days sleeping, leaving only to attend Bob's New Year's party.

Bob had always kept her spirits up with wicked jokes and wild pranks. He was a movie buff and used them as inspiration. The year *Star Wars* had come out, he'd spent the *pas de deux* whispering lines about the Force being with her. The year of *E.T.*, he'd hidden a phone onstage during party scene and mimed phoning home. At the end of the run, he'd always given her an extravagant gift like a hand-tooled piece of luggage or a full-day appointment at a spa.

"You're the only woman in my life," he'd say when she protested. "I have to take care of you."

Last year, though, he'd returned from Thanksgiving with a purple splotch on his face.

"It's nothing," he said when she asked.

By the end of the run, he'd developed another one on the bottom of his foot.

He'd attempted a smile as he passed her that year's present—a designer silk scarf—but his eyes were pained.

She hadn't bothered to object, fearful this would be the last Christmas gift she'd get from him.

It was as it turned it out.

While she missed Bob, felt his absence in every note of the music, Mark was there to fill the emptiness. Mr. D had declined to cast Mark in any of the showy roles.

"I am keeping you hidden in plain sight until *The Maiden and the Mountain*," he told Mark. "Get used to the stage. Practice when you find a spare minute."

Mark had opened his mouth to argue, but Mr. D cut him off. "I want you to be fresh for the critics with their sharpened quills to know nothing about you and be pleasantly surprised when they do get to know you."

So Mark moved presents as a footman during party scene and marched as a soldier and stood bare-chested next to the snake charmer's basket during Coffee.

It was a waste of his colossal talent and Mark was restless, but Peri talked him around, and he handled his featherweight duties with resigned grace.

"I know Mr. D's right, but still." He groaned. "Couldn't I at least dance Trepak or something? It's boring to do nothing but stand around."

Peri stood on tiptoe and kissed his forehead. "It'll be worth it in the end."

For her, this was the first time in years the holiday season didn't drag. Mr. D had partnered her with Glenn, who wasn't as good as Bob had been nor as good as Mark would have been, but he was dutiful about hitting his marks and he had a big, fake smile that read as real to the audience.

During rehearsals, Glenn developed a crush on her, which would have been flattering if it hadn't been so annoying. He trailed her out of the studio to talk about Mr. D's notes, and he sought her out to request a few minutes of extra practice.

"I want to be perfect for you," he said, his cheeks matching his ginger hair as he gazed at her with lovesick eyes.

One time, he called her at home to ask if he should assume a deeper plié before the ending shoulder sit. She and Mark had been making a chicken potpie for dinner.

Peri couldn't keep the frustration from poking out of her response until Mark did an exaggerated imitation of Glenn, who had a swayback. Mark stuck his butt out as he bent his knees in a deep plié. Through her giggles, she assured Glenn that the volume of his current plié was just fine.

Although he had big ears and plain features, Glenn was popular with the girls of the company. He drove a motorcycle and had a pompous way of talking. Plus, he was tall and, after Mark, the best male dancer in the company. He never failed to dazzle some naïve apprentice when he whizzed out of the parking lot on his bike, his impression faint through the smog of L.A. and his bike's exhaust.

Peri found him ridiculous and insincere. The motorcycle and the grandiloquence seemed like affectations to attract girls. That, though, was clearly just her, considering the dirty looks thrown her way now that Glenn had winnowed his attention to her rather than the entire corps de ballet.

She couldn't mask her disinterest, which Glenn interpreted as a personal challenge. He doubled up on his compliments and knelt with a Tab in his outstretched hands at the beginning of each rehearsal.

She gave what she could where she could to be nice, but why couldn't Mark have been cast as the Cavalier? They knew each other's bodies, each other's personalities. Mark kept her steady on her feet with his warm, comforting grip, and he lifted her spirits with jokes and grins. Glenn, however, did not know her body, and she was always asking if he could lower his hand here, raise his arm there. He also didn't know her personality, which meant he often said the wrong thing in his desire to say the right thing. He treated her as some rare work of art, using big words and chivalrous gestures to win her over. "Will the beauteous lady do me the honor of accompanying me through the *pas de deux*?" he'd ask, extending a sweaty hand. Peri would disguise her eye roll and accept his wet grip.

During the run of *The Nutcracker*, Glenn wrote her little notes that he shoved under the door to her dressing room.

You looked radiant during the piqué turns, Peri read. *Your balance in first arabesque was stunning.*

Unlike Mark, Glenn could spell, and unlike Mark's smeary swoops, he had painstakingly neat handwriting. She read Glenn's notes aloud to Mark, so he would know she wasn't keeping secrets.

"Glenn is right," Mark said. "You did look radiant in the piqué turns." He pointed to the note "Do you like this?"

Peri shrugged. "It's cute, I guess."

He looked at her with blue eyes graying with worry. "Should I . . ." She squeezed his hand. "Just be you."

Maybe if Peri hadn't met Mark, these efforts would have charmed her, but all she could do was compare Glenn to Mark. Mark was always himself, had never employed a faked word or deed to win her over. Glenn was all polished, desperate adoration, which just made her like Mark more.

Disingenuousness was the weapon of the poor lover, and it, when brandished, couldn't slay earnestness, kindness, and cheerfulness— slender, inconsequential arrows on their own, but powerfully precise when grouped together and leveled at her heart.

Mr. D seemed fine with Glenn's performance, and Peri took comfort that she wasn't worse than last year, so she ignored the *Nutcracker*-less future looming in front of her. Instead, she set to enjoying Mark, who'd become delightfully omnipresent. Her heart thrilled to his presence before freezing mid-thump because, obviously, it wouldn't last. It couldn't.

Mark would tire of her sooner rather than later, realize the impossibility of their age difference, and move on to someone else. Her heart would be flattened, but she couldn't make herself care about that now. She was too overwhelmed by him and his vitality, his virility.

After Mr. D, who wanted so much from her, it was gratifying to spend time with someone who wanted nothing from her beyond simple, pleasant things she enjoyed giving: smiles, kisses, quips, her presence.

Mark found ways to approach her during the party scene to stroke her back or whisper a quick greeting in her ear. When she danced the Sugar Plum Fairy variation, he hung out in the wings, sticking his thumb in the air as his bare chest glowed in stage lights. At intermission, they met by a cluster of furniture from the party scene. Behind the cover of a heavy velvet sofa and two straight-backed chairs that were reminiscent of 19th-century Germany, she sat in Mark's lap.

She left open the hooks and eyes of the tutu's bodice to prevent her rash from getting too itchy, and he tiptoed his fingers up and down her spine. They exchanged silly stories about that evening's performance, and then, when five minutes was called for Act II, they lightly kissed each other on the lips so as not to mess up their makeup.

Once, Glenn caught them pulling away from a kiss that had gone on longer than their typical peck. Mark had been faster than she, her brain foggy, her heart still stuck to his.

"Just making sure she's buttoned up," Mark had said as he latched the hooks and eyes of her tutu.

Glenn squinted, but he'd come too late to see anything. "Will the beauteous lady—"

Peri leaped to her feet. "She will." She slammed her shaking hand into his slick one.

Kissing Mark in public was reckless, but Peri didn't care, couldn't care about any of it: the half-filled houses, the stomach flu that took out half the cast of "Waltz of the Flowers," the whispers from the company about Mark and her—the girls in the corps de ballet had nicknamed her "cradle robber." She only cared about the moments she spent with Mark. Everything that happened in between those was a distraction.

The last performance rolled around, and she couldn't wait for it to be over. She and Mark would have ten glorious days to do whatever they pleased with no class and no rehearsal and no outside obligations beyond one Sunday lunch with Mr. D.

Then, she had to care. Mr. D knocked on the door of her dressing room as she was changing out of her tutu. Peri slipped her arms into a pink sweater and was tying the ends together as he entered. Mr. D had seen her naked hundreds of times before, but if he never saw her naked again, she would only be grateful.

"Peri-jan," he said.

She smiled to cover her irritation.

She'd known Mr. D for fourteen years and been his lover for most of them, yet she never could relax around him. Even their most banal exchanges felt like a performance where he'd cast her as his muse.

Her choreography?

Inspire him with her lightness and brightness, her utter devotion to him and only him, so he could make dances that he, and only he, would receive credit for.

The show had been going for a long time, and the curtain needed to come down.

"You were lovely as always," Mr. D said as his eyes flickered around the dressing room.

Peri flinched although there was nothing incriminating in sight. Her vanity looked the same as it always did. Small tablets of powder and slender tubes of paint were arranged in neat rows. She'd taped holiday cards from various children in the production to the mirror. Her party scene costume, an ornate dress of lilac satin, hung on a rack next to the white-sequined, sweetheart-necked dress she'd wear to the after party tonight. A beribboned box of French chocolates rested on a footstool that Glenn, after pushing down his cowlick, had pressed into her hand as he recited a speech about how the beauteous lady had made this the most special *Nutcracker* yet.

She was all clear.

She managed a tight smile at Mr. D. "Thank you."

Please let this be quick, she thought.

Her gaze drifted over to her dance bag, which held Mark's Christmas presents. Even if Mr. D had X-ray vision and could see it, there was nothing to arouse his suspicion. She was allowed to give Mark something, and a gift certificate to a restaurant that served enormous steaks and a cookbook were hardly romantic although Mark would like them.

Mr. D gestured to her chair. "May I?" Peri jumped up. "Of course."

He settled himself into the chair. "I have bad news."

She cocked her head at him, her heart racing. Bad news?

"Our *Nutcracker* run fell short—very short—of my expectations. The company does not have the funds to do *The Maiden and the Mountain* justice." Mr. D paused. "And *The Maiden and the Mountain* must be done justice."

"Okay," Peri said, unsure as to where this was going.

"And it must be done justice this March." He looked at her, his black eyes opaque. "I may not have another opportunity."

She murmured something comforting. "I have to raise funds immediately." "How?"

"In two days time, I will attend a dinner thrown by our board president where I will solicit the Armenian community."

Mr. D had founded his company in Los Angeles because of the large Armenian population in Glendale, the neighborhood bordering Hollywood. They used to come out in droves to support their fellow countryman, but in the last few years, as Mr. D had stopped making new ballets, they'd dropped off, and the company's fortunes had declined as a result.

Mr. D leaned forward. "You must accompany me. A ballerina in a beautiful dress will be a great asset to my appeal."

Peri counted forward. Two days from now was Christmas Eve. She and Mark were going to decorate a tree and make a pot roast. She had the list of ingredients they needed to purchase tucked into her purse.

"That's Christmas Eve," she said.

Mr. D shook his head. "Not for Armenians. Christmas Eve is January 5."

"I . . ." Her voice faded. She searched for something to say that would get her out of going, but there was nothing beyond the truth, which was that she wanted to spend Christmas Eve with Mark.

Peri's shoulders sagged. She had to go help him raise money. Even if she could find a coherent, believable excuse, how could she say it? It wasn't like Mr. D ever asked. He only issued instructions. Plus, she was dependent on him for her livelihood. Saying no could throw her whole life into a catastrophic tailspin that she, at present, was unequipped to confront.

His gaze flitted over her as if trying to divine her secrets. After a moment of uncomfortable silence, he said, "The car will come for you at seven."

"Okay," she said flatly, unable to disguise her disappointment.

Mr. D hoisted himself to his feet. He cocked his head toward Peri's white cocktail dress. "Enjoy the party with the other children."

12

À la Seconde

(TO THE SECOND)

MARK EXITED THE JEWELRY SHOP, his skin tickling with excitement. He traced his finger over the tiny cube in his jeans pocket. Tucked in its dark velvet was a pearl the shape and color of a full moon, hanging from a skinny gold chain.

The store was four doors down from the studio. He'd seen the necklace a bunch of times in the window, shyly glowing among all the loudly winking diamond rings and bracelets. He stopped to gape at how it reminded him of Peri: small, pale, and perfect.

Today, he'd screwed up his courage to walk in and ask the price. It'd been a little, but not a lot, out of his range, so he shoved a bunch of bills across the counter.

He wanted to throw off some *tour jetés*, change his legs like a switchblade in the air, as he pictured her opening the box, seeing the pearl, a big smile spreading across her face.

Cold sweat dotted his upper lip. What if she didn't like it?

Mark was pretty sure there were no returns or exchanges at the shop. Even if there were, he couldn't imagine going back, admitting he'd messed up, asking for the paltry number of bills back.

She'll like it, he told himself. *She will.*

He turned toward his car to run errand number two—getting the Christmas tree and ornaments—but someone bumped into him, hard. Mark stumbled before catching his balance.

Dancer reflexes.

He turned to find out who'd been so rude.

It was Glenn, scowling at him, his cheeks and hair the color of a Santa hat.

Mark groaned internally. Glenn had started sniffing around Peri during *The Nutcracker*. A couple of times, he'd followed Mark and Peri, and once, they had a near miss when they had to pretend they hadn't just been kissing.

Glenn suspected that Mark and Peri were more than just friends. At this point, the whole company suspected. While the rest of the company didn't care, just looked at them as something fun to gossip about, Glenn did care and he wanted to prove his suspicion.

Mark tossed his hair out of his eyes. "Hey, man."

Glenn pointed to the jewelry store. "What did you buy the beauteous lady?"

Mark thought fast. "What beauteous lady?" He adjusted himself, so the pocket with Peri's present was turned away from Glenn.

Glenn pulled himself to his full height. He was a couple of inches taller than Mark, but Mark didn't feel intimidated. Maybe it was because Glenn, even when he was mad, looked like a goofball with his round face and big ears. Mark didn't look like a ballet dancer out of the studio, but Glenn did so even less.

Glenn was wearing a leather jacket and boots with thick soles. He was about to hop on his motorcycle, a ride Mark thought was dumb— one accident would be all it took to end his career, maybe even his life. But Glenn didn't seem to care. Instead, he made a big deal of carting his helmet around the studio and revving the engine when he left for the day.

Glenn loved to showboat about his bike. He was always buying a new part or waxing poetic about a dangerous trip he'd taken.

"Between Death Valley and Panamint Springs, it's an eighty-five-mile two-lane highway with extreme peaks and valleys." Glenn sketched big zigzags with his finger through the air. "Imagine the cardiogram of someone having a heart attack." He paused for dramatic effect as a few girls leaned in breathlessly. "The first time I made a trip on my bike, the night was so black that it made the inside of a coffin look like high noon."

"So it was hilly and dark," Mark said under his breath.

Glenn glared and opened his mouth to say something to Mark, but Glenn got sidetracked when one of the girls asked about his trip to Bear Valley.

Glenn sounded conceited to him, but the girls in the company dug it, which might be the point, because Glenn was always chasing after this or that girl.

Although Mark and Glenn weren't friends, would never be friends, Mark spent plenty of time alongside him, thanks to the small footprint of the studio, and he had a pretty good read on Glenn's personality. Glenn used his bike like armor. The shiny chrome attracted girls while the booming noise repelled guys who might otherwise try to find his chinks.

Now, Glenn had a crush on Peri, and he seemed pissed that the usual tricks weren't working. Glenn thought—correctly—that Peri wasn't interested in him because she was interested in someone else, to be more exact, Mark, the person Glenn hated.

Mark glanced at Glenn, who hadn't lifted his eyes from him. Glenn's lips were pressed into a hard, angry line although his eyes looked big and hurt. Mark shrugged and turned to go. This showdown with Glenn was stupid. Plus, he wanted to get home before Peri left, so he could see how pretty she looked in the tight silver dress she'd be wearing.

"Are you dating Peri?"

Mark's mouth plunged open. "Uh . . . no, man." He scuffed a foot. "We're just friends."

Glenn tilted his head. "Friends don't hang out behind the party scene sofa, so they can sit in each other's laps. Friends don't look guilty when someone walks in on them after they've been kissing." He gave Mark a knowing look. "Friends don't buy friends jewelry for Christmas."

"I told you. We're just friends." Mark managed a stern tone through the dryness in his mouth. He hated lying. Telling one was like buying something using a credit card. He'd just end up paying more down the line.

Mark stood still and met Glenn's eyes although his heart, smacking inside his chest like a ball in a batter's cage, was probably giving him away.

Glenn dropped the tough-guy posture and pushed down his cowlick. "Hey man. Has she mentioned anything about me to you?"

Mark swallowed. His whole body felt as red and ruffled as Glenn's hair. "Uh-uh."

"Nothing?" Glenn's face was bright and shiny with hope. "We don't talk about stuff like that."

"So what do you talk about?"

"Ballet, the news." He stopped for a moment. "We both like to cook."

Mark searched the strip mall for escape. This conversation was heading toward a bad place because he would slip up sooner rather than later, which was what Glenn was waiting for. He'd made a promise to Peri that he'd keep their relationship a secret, and he didn't want to break it.

Glenn leaned toward him. "Is she still with Mr. D?"

Mark almost whistled with relief. He had an out. "Yeah, man."

Glenn made a noise in the back of his throat. "That would be just my luck." His voice dropped to a whisper. "What does she see in him? He may be the boss, but he's a decrepit old despot."

Mark made a your-guess-is-as-good-as-mine face. He certainly wasn't going to tell Glenn about how Mr. D had tricked Peri into sleeping with him by getting her drunk when she was fifteen.

Neither of them said anything, and the silence between them stretched on and on, like that highway between Death Valley and Panamint Springs.

"You did a great job in *The Nutcracker*," Mark said, just to say something.

And Glenn had, with only minor errors and major smiles.

Glenn's family had flown in for opening night. His dad was a state trooper, and when Glenn brought everybody backstage, Glenn's dad had stood off to the side with crossed arms as Glenn showed his mother and sister around.

Glenn had been thrown in ballet classes when his sister got the bug, but he'd been the one with the talent and the drive so he continued when she stopped. At nineteen, he'd traded the ten thousand lakes of Minnesota for the one giant ocean of California.

Mark's eyes felt hot and itchy. Glenn's dad might not approve of ballet, but at least he'd shown up for his son's big debut. Mark's dad wouldn't be making an appearance for *M+M*.

Glenn half-laughed, half-groaned. "Yeah, man. But not as well as you would have done."

"I didn't mean it like that," Mark said in a rush. He tried to figure out what to say next, but he couldn't think of anything because Glenn had spoken the truth.

Glenn's forehead creased. "Tell Peri I said Merry Christmas."

Mark opened his mouth to respond, but it didn't matter because Glenn was stomping to his motorcycle. He pushed on his helmet and then gunned the engine. The noise spanked Mark's ears, and he had to stop himself from throwing his hands over them.

As Glenn zoomed out of the parking lot, Mark scratched his head, trying to understand their conversation that had corkscrewed from aggression to confession and then back to aggression. Plus, they'd kept calling each other *man*, like it was some weird pet name.

What had Glenn wanted him to say? That Peri liked Glenn back, even though Glenn knew she didn't? That, duh, of course Glenn was right that friends didn't kiss friends behind party scene furniture? That in the battle of sparkly tunics, Mark was always going to win and that wasn't Glenn's fault? That Mark was jealous that Glenn's dad had come all the way from Minnesota to watch Glenn dance when his dad wouldn't drive the handful of miles to see Mark in *M+M*?

It felt like they'd had two conversations. There was the one with words where they'd acted like a couple of billy goats locking horns over the same nanny goat. Then, there was the one with no words where they'd tried to admit how uncomfortable and hard it was to be a man with a job that people assumed made you not a man.

Talking was like music. The notes told the story, but the silences held the truth. He and Glenn had talked about Peri because if they talked about the other stuff, then everyone, themselves included, would wonder if they were real men.

Mark's shoulders slumped. He was doing everything a man did. He was going to a job he liked, doing well at that job, coming home to a great girl, buying jewelry for that great girl. He was on top of his bills, even saved a little, hadn't made any big mistakes beyond falling for Peri, who was still Mr. D's girl.

Yet Mark didn't feel like a man because ballet was what made all those things possible.

Maybe that had to do with his dad, who not only hated that Mark did ballet but, if he knew, would also hate the life Mark had built outside the studio.

His dad had strong ideas about what a man should and shouldn't do. A man shouldn't cook, make beds, or do laundry. Mark's dad didn't even know how to work the microwave, and once, when Mark's mom had a bad case of the flu, he let the laundry pile up. When they ran out of clean socks and underwear, his dad went out and bought more for Mark and him.

But Mark liked cooking dinner with Peri, didn't mind making the bed since he was the last one out of it, felt good that Peri trusted him to wash their clothes. He didn't feel like less of a man doing these things. Plenty of men—pretty much all single men—did these things too, and Mark doubted they felt unmanned by them.

To Mark's dad, men had one job, which was to bring home a good paycheck. His dad was a man because he brought home a paycheck by playing baseball, which was something a man did, and even more important, something other men approved of.

Ballet was not something other men did, and it was definitely not something other men approved of. Mark learned early to keep his mouth shut after blabbing, once, to a guy in his social studies class who seemed cool. Mark talked up the high points of ballet. The rows of girls in skimpy clothing he got to stare at. The high jumps and fast turns he got to do. The grand music he got to listen to. The guy, though, had sneered at Mark.

"Dancing is for fags," he said.

The sneer reminded Mark of his dad, who'd do it anytime he saw a man doing something that seemed unmanly.

"What type of guy plants tulips?" his dad would say, pointing a finger at one of the neighbors who took pride in his flower bed.

His mom's brother baked wedding cakes for a living, which his dad found hilarious.

"He must be gay," his dad had commented more than once even though his uncle had been married twice and had three kids.

But for all his jeering, his dad didn't seem much like a man, sitting in his easy chair, watching television, yelling at Mark's mom to bring him another beer. Although his dad had been unemployed for years, he fulfilled his job as a man by growing the money he'd made from playing baseball.

"I'm working," Mark's dad would say if Mark made a sound during the morning hours when his dad was still sober. "Someone's got to keep this family going," he'd say as he traced his finger over rows of numbers on financial statements.

It was convenient, really. By making being a man this small, easy-to-perform role, his dad could be a man without doing much or risking anything, the things that made a man, a man.

Why was his dad like this?

Maybe it had to do with Mark's dad's dad. Mark only had faint memories of his grandfather, who died of lung cancer when Mark was four. Mostly, he remembered him as a big guy with a cigarette dangling from his lips and a laugh sticky with mucus. Mark's dad referred to Mark's grandfather as Daddy Asshole, after which, his mom would shush him. Supposedly, his grandfather was a big believer in unbuckling his belt anytime his dad stepped a toe out of line.

But that couldn't explain everything. Because if anybody deserved the title Daddy Asshole, it was Mark's dad, and yet Mark didn't act like his dad. To be more exact, Mark tried not to act like his dad.

Maybe it had to do with the world of baseball where a bunch of dudes—whose sole goal was to win games against a bunch of other dudes—spent months on the road with only each other for company. It had to get tense, weird, lonely. Maybe being an asshole was his dad's way of coping with other assholes. And once his dad started being an asshole, it was too hard to stop being one.

But that couldn't explain everything. Mark had met some of his dad's teammates, gone to their kids' birthday parties, and they weren't flaring up at the smallest, stupidest things. Some of them were even nice, chatting with Mark about school, making sure his mom had a choice slice of cake.

Maybe it had to do with bad luck. A foul ball smacked his dad upside the head. Not his fault. His dad tried hard to get better, but he couldn't get his balance back. Not his fault. His dad finally had to quit playing baseball. Not his fault.

But that couldn't explain everything. Injuries were part of sports, just like ballet. Guys were sidelined for weeks, months, sometimes years with issues. They found other things to fill the time, the space. The shortstop who used to be his dad's best friend had torn his ACL while diving for a ball. He was older, in his late thirties, so after the injury, he cashed out and ran toward retirement like it was home plate. He enjoyed cards, got good at poker, went to Vegas every couple of months to win fat stacks of cash. When Mark's dad got injured, he did the opposite. Froze everything and everyone out.

Maybe it was all these things. Maybe it was none of these things. Who knew why his dad was the way he was? And, really, why did the *why* even matter? His dad was awful, would probably always be awful, because he thought he had a right to be awful as long as he had a decent chunk of change to his name.

Mark looked toward the sky, which had turned light purple. He elbowed his thoughts from his head. He had to get going if he was going to buy a tree and get home in time to give Peri a goodbye kiss before she left for the *M+M* fundraising dinner.

13

Coupé

(CUT, CUTTING)

THE FUNDRAISING DINNER WAS ENDLESS, one of those affairs where everyone knew everyone else and had so for decades. Peri twirled a squishy hunk of crème brûlée around her fork as she made polite chitchat with a doctor in his sixties on her left and a lawyer in his seventies on her right.

The questions were always the same. "What's your favorite ballet?" "Where did you train?"

"Is this your only job?"

"Really?" They always asked the last with big, surprised eyes. Her answers were always the same.

"I love all of Mr. D's ballets."

"A local studio in Pittsburgh and then a top school in New York." "This is, in fact, my only job."

"Really." She said this firmly.

As the evening wore on, the doctor, who wore a wedding ring, leaned in close to find reasons to touch her. She deflected as best she could, turning her attention to the lawyer, who, blessedly, was not creepy. They talked about his upcoming trip to London and their mutual dislike of shellfish.

When she had nobody to talk to, she gazed around the hotel ballroom, ordinary in its grandeur with chandeliers roped with crystals and an ornately patterned blue carpet.

Inside, Peri's patience was shriveling. She wanted Mr. D to make his speech, collect the checks, and call for the car, so she could go home. It wasn't that late. Mark might still be up, watching television or listening to the radio. She could wash her face, hang up her dress, and snuggle with him while having a conversation that she would enjoy.

She adjusted the slashing neckline of her dress, a slippery column of silver with one long ruched sleeve. Mark had returned home, right as she was leaving, kicking off his sneakers, his cheeks rosy, pine needles sticking out of his hair.

After giving her a catcall, he'd said, "There was a battle between the tree and me, but I won." He widened his eyes. "But barely. I had no idea those things were so hard to carry." He mimed carrying a tree that kept slipping out of his hands. "And so prickly."

Mark hadn't been pleased that their plans for Christmas Eve had been foiled.

"Can't he ask someone else?" he asked. "We have plans." "Who else? I'm the Maiden."

"You're not going to . . ."

"Of course not," she said although her mouth went dry. She wouldn't have to, would she? It'd been at least a year since Mr. D had ushered her into his home.

He shrugged. "So we'll make up for it on Christmas Day," he said, his grin lifting her frown.

Peri kissed Mark lightly to keep from smearing her lipstick, grateful for his good humor, even more grateful for him.

She twisted a lock of hair that had escaped from her French twist. She needed to rein in her feelings for Mark. Because it wasn't a question of if but when Mark realized she was too old for him. She'd tried to police her heart, but it refused to cooperate. How could it when it was so easy, so fun, so natural to be with him?

She was roused from her thoughts by the ballet's board president, tall and slender like a reed, tapping a spoon against his wineglass. He swept through his opening marks, hitting the high points of gratitude and light humor before introducing Mr. D.

"When people hear the name Levon Dektember, they think of the choreographer whose decadent ballets have entranced audiences for half a century. But Levon is an Armenian first, and tonight, he approaches you, Armenian to Armenian, to discuss his latest project."

Mr. D limped to the podium, pushing his cane deep into the floor with each step. He'd arranged his face into a pleasant expression, but his knuckles were pale from clutching the cane so tightly.

At the podium, Mr. D twisted the microphone toward him. He

tried to take a sip of water, but it splattered on the lapel of his white suit. He dabbed at the drops and then took a deep breath.

Mr. D was nervous.

But why? He'd done these appeals before.

"I have often been asked why I became a choreographer," he said, his voice shrill through the mic's amplification. "I have never told anyone the truth. Instead, I lied and said there was no better place to spend my time than in a studio with beautiful women." He looked out into the crowd. "But tonight, surrounded by fellow Armenians, I will tell you why."

Peri blotted her lips and prepared her best listening face.

"Growing up, I could see Mount Ararat from my home. The river Tigris flowed through our village. My family didn't have much, but we had enough. My father was the town's tailor, and my mother was a seamstress who took in odd work. Our bellies were full more times than not, and there was plenty to occupy a curious child like me. At night, my mother would tuck my younger sister into bed and tell us folktales. *The Golden-headed Fish. The Clever Weaver.* And the one my sister requested every time, *The Maiden and the Mountain*," he said in a flat voice.

Her scalp prickled. What terrible thing was he going to tell them? "In 1915, two days before my thirteenth birthday, the Turkish gendarmes in their bucket-shaped hats came to exile us. There was no time to pack, only to panic," he said. "I walked alongside my mother. My father carried my sister on his shoulders as she was recovering from a bad cold. While walking and walking, we were beaten with sticks, whips, and clubs. They shot people who were slow, anyone who tripped. Although my sister was small, my father struggled because he had a weak back. He carried her until he couldn't. He took her off his shoulders and told her that she had to walk like her mother."

Mr. D gazed off into the distance as if reliving the scene. "He made it another half mile before his back had a spasm." He paused. "He tripped."

Peri's jaw dropped. Around her, people were reacting in one of two ways. The younger ones, like Peri, clasped their hands over their mouths and stared at Mr. D with horror-filled eyes while the older ones nodded in grim agreement.

"Eventually, we reached the northern part of the desert near the town of Mardin, where the trains passed to Aleppo."

Mr. D looked down and then up again. Peri's mouth went dry, her knees weak.

He was going to tell them something even more awful.

"The gendarmes made us stop in a field." He paused. "It was green, quiet, peaceful. They separated the adults from the children. There were about three hundred adults, perhaps four hundred children. The adults were made to strip out of their clothes. My mother, ever enterprising, had sewn a few gold coins into the hem of her dress."

Mr. D's voice faded.

"Although we were divided from our mothers, the field was flat enough that we could watch what was happening. They stripped the women one by one, cut off their heads with an ax, and then threw them into the valley."

Peri gasped.

"My mother was at the end of the line. She kept running to where I was to kiss me and to tell me to look after my sister. She could do this because she gave her gold coins to the guards. The fourth and final time she was in her white underwear. She kissed us over and over. She made me promise I would do everything to keep my sister safe. Although I was only thirteen, I knew it would be the last kiss I'd get from her." He didn't say anything for a long while. "It was." His voice maintained the same cold, gray tone as if he were reading lines from a history book.

Peri wanted to shut her eyes, throw her hands over her ears, so she could tune out Mr. D's story.

"They killed her," he said. "Not more than two minutes later, there was an uproar. Armed Persians appeared and slaughtered the Turkish gendarmes. The Shah had issued a decree that whoever brought an Armenian, be it child or adult, would receive a gold coin. The soldiers gathered the children and the few adults who'd found enough favor with God to escape death. They were going to take us to Persia, so they could get their gold coins."

Peri sat rigidly in her seat. *This has a happy ending, right?* she thought. *You ended up here, in Hollywood, making ballets.*

Mentally, she smacked herself. Her words were ridiculous. He'd watched the murder of his mother and father. There was no happy ending after that, just a lifetime of trying to forget.

Mr. D continued his story, no emotion rippling beneath the surface of his placid face. "As they lined us up, an old sheikh with a beard halfway down his chest came to us. He asked if anyone could sew. He promised wheat for lavash, milk, a place to sleep if someone would sew dresses for his women." Mr. D's shoulders drooped. "No one said yes, so I did. I'd grown up sewing alongside my mother and father, and while I wasn't a master, I could sew well enough to fulfill my promise to my mother and keep my sister safe."

A corner of Peri's heart chipped off and sank where it buried itself in a fold of her guts. Mr. D had made all those white suits he wore.

She pictured them in their respective homes, feeding fabric through their machines, taking ordinary things—color, texture, effort, skill—and making them into something beautiful, their loneliness stitched into silhouettes that belied their inspiration.

Peri hadn't been sewing as much since Mark had become her—

She cut off her thoughts. She'd been about to say boyfriend. Mark wasn't her boyfriend. He was her . . .

She pressed her lips together. She didn't know what Mark was beyond he gave her the elusive, precious gift of happiness.

Thank you, she telegraphed to him, imagining him asleep on the sofa, hair hanging in his eyes, arms flung wide so he could embrace the world.

"The sheikh laughed."

Peri roused herself from her thoughts of Mark, so she could pay attention.

"As he should. I was a boy of thirteen. How could I possibly know how to sew? So the sheikh repeated the offer. No one volunteered. Finally, frustrated, he threw a few gold coins at the Persian behind me and gestured for my sister and me to follow. So we did."

Mr. D sipped water. "For months, I sewed for the women. The sheikh kept his promise. We ate, not enough. We slept, not well. But we stayed alive as long as I kept sewing. It is why my spine, after years spent in the ballet studio, bows. It is looking for the sewing machine," he said. "My sister helped where she could. She did simple embroidery, brought me fabric and thread, made fava beans in oil for breakfast, and dzhash for dinner." Mr. D closed his eyes, silent for a moment.

Peri wanted to throw her hands up, prevent him from telling another horror, but he continued.

Mr. D opened his eyes. "Then, the sheikh died."

He looked at Peri, whose heart stuttered in panic. What did he want from her? A smile? A sympathetic frown?

Lightness and brightness, Peri-jan, she heard him say in her head.

That is what I need from you. She cocked her head at him and lifted her lips in the best approximation of a smile she could manage. He nodded and continued.

"With nowhere to go and no way to get there, we were swept into a convoy of women and children passing through Mardin. Our destination? The Deir ez-Zor camps." Mr. D's voice went low. "You have heard of Auschwitz, no? This was the original Auschwitz. Except there was no camp planned for us, just open air and our own wits. We cooked grass, ate dead birds, drank from puddles. The governor general was the loyal Zeki Bey—an Ottoman barbarian. The guards of the camp were no better. They denied us everything unless we could bribe them. I had a few coins from the sheikh, and I used them whenever our situation became dire."

Peri's faux smile split into an appalled *o*. Around her, the audience issued a collective gasp. Desperate to look at something other than Mr. D, she gazed around the hotel ballroom, a place that, just a handful of minutes earlier, had seemed ordinary. Now, its elegant corners were soiled by the story unfolding within them. Maybe the next event, a corporate dinner or a fiftieth-anniversary party, wouldn't notice, but the pall had been cast.

"Then, something even more terrible happened. My sister went through puberty. She had always been a beautiful girl, but now, she was a beautiful woman. Everywhere she went, men were staring, following her. She did what all young, beautiful women do. She fell in love. At any other time this would have been cause for celebration. He was a young medical student from a good family. He had managed to stay alive thanks to his ability to set a guard's broken arm or mix an ointment to ease a rash." Mr. D fiddled with the button on his suit jacket.

"But my sister had another admirer. One of the guards. He would slip us food and tell us the news about the war. I begged her to avoid the medical student and submit to the guard, so we could stay alive." For the first time since Mr. D had started speaking, his voice registered emotion—anger and regret directed at himself. "But we had been through so much that I relented. She managed for a while, but the guard discovered her kissing the medical student." Mr. D stared into the distance.

Peri's heart felt like a black hole, dark and overburdened, knowing where the story was going but wishing it would go anywhere else.

Next to her, the lawyer held his head in his hands. "He lost his family," he said. "That is a fate worse than death to an Armenian."

"He killed them. A gunshot to each of their hearts." Mr. D's voice dropped. "I had failed my mother, but I could do one thing—avenge my sister's death. So I used the last coin I had and paid another guard to do it. He thought it was great fun. He brought me the body. I removed the uniform off the guard and hid it. Although I did not know at the time, God was directing my actions because Zeki Bey was planning to kill us Armenians. He did not have enough men to do it himself, so he recruited those who had committed massacres in Ras-ul Ayn. They would lead a few thousand men to the hills to kill them or to take them to the caves to burn them."

Peri flinched, overcome by Mr. D's story. How had she never heard about this? Her grasp on history was slight, but still. Was this a chapter of World War I her teachers had never gotten to?

"When they came, I put on the uniform of the slain guard and looked official. I rarely spoke, and I never drew attention to myself. The uniform had blood on it, so I can only imagine they assumed I was spooked from being wounded. It worked, time and time again."

Mr. D lifted his cane and slammed it down. "They killed Armenians because it was profitable. Because the scent of money was stronger than that of blood. They took clothing, jewelry, what few coins anybody had—like it was payment for slaughter."

Peri hadn't stopped listening, but she had stopped processing. The horror was too great to comprehend.

"In 1918, the victorious British forces entered Syria. At that point, there were only a thousand of us Armenians left. I took off the uniform, stole a donkey, and set off toward Mardin. I found the field where they had slaughtered my mother. I looked into the pit, which was piled high with bones from the victims. I could not cry. I would not pray. Instead, I stood for a long time like a stone. Then, it began to rain, so I walked into town. There, an American soldier asked me if I wanted to move to his country. I said yes immediately."

Peri threaded her fingers through each other. *Please let the story get better*, she prayed.

"I spent five years in New York, working in the garment district, trying to find my place in the world, until I followed a girl to Paris. She did not work out, but Paris did. A few months later, a friend took me to the ballet."

He smiled for the first time. "I met God again, who showed me a way forward. Because I had seen so much ugliness, I knew it could only be fought with a powerful weapon—ballet. So I devoted myself to it. I shed my old name and identity, renamed myself Levon Dektember. I was too old and broken to ever be much of a dancer, but

I could make dances that would combat ugliness with beauty." Mr. D made eye contact with several people in the audience. Peri guessed they were the ones with deep pockets. "Because beauty is the most potent weapon of all."

Around Peri, people were nodding.

"So I have made beauty, feeling that I have tried to do my part, until I ran into a new ugliness."

Peri closed her eyes. Mr. D was going to talk about Bob, about AIDS. Her heart, already heaving after Mr. D's story, wasn't steady enough to handle this.

I wish you were here, she said to Bob, wherever he was. *You would know how to handle this. How to make it better.*

"In November, we lost Robert Winslow, a talented dancer and wonderful man, to a different type of genocide—AIDS. One that, much like the Armenian genocide, many would prefer to sweep under a rug and pretend does not exist." Mr. D tilted his head in her direction. "His dance partner, Peridot Jones, is here."

Peri waved. She tried to smile, but her lips refused to lift.

"Bob danced the lead in every piece I made over the last fourteen years. Now, I want to honor Bob." Mr. D paused. "And my family." Mr. D looked into the audience. *"The Maiden and the Mountain.* Perhaps you know the story?"

"My mother used to tell it to me," the lawyer on her right whispered. "It is a wonderful fairy tale, one of my favorites."

"This ugly world needs beauty more than ever. Tonight, I am asking if you will . . ." Mr. D trailed off. Women were reaching into their handbags, men into their wallets.

He was going to get the money. More than enough.

Around her, the world slackened and blurred. In slow motion, people approached the podium, their hands laden with cash and checks or promises of a donation scrawled on a cocktail napkin. Mr. D shook hands, kissed cheeks, bowed gratefully over their contributions. Peri's stomach coiled around itself, troubled by the tawdry commerce of the last hour. Mr. D hadn't wanted to tell that story. But he'd excavated his darkest secret and exhibited it for everyone to see in exchange for money, so he could make what might be his last ballet.

And then what? He died, and his ballets faded into the ether, his weapon against ugliness too fragile to resist the erosion of time.

The crowd thinned until it was just Mr. D, Peri, and a few younger Armenians huddled at a table. Mr. D gestured to her. She followed him to the waiting car, each step a numb thud. She couldn't wait to get home, away from him, his past. Although none of the terrible things had happened to her, she felt, by association, their witness, the person who could give testimony to exactly how god-awful one person could be to another.

Mark would be asleep, but that was okay because she was shattered. She wanted nothing more than to slip into his arms and succumb to an empty sleep where she could forget tonight.

Mr. D had other ideas. His black eyes, normally opaque, were shiny with desire for the comfort that one body could offer another.

When the car reached his home, he bowed and extended his hand, the decorative cross he wore poking out of his dress shirt. "Come, Peri-jan."

Peri fought back the bile that was forcing its way up her throat. She turned her head and rustled through her purse, pretending she hadn't heard.

"Peri-jan." Mr. D's tone was flinty.

She didn't want to, but how could she not? She struggled for an excuse, but there was none, just Mr. D with his hand out, frowning, displeased at her.

She placed her hand in his as an image of Mark, pine needles stuck in his hair, flashed in her head.

14

Entrechat

(INTERWEAVING OR BRAIDING)

MARK BLINKED HIMSELF AWAKE, pushing back the hair that was flopping in his face. The pop of the front door opening had woken him up. He'd been having a dream, a good one, about him, Peri, and a beach. She'd been in a bikini, laughing, as they raced toward the ocean.

He pushed himself to a sitting position. Peri's sofa, a hard hot dog bun of beige, was like sleeping on a board.

He massaged his neck. *Boards might be more comfortable*, he thought. Peri came into focus. Her mascara was splattered on her cheeks, her lipstick chewed off. Her hair had pulled loose from its twist, and it hung around her shoulders in chunks.

"What time is it?" he asked, as his brain frantically tried to assemble the facts.

Peri dropped her purse on a table near the front door. "Four in the morning."

"Did the party go that long?"

She walked over and perched on the arm of the sofa. "No." Mark stood. "Then where were you?"

"I was with Mr. D."

Mark took in her messy appearance again. The gears of his brain rolled into understanding. "What?" he shouted. "Did you . . ."

"I had to," she whispered.

Red heat was rising from deep inside of his gut, blurring his judgment, tempting him.

"Goddammit, Peri. You're my . . . " He trailed off. He wanted to say girlfriend. That's how he thought of her although he'd never asked.

She looked at him, her pixie features white and pained. "Technically, I'm Mr. D's."

The heat had risen to his eyebrows, and Mark couldn't feel anything beyond its warmth. He was going to suffocate if he didn't fight his way out.

Not thinking, just acting, he punched one of the stiff cushions on the sofa. It felt so good he did it again. He raised his fist to do it a third time when Peri called out.

"Mark!"

He looked up. Peri had run from the sofa and was cowering next to the Christmas tree he'd wrangled into the car, up the steps, and through her apartment door. He'd decorated it with a strand of colored lights, three-dozen silver balls, and a star that was listing like a drunk. His present for Peri, clumsily wrapped in paper printed with cartoon Santas, lay under the tree.

A memory unglued itself and whizzed to the front of his head. He was eleven and it was Christmas and Mark had been waving around the lightsaber he'd gotten as a present and he accidentally swiped the tree with it and a bulb had tumbled off and it hit the floor with a crack and shiny glass sprayed everywhere and his dad was screaming about what an idiot Mark was and his mom was saying she would clean it up and Mark was trying not to cry because he hadn't meant to do it and then his dad shook his fist at Mark and he told Mark that he'd ruined Christmas.

The red heat vanished. He dropped on the sofa, crossed his arms, and clamped his lips together.

I'm not turning into him, he told himself. *I'm not.*

"I'm going to take a shower," Peri said. She came up behind him and kissed the top of his head. "Don't leave. Please."

Mark sat on the sofa, trying to organize the runaway horses of his thoughts into something logical. After a few minutes of frantic thinking, he reached some order.

Peri had slept with Mr. D tonight.

She'd slept with Mr. D before.

Mark didn't want her to sleep with Mr. D.

He wanted her to sleep only with him.

They had to be open with their relationship.

Mark breathed out, his mood lifting. Being open sounded great. He could ditch his crappy room and officially move in with Peri. They would come and go from the studio as they wanted, in one car. There'd be no more weirdness with Glenn following them and trying to get Mark to admit he was dating Peri. Peri could stop having those lunches with Mr. D, and they would start doing their own things together on Sundays like lounge in bed until noon, go out for their own lunches, or hang out at the beach where maybe Peri would wear that bikini from his dreams.

He elbowed the cushion, which refused to fluff. Maybe they could even pool their cash and buy a new sofa.

The bathroom door opened, and he turned. Peri was walking toward him in a silky blue robe, a towel wrapped around her hair. She was carrying a brush.

Peri had three brushes. One was for when her hair was wet, and she didn't want it to tangle; another was for when she blow-dried her hair, and she wanted it to be wavy; the last was for when she'd put her hair in a bun, and she wanted to smooth down wisps.

"Wetty, Wavy, and Smoothy," she'd explained, naming each brush as if it were a favorite doll.

Girls.

Mark had a comb. As in one.

Peri sat beside him on the sofa. She removed the towel and shook out her hair. Something wet and pink rushed up his nose.

Roses after the rain, he thought as he shifted uncomfortably, embarrassed by his bad poetry and Peri's effect on him. He'd liked plenty of girls before, but it'd never been like this.

"I'm sorry," Peri said. She took the brush—it was Wetty—and hiked trails through her hair. "I really am."

"Do you love him?"

She stopped with the brush halfway through her hair. "No." "How do you feel about him?"

"When I was younger, impressed. Now, sad." She hesitated. "He's old and he's lonely and he's scared. He's made all these ballets, but what's going to happen to them when he dies? He thought he was making things that meant something, but nobody is going to care in the future. Even if someone does care, they're not going to care the way he cares." She finished the brushstroke with emphasis.

Her face scrunched up as if she was going to cry. Mark reached out an awkward hand and patted her knee. He connected with more force than he meant to because he was still pissed. He inhaled, blowing his anger to the sidelines. He patted her knee, this time gently, carefully.

"Did he get the money?" Mark kept his voice neutral.

Peri nodded. "But only because he told this awful story about his childhood. It was like the Holocaust, but thirty years earlier and in Armenia."

"Does he love you?"

Peri lifted her eyes to him, more gold than brown now. "I don't think he can love."

She didn't say anything for a while. Then, she slipped out of her robe and stood before Mark, naked and helpless. "After the class he watched in New York, he pulled me into an empty studio. He asked me my name. I told him, 'Peridot, but I go by Peri.'"

She turned, so she was backing him. She traced the outline of her shoulder blades, pale and sticking out like snowy peaks. "As he was doing this, he said, 'Peri means fairy in Armenian. I have been looking for one all my life.'"

She faced him, her chest shaking. "I felt so lucky. This brilliant choreographer had picked me out of a class full of girls. I was moving to California where it would be warm and sunny. I was going to be paid to dance." Peri didn't say anything for a while. "But I didn't know what being Mr. D's fairy meant."

Mark leaned toward her. "I want us to be out in the open. No more taking two cars, no more kissing behind party scene furniture, no more pretending like we're not together when we are."

He froze as Peri's mouth dropped open.

"Are you asking me to be your . . ." Her voice faded. Mark tossed his hair back. "Yes."

Peri pushed her arms into the robe. "I don't know." She looked at Mark, biting her lip. "I'm eleven years older than you."

"I don't care about that." "You will one day."

"This isn't one day. This is today," he said.

I don't care about the age difference, Mark thought. *I'll rise up to its challenges. I won't ask you to come down to me.*

"Don't you want to date someone your age?"

He shook his head. "I want to keep doing what we're doing but without pretending we're not doing it."

"Mr. D . . ."

Can bite me, Mark thought. He didn't want to say this to Peri, so instead, he said, "Mr. D will come around."

She opened her mouth to give him another reason why it wouldn't work even though it was working. To cut her off, he leaped up and kissed her. In that kiss, he told her that everything was going to be okay, that he meant it when he said he didn't care about the age difference, that he didn't want to be with anybody but Peri. She seemed to understand because they kissed for a long time. When they pulled away, Mark's heart was going in crazy circles like a Tilt-A-Whirl. He tipped his head toward Peri.

Please say yes, he telegraphed to her.

"After *M+M*." She laid her head on his chest. "It might be Mr. D's last ballet."

Mark wanted to high-five himself. He'd have to wait until March for it to be official, but still. Peri was his girlfriend.

He held out his pinky to her. "Swear?" She hooked hers around his. "Swear."

$\sim$

Mark burped, too full and sleepy to care.

That was one good meal, he thought.

He and Peri had made their first pot roast, and it'd come out surprisingly tasty. He ate way more than he should, but how could he say no to seconds and thirds and even fourths when there was that much food and it was that good.

Mark rubbed his stomach, which was sticking out. It'd been a great day. They slept in, and he woke up to find Peri on top of him, her braid tickling his neck.

"Merry Christmas," she whispered.

It was a *Merry* Christmas. He flung his arms around Peri.

They ate breakfast listening to holiday music on the radio and then opened presents. His mom had managed to get him a package of new T-shirts via his dance teacher, white for the studio and bright ones for the streets, plus she'd included a hundred bucks. Her signature was the only one on the card, which was fine by Mark. If his dad knew where Mark was and what he was doing there, he'd freak out.

Asshole.

Mark's lips drooped.

He hated that he couldn't see his mom. He missed her, but they couldn't take the risk of meeting up. His mom couldn't tell a lie, no matter how much she wanted to. Even if she managed to squeak out some untruth, her face would give her away. Supposedly being honest was a good quality, but his mom would be better off if she could tell a lie. Then, they could see each other, his dad wouldn't find out, and his mom would be safe from the worst of his dad's temper.

Since she couldn't keep it from his dad, Mark wouldn't take the risk. He didn't want her dealing with the screaming that would go on for hours; the insults about Mark and his lack of masculinity; the threats to hurt her, to hurt Mark, to hurt himself.

His mom thought his dad would eventually miss Mark and accept Mark's career as a ballet dancer. Mark doubted that. His dad hated anything that seemed gay, and ballet seemed gay to his dad, even though Mark was not gay when he started ballet and was not gay after doing ballet for years. And, even if he were gay, it wouldn't be ballet that had made him gay.

I enjoy dancing, he wanted to tell his dad. *Just like you enjoyed playing baseball. Because we both like sweating, moving, challenging ourselves to do hard things. Ballet may be an art and baseball a sport, but they're not that different. They're both about being the best and making the people who are watching happy.*

He pushed thoughts of his parents out of his head. It might be the first Christmas he'd spent away from his mom, but Mark couldn't complain. He had a lot to be thankful for, to be more exact, Peri and his job, both thanks to ballet.

Mark picked up the paper and flicked through it, searching for a story about the teacher who was going into space in January on the Space Shuttle Challenger. He and Peri had been following it for the last month. Hopefully, they'd be able to watch the launch in a few weeks. He sighed when he got to the last page—nothing.

He turned on the television and flipped through the channels, looking for a show that wasn't Christmassy. Mark froze, the remote hanging limply from his hand. Something yellow moving in a box of black had caught his eye.

In costumes the color of dandelions, dancers lined the perimeter of a stage, standing stock-still. One couple in center posed with the woman in profile, her leg extended in a *tendu derrière* while, behind her, the man had his legs apart in second position. A violin squealed.

He sat up. "Peri, come see."

She exited the kitchen, wiping her hands on a dishtowel. She preferred to dry since hot water irritated her skin. That was fine with him. He liked to wash, scrubbing and scraping the plates until they shone.

"Ballet!" she said as she touched the tiny pearl at her neck. She'd done this a few times already as if reminding herself it was there.

Mark wanted to jump up-and-down. She liked it. For real.

From the television, a British voice was saying, "Choreographer James Prescott has always loved dancing. He grew up in a suburb outside New York City where his first memory was imitating Fred Astaire. Later, to make friends in high school, he entered dance contests, impressing his classmates with the Twist and the Mashed Potato. It wasn't until he went to college in Florida that he received formal ballet training. He danced with companies in New York before following his wife to West Germany. He premiered his first piece soon after where he displayed his signature ethos of mashing, smashing, and twisting ballet's rigid perfectionism. Prescott was recently installed as the artistic director . . ."

Mark stopped listening, so he could watch.

Two guys led two girls to whack out grand battements, their pointe shoes smacking the air. Then, the guys helped the girls slice into fast *penchées*, where their legs struck six o'clock. Around them, the army of dancers gestured like graceful cheerleaders.

Then, stuff started happening that his ballet vocabulary couldn't name, so Mark reached for simpler sports terms: slide, punch, lean, turn, kneel.

This was ballet on steroids. Everything was angular or off-balance or lightning quick. Nothing was polite or calm, no pomp, no circumstance, just the human body pushed to its limit and then past it. The partnering was angry, violent even, the girls giving back what they took from the guys.

His brain struggled to keep up with the actions that were exploding like a hail of fire where the body was both bullet and gun. The two couples were in the air and then on the floor or maybe they'd chewed a pathway from one side of the stage to the next.

It was their spines. They weren't the up-and-down spines of ballet where the head was always the highest point. These went every which way. The floor was the only line that didn't change.

The dancing dissolved into James Prescott's face. He had hangdog features and thinning brown hair. His eyes sparked with intelligence behind horn-rimmed glasses.

"Choreography is not about the actuality or the specificity of a movement," James Prescott said. "It's about arranging. Arranging bodies. Arranging bodies with other bodies, against other bodies. To music, against music. Layering and splicing and collaging."

Mark tried to repeat the words back to himself, but he got confused because the video had cut to a clip of James Prescott dancing by himself in an airy studio, his arms swinging, his torso swaying, his legs sometimes doing ballet steps but plenty of times just sticking out at awkward angles.

"Improvisation is a cornerstone of Mr. Prescott's process," intoned the voice-over. "Using the points and lines of the human body, he has created a movement vocabulary that operates as a system of numbers. This numeric vocabulary can be organized into an endless array of problem-solving operations. He says, 'It's how he subdues ballet rather than having it subdue him.'"

On screen, James Prescott pressed his wrists together and then wound and unwound them to make hunks of space between his arms and his torso. "Using the pressure of one body part on the other, I rotate them as far as I can," Prescott said.

Mark took his wrists and pressed them together to recreate what James Prescott had done, but he got distracted and his arms went limp. On screen, one of the couples in yellow was oozing through a slinky *pas de deux* as the corps de ballet lay on their backs like a row of paper dolls.

The program broke for a commercial.

"Wow!" Peri said. Both of them were leaning forward, barely breathing.

Mark couldn't find any words, so he got up and did what he'd seen. He pushed his hips forward and flexed his wrists. He made himself move faster yet maintain the size of his steps.

Crack.

While arcing his leg like a curveball through a *grand rond de jambe*, he'd knocked a glass off the end table. He stared at the shards scattered in a puddle of Tab and ice. Their jagged edges and jumbled positioning gave him ideas, things to try with his body, with other bodies.

It's about arranging. Arranging bodies. Arranging bodies with other bodies, against other bodies, he said to himself, pasting James Prescott's words in his brain.

"Are you okay?" Peri asked.

He took a mental snapshot of the broken glass and forced himself to return to reality.

"Sorry," he said. "I got excited."

She smiled although it didn't reach her eyes. "It was exciting." She jumped up. "I'll clean this up. Keep dancing, Mark."

15

Balancé

(ROCKING STEP)

PERI LOCKED eyes with herself in the bathroom mirror as she prepared to begin her morning ritual, something that had once taken a few minutes but had since expanded to close to an hour. She'd always cared about her appearance, but now, with Mark in her life, she took special pains.

Under the harsh fluorescent light, she guided her face toward the mirror's silvery surface to confront her reflection.

"Mirror, mirror on the wall," she said. "How far will my face doth fall?"

She smiled. Pitchforks of delicate lines radiated from the corners of her eyes. She frowned. Furrows sprung up between her eyebrows. In neutral, her face was wrinkle-free and blemish-free.

It wasn't bad for almost thirty; it was good even. She looked younger than her actual age, thanks to spending her days in the studio rather than the sun.

But for how long?

She could hold time at bay, but it would come for her sooner or later. She would wrinkle and go gray and gain weight, no matter how hard she tried, because gravity would always be stronger than her will.

Peri sighed and reached for her moisturizer. It was expensive and probably not much better than what she could buy at a drugstore, but she'd been seduced by its promise to reverse aging. She shook the slender tube, squirted a globule on her finger, added another spurt for good measure, and then massaged it into her skin, using the gentle strokes the woman at the cosmetics counter had shown her.

It was less than forty days until the premiere of *M+M*, and everyone was excited. Or, if you were Peri, on edge. It was the first piece Mr. D had choreographed in years, so the company had caught a second wind. Ticket sales were strong. Expectations more so.

A reporter from the paper had swung by the studio to chat with Mr. D and to take pictures of Peri and Mark. Although she paid perfunctory attention to Mr. D and Peri, she spent most of her time sniffing around Mark. At the end of rehearsal, she steered him toward a quiet corner, so she could interview him personally.

"Are you the son of Mark Maroulis, Sr., the baseball player?" she asked as Mark threw a please-help glance over his shoulder.

Peri gave him a thumb's up. *You'll do great,* she telegraphed to him. And he had. Mark might be eighteen, a fact she forgot regularly, but he hadn't flinched from any challenge thrown his way.

She examined her face. She looked the same as she had before applying the moisturizer. If anything, the moisturizer emphasized the mauve half-moons under her eyes and her pale cheeks.

Because she, unlike Mark, was flinching. Specifically from Mr. D, who was placing more and more demands on her. He took her to dinner with him after rehearsal, insisted she come over after lunch on Sunday for tea, escorted her to his office to look at costume samples and mock-ups of props. She dug in her heels, made up excuses, pleaded exhaustion, but more times than not, she found herself stuck with Mr. D. Fortunately, there'd been no repeat of the night after the fundraising dinner.

Although he never admitted it to her, Mr. D was nervous. It was his last chance to make something important, something memorable. He was leaning on her because she was the only person he could lean on.

Mr. D's health was also declining. Telling that awful story in exchange for donor money had taken its toll. The warm beige of his skin had taken on a whitish cast, and his frame, never meaty to begin with, had shrunk. The hand pressing on his cane looked gnarled, like old tree roots. Several times, she'd caught him clutching his abdomen, as if in intense pain.

When she asked him about it, he put her off with vague assurances.

She made herself be sympathetic, remembering what he'd survived, intuiting how little time he had left, but his impositions were rubbing holes in her patience, which was thin to begin with. She wanted to be with Mark. She was with Mark, if not every time physically then always emotionally.

Mark wasn't taking it well.

"Do you have to go?" he'd ask in a grumble.

"I do."

Mark would grab her and whisper how many days until *M+M* was over as she pressed her head against his chest, enjoying the warmth of his skin, the cleanliness of his T-shirt, the regular thump of his heartbeat. Then, she'd pull away to go deal with Mr. D.

She reached for her silver tackle box of makeup in a futile attempt to camouflage her exhaustion and frustration. Makeup was tricky. A flick of mascara and a swipe of gloss were the most she wore since the sweat from dancing would send anything else streaming down her cheeks. Today, though, she unscrewed a pot of concealer and dabbed it under her eyes and on a few ruddy splotches around her nose.

She glanced at her watch. She had a few minutes before she had to wake Mark up. Maybe he'd get up less grouchy than he had yesterday.

Mark's mood extended beyond the demands Mr. D was making on Peri's time. He was dancing well, his technique acquiring luster from the influx of new information he'd received from Stick and Stone, the former of whom had made Mark her pet.

Stick kept Mark after class to work on his transitions between jumps, making him cross his fifth position toe to heel and land in a deep, plush *plié* that would rocket him into the air again. Peri watched from the sidelines, so she could make mental notes that she'd remind Mark of when he wrote down Stick's corrections.

Stick knew he was going places. She wanted to get everything she'd learned into his body, so Mark could pass it down later. That was dance—folklore physicalized.

Mark was dancing far and above any of the other men in the company, a feat he paid for dearly by having no one to talk to beyond Peri.

"Everyone treats me like I don't exist," Mark said last night as he passed a plate to her, its surface smooth and sparkling, not a speck left from the turkey meatloaf they'd made. His shoulders sagged. "To be more exact, Glenn treats me like I don't exist, and since he's the king of the dressing room, no one else says hello or even pardon when they bump into me."

Glenn's crush on her had evaporated by the time the company had reconvened in January. She would have been relieved except the infatuation had left a residue of resentment. Glenn's envy of Mark had hardened into hostility, which he, as a popular dancer, exploited to shun Mark.

"They're jealous," she said.

"I know, but still. I'm tired of the dressing room going silent when I walk in."

She swept her dishtowel around the plate in the same action she used to apply moisturizer. "It's the cost of talent."

Mark emitted something between a laugh and a groan. "People are weird." He looked at her. "Did you ever have friends in the company?"

She shook her head. "I came in as Mr. D's protégé." She paused, the plate still in her hands. "It got better when Mr. D partnered me with Bob because Bob was friends with everybody. Even if someone didn't like him, Bob went out of his way to be nice. He'd stand next to them at barre, buy them coffee, make them laugh."

"How did that help you?"

Peri put the plate in the cupboard and held out her hand for the next dish. "Bob was protective of me. He considered us a package deal. If someone was friends with Bob, then that person had to be friends with me."

"Were they really your friends?"

"They were nice to my face. And I had Bob, so it was okay. He saved me a spot next to him during lunch, and he'd confront anyone who said nasty things about me." She wiped her eyes.

Mark flushed. "I didn't mean to make you upset."

Peri hugged herself. "Talking about Bob is nice, even if it makes me tear up."

He scuffed his feet. "I wish I could do what Bob did for you."

"You do plenty for me." She kissed him hard, feeling sad and happy at the same time. If Bob hadn't gotten AIDS, then she might never have met Mark. That was the cruel equation of life—one person taken, another given.

His mood had shot up after their conversation, but it'd probably be back to zero by the time today was over.

Peri rummaged through her tackle box, perfect for makeup with its many small compartments. Her fingers closed over and then released compacts of eyeshadow and blush. Anything powdery was a bad idea. It would clump in her wrinkles, and her sweat would drive tracks through it. After rooting around, she unearthed a tube of lipstick the color of peonies. She painted circles on her cheeks and filled in the contours of her lips. Then, using the tips of her fingers, she blended it in.

She stepped back to judge her handiwork. Better.

It gave her a youthful glow that looked almost natural.

Mark was chafing against another problem—Mr. D, who ignored Mark.

"Peri-jan," he'd say as Mark stood in front of Mr. D, flushing. "Can you show Mark—"

Mark interrupted, trying to get Mr. D to address him personally. "It was the finger turns, right? I led them too early before Peri could extend her leg."

Mr. D wouldn't even acknowledge Mark. Instead, he'd repeat exactly what Mark had just said, his eyes glinting knowingly.

It was emasculating for Mark and unpleasant for Peri, but they didn't have much choice. Mr. D was the boss, and their job was to do what he told them to do.

Mr. D knew. And there was so much to know.

Peri pitched her body forward to stretch the backs of her legs as she reached for her mascara. Luckily, she hadn't felt even a twinge of pain in her calf. The nerve in her back was holding up. The choreography in *M+M* was showy and technically challenging, but at least for her, there wasn't that much of it, which meant she could do it well without overdoing it. Mark was carrying the show, but he had youth and optimism to push him through the thorny, arduous phrases.

"You seem revitalized, Peri-jan," Mr. D had commented more than once after they'd run the *grand pas de deux*.

"I love the choreography," she said hurriedly as she stood beside Mark, her cheeks hot, her heart thumping, sure her body had betrayed her secret. There was only one reason she was revitalized, and it had nothing to do with Mr. D's choreography.

Mr. D had smiled with knowing eyes.

She twisted off the top of her mascara and positioned the wand near the base of her lashes.

Plus, although she and Mark had been discreet, they'd stopped trying to pretend when they danced, and their passion ignited the artifice of movement into truth. It was easier to give in to her feeling, let it power her through the movements her body protested at every turn.

"Mr. D knows," Mark said last night as he settled himself in bed.

He held out his arm to her. "I keep forgetting to hide it." She snuggled against his warm chest.

"I can't wait for M+M to be over." He pulled the coverlet over her and kissed her as she threw her arms around him, her heart warming while her stomach wobbled.

She sighed as she stroked the mascara over her lashes, making sure that it didn't clump. She considered adding another coat, but she didn't want to look like Trish.

She'd promised Mark, and she intended to keep that promise. She wanted to keep it. But Mr. D was not going to take it well. If he took it at all.

Mr. D considered her to be his—a pretty little bauble he used as he pleased. Yet she was a person, not a thing. Losing Bob and meeting Mark had roused her from her dutiful passivity. She'd always done what she was told to do, but she was done doing that. She could—she should—make her own decisions about her life, and the decision she was making was to be with Mark openly.

That meant she had to break it off with Mr. D, which she wasn't sure how to go about doing. He would retaliate. But how?

He couldn't do much to Mark and her. Or could he?

They had contracts that would see them through the season. That bought them time to figure out . . .

She frowned, distracted by something flashing in her hair. She pushed the strands aside until her fingers closed over the offending one. She yanked it out, wincing at the sting, and then flushed it down the toilet.

Peri closed her eyes. It was one hair, but still. She was going gray.

The back of her throat tightened.

What, exactly, were she and Mark figuring out?

She brushed her hair into a ponytail and looped a rubber band around the sheaf.

There was nothing to figure out. She was a decade-plus older than Mark. They both knew how their story ended. She was the old car, good for practicing on, but no big loss when totaled. Because it was the opportunity to find a newer, shinier model that hadn't been around the block and back again.

She coiled her ponytail into a bun.

Maybe it could work if there were a paradigm for their relationship that wouldn't cause society to lose its collective marbles. It was dumb, really. She and Mark were happy together, not doing anything immoral, but age differences only worked one way.

Men could do it, marry a woman a decade and even two or three their junior. Women, if they had the guts to fall in love with someone younger, were supposed to stick to small, discrete increments—a year, maybe two or three, for the bold. Enough to be racy but not unsettle anyone's view of how men and women should behave.

Peri stabbed bobby pins around the bun's perimeter, not caring when the plastic tips scraped her scalp.

She'd told herself this before, but she couldn't seem to listen. Her feelings, two freight trains, one of reason and another of passion, kept racing toward each other in their dangerous bid to outrun the other. Passion, propelled by the warm pump of blood, always flattened reason because the head, when defied by the heart, had no power.

Peri gazed at herself in the mirror. Her eyes were still tired and worried, but she looked as good as she could otherwise.

She peeked into the bedroom. Mark was asleep, his limbs flung every which way, the sheets bunched around his waist. His mouth gaped a little, and his hair was dangling in his face. In sleep, he was as honest and endearing as he was awake.

How did I ever think you were ordinary? she asked herself, remembering her dismissal of him at his audition. She tiptoed toward the bed and placed a light-as-air kiss on his forehead.

I love you, she said silently.

She would never say the words aloud, but in the morning, when everything was rosy gold with possibility, she couldn't stop her tongue from tapping out the rhythm.

She couldn't tell him because it would be a burden for him, and he was already shouldering so much. Mark would stay with her long after he was ready to leave because he was loyal. She should save them both that drawn-out misery. She would love him and let him go when it was time, so he could go do the things that he should go do.

Mark wasn't going to be happy dancing for Mr. D for much longer. Not after seeing that show about James Prescott. He would want to go to a better company where the repertory was varied and complex.

And, after *M+M*, when the reviews came in, he'd be able to do just that. Peri, though, was in the sunset of her career. No company would want her. She'd danced Mr. D's repertory her whole professional life, and she couldn't—not at her age—pick up a new style, maybe even multiple new styles, with the thirst and fervor of a young dancer.

So she took each day with Mark as if it would be the last, making an effort to encase each moment in amber. When her mind become jumbled and overloaded, she took to writing in a journal all the silly minutia of their day that might, in retrospect, feel epically important. What they made for dinner. When they made love. The color of Mark's T-shirt. She hid it deep in a drawer of her dresser, terrified he would find it, but even more terrified she'd forget. It was her small gesture to lessen her future sadness.

At least she'd have the memories.

She stroked Mark's cheek. "Time to get up."

His eyes flitted, and then he groaned. "I feel like I just fell asleep."

"That was hours ago."

Mark sat up. "Good morning, then."

She pushed the hair out of his face. "Good morning."

"You look pretty."

"Thanks," she said casually. She kissed him and then bounded out of the bedroom to execute a thousand small tasks to fill the time until they would leave for the studio.

As M+M got closer and closer, the wobble in her stomach spread through her body until it felt as if she were in a perpetual teeter. Sure everyone could see her nerves vibrating beneath her skin, she stayed in constant motion to conceal it.

Her perpetual flurry provided another benefit. When she was doing, she wasn't feeling that something terrible was going to happen after M+M. She just knew it.

"How do you have this much energy in the morning?" Mark shuffled into the living room, his eyes still bleary.

Peri was whizzing around the apartment, gathering tights and leotards to toss in her dance bag, writing a list of ingredients for tonight's dinner, shoving a bowl of cereal into Mark's hands.

He dropped into the sofa and then winced. "Do you think we could get a new couch after M+M? You know, to celebrate."

Her mouth fell open. "A new couch?"

Mark poked the back cushion. "Sitting on bricks would be more comfortable."

"I . . . sure," she said. "I know a couple of good thrift stores." Then she headed into the kitchen, so Mark wouldn't see her expression.

She pressed her fingers against the corners of her eyes, overwhelmed. *Mark is living in the moment,* she told herself. *He doesn't know what buying a sofa together means.*

Because he was eighteen. Something she needed to remember.

She arranged her features into a neutral mask and walked back into the living room, after grabbing a can of soda. She tossed it to Mark, who was still fixated on their future sofa.

"A soft, squashy one," he said. "Maybe blue. The color of a swimming pool." He looked around the living room, where everything was white and beige, like toast with butter. "We could paint too. Make it feel homey."

He pulled back the tab and lifted the soda to his lips. After he took a sip, he spied her face. "Oh geez, Peri." He raked a hand through his hair. "I didn't mean it like that. Your apartment is great. It's just I'm here all the time, and I like color." He pointed to a stack of his T-shirts, their bright shades like a package of highlighters. She'd ironed them last night in an attempt to burn some of her excess energy.

Peri followed Mark's gaze around her living room. She'd lived here so long that she'd stopped noticing her apartment. It didn't look like much, no personality, no vibrancy, and nothing to mark it as anything other than what it had been for fourteen years—the layover from dancing.

The only thing that labeled it as hers was a picture of Bob and her, their arms thrown around each other, taken a decade earlier, after a sold-out run of Mr. D's first big ballet. A couple of years ago, she'd buried all the pictures of her childhood in a box and stuffed it in her closet. As for Mr. D, he'd never given her anything, which was fine by her. At least his presence hadn't breached the one place she could call her own.

She peeked at Mark. The place she wanted to call theirs.

Feeling her eyes on him, Mark looked up from the newspaper that he'd been skimming. "Guess what? They're finally going to launch that space shuttle."

They'd followed the story since the first article Mark read out loud. They learned about the teacher's preparations at the center in Texas, giggled that the training plane was referred to as the vomit comet for its ability to induce nausea, and groaned at the regimen that astronauts went through to learn how to pee in space.

"9:38 a.m.," he read from the paper. He glanced at the clock. "We missed it because of the time difference."

"Maybe not," Peri said. "With all the delays, I bet there was one more today."

Mark flipped on the television. On screen, someone was counting down. She parked herself beside him. "Must be our lucky day."

Five.

Four.

Three.

Two.

One.

LIFT OFF!

They cheered when the shuttle went blasting into space.

How amazing, Peri thought. *I hope that teacher has the time of her life.*

Mark stood and reached for the remote. They had to hightail it to the studio, so they could warm up before class. On the television, the shuttle was pushing into a wall of blue. Then, fuzzy white smoke and shiny gold flames filled the screen.

"My god," said the horrified announcer. Both of them froze.

She screamed. "Did it . . ."

He dropped beside her and pulled her body, stiff with shock, toward him. Debris tumbled toward the earth, trailed by fuzzy plumes. "It exploded."

Peri's stomach contracted. "Did they . . ."

"They had to have. How can anybody survive that?" "That poor teacher. Her family. Her children," she cried. Mark rubbed her back as she held him tight.

Why? she asked God. *Why was that necessary?*

God didn't respond.

16

En Face

(FACING THE AUDIENCE)

MARK WAS STANDING in the wings as the overture to Act II played. He moved closer to the filthy black curtain. It was dress rehearsal, and the dancers milling in his wing were reviewing the fancy walks and bows they were about to do.

He didn't need to join them thanks to writing down the choreography in that journal from Peri. Although he'd hidden the journal under one of the wings, he didn't need to check it. Mark knew his steps backward and forward. He still couldn't spell the names of any them, but no one in the audience was going to care about that.

Using one of the lighting rigs for support, Mark slanted his body forward to stretch his calves. He had plenty of time before he danced.

Act I had gone well although he'd overshot a *grand jeté* and ended up swallowing a mouthful of papier-mâché leaves hanging from a tree. A slippery spot downstage had almost sent him spinning out of control on a pirouette, but he saved it at the last minute. The gigantic mountain backdrop made him feel small, so he leaped higher than normal, which caused him to get behind the music. He'd get a note about that for sure from Mr. D.

Oh well. He'd been good otherwise.

The stage curtains swept open. In the wings, everyone stood up straight, pasted smiles on their faces, and pointed their feet in preparation for their entrance.

"Excuse you," someone said to Mark.

It was Glenn, walking by him, rattling his jester hat at Mark.

Mark wanted to laugh. Glenn was hardly threatening in the bright hat with bells, but Mark bit back his *haha*. Instead, he flattened himself against the wing and gave Glenn a tight smile. "It's all yours, man."

Glenn lifted his chin and sauntered past him.

Their conversation outside the jewelry store had led to nothing. If anything, it made it worse. Glenn took it personally Peri hadn't liked him back, and he blamed Mark for it, which, while true, had nothing to do with the facts Glenn was basing his hate on.

Glenn had been cast as the first son in Act I and the jester in the second where Mr. D had made a funny variation for him with lots of small beated jumps that Glenn was supposed to dance as if he couldn't do them. It was harder than doing the steps right. Glenn looked happy enough during rehearsals when he wasn't shooting dirty looks in Mark's direction because, if it weren't for Mark, then Glenn would have been the seventh son.

Mark shrugged. That was Glenn's problem, not his.

Onstage, the company promenaded in costumes of red or green with embroidery based on traditional Armenian designs. As the grand music swelled to a climax, the company lifted their arms and bowed to each other.

This act was totally different from the first one. Act I was all story. Act II was all dancing. *M+M* was pretty much *The Nutcracker* but with scenery and costumes based on Armenia rather than 19th-century Germany.

Mark gazed across the stage as he glimpsed Peri through the throng of dancers, her crown of pearls and rhinestones catching the light.

You look pretty, he telegraphed to her.

And she did. He scrunched his brow and counted backward. If today was dress rehearsal, then that meant only four days until they were official. The bottom of his stomach sparked.

Four days was nothing.

He'd been counting down since Christmas. He used the calendar in his checkbook register to tick off the days. When Peri took her shower after dinner, he'd pull it out and swipe his pencil across the date. He didn't want her to know, so he put it back quickly, his cheeks hot.

Sometimes, he got weirded out by how things had changed so fast. Last year, he'd been in high school, living at home, sneaking around his dad so he could take ballet classes. Now, he was on his own, about to take the stage as the lead in Mr. D's new ballet. He was still sneaking around though, this time with Peri.

He couldn't wait to be out in the open with her, for everyone to know she was his girlfriend. It felt like forever at first. But they were busy. At work, dancing their way through hard classes and long rehearsals and at home, cooking up new things in the kitchen and in the bedroom.

It was the same thing that millions of other people were doing—going to work, making dinner, having sex, nothing special—but doing it with Peri felt better than great.

Mark always thought big, important events led to happiness, but with Peri, it was the smallest, simplest moments. Making a new recipe together. Twisting her braid around his finger as she slept. Listening to the sound from her sewing machine as she fed sheets of fabric through it.

She'd started making robes and hospital gowns for AIDS patients in cheery colors that would fit their bodies, which had shrunk like cotton washed in hot water. He cleaned the fabric before she sewed the outfits, and as the tangle of egg yolk and hot pink and jade green rolled in lazy circles in the dryer, he'd have to stop himself from tapping the old lady reading a romance novel beside him, so he could tell her about Peri.

My girl is incredible, he wanted to say.

His breath still went missing when she wrapped her limbs, thin and stretchy like the stitching on a baseball mitt, around him, and if the only thing he did with the rest of life was kiss her, then that sounded pretty good.

Mark looked across the stage where the good fairy from the first act was welcoming everyone to the wedding celebration. Peri wasn't watching the action. Instead, she'd pressed her head to her shins, her white tutu sticking up like a fan from her butt. He rubbed his forearms.

When was she going to wise up? Realize she was out of his league?

That he was making it up as he went along?

But Peri didn't notice, or if she did notice, she didn't care. She treated him like her equal. She asked for his opinion, listened to it, and then went along with it if she thought it was worthwhile.

Take that new couch they were going to buy after M+M. One evening, they'd gone poking around a few thrift stores. Mark had his eye out for one thing—comfort. After a long day of dancing, he wanted to veg out on something that would comfort him like a hug.

Peri, though, was more concerned with appearance. She wanted a pretty sofa. Something with curved arms and a high back and scratchy fabric that looked expensive.

"I feel like I'm being punished," he said as he sat stiffly on a sofa the shade of mint ice cream. "Come try this one." He'd dragged her to a soft, welcoming one with squashy cushions and nubby fabric.

He sank into the couch, spread his legs, and threw his arms open with a happy sigh. "Yes." He looked at Peri who was perched on the edge, her nose wrinkling.

"It's plaid," she said. "Brown-and-orange plaid." She stroked the fabric with her fingers. "It feels cheap."

He extended his hand to her. "Give plaid a chance."

She'd settled beside him and snuggled into his outstretched arm. "It's better than a bed," Mark said.

"Maybe." She hesitated. "But I hate plaid. It makes me think of lumberjacks."

Mark sat up. "Could you make a . . ." He tried to remember the word but failed. "Something to go over the plaid?"

"A slipcover?" she asked. "I guess I could."

"You pick the color and fabric." Mark squeezed her hand. "But something soft. Please."

She smiled. "It's a deal."

And just like that, they'd picked out a couch. They were going to come back the weekend after M+M and buy it.

"Are you sure it's safe?" Mark asked as he shot the sofa a longing look over his shoulder.

"Look." Peri pointed to a woman who was giving the couch a wide berth, her mouth dropped in a small, horrified O that something that ugly existed.

As he got more and more excited about M+M being over, Peri got more and more anxious. She tried to keep him from feeling it, from seeing it, but tension had bunched up her muscles, skinny lines threaded their way across her forehead, and worry had dimmed her eyes.

Because Mr. D wasn't going to take it well.

But what could Mr. D do? They had contracts through the end of the season. That gave them plenty of time to figure out what was next.

Mark had some ideas about what could be next. He wanted to go to a different company that had a varied repertory—the classics plus contemporary pieces. He'd start at the bottom; he didn't care as long as he was dancing.

Onstage, the company had arranged themselves into small,

decorative knots in preparation for the string of solos and duets that would end with the *grand pas de deux* of the maiden and the seventh son.

M+M was shaping up to be a good ballet, but it was going to be Mr. D's last. Mr. D's health was going bad, fast. He'd lost a bunch of weight, and he had a hand stuck to his stomach all the time. It was only a matter of time before he got too sick to work, and the company folded. They could get out ahead of the crash. Peri was coming to the end of her career anyway. She should leave on a high note.

Come with me, he would say to Peri. *You can guest with a few companies or teach classes. And if you want to stay home and sew pretty clothes while you figure out what's next, that's cool too. I'll take care of us.*

He ran his hands through his hair, suddenly feeling doubtful. He could do that, right? Take care of Peri and himself?

I can do it, he said to himself, pushing aside his worry. *I'll make a good life for us.*

Although Mark hadn't been on his own all that long, he had life's number. It was a grab bag of happiness and disappointment no matter how rich or how good looking or how talented or even how lucky you were. You either ranted at the bad or appreciated the good. Thankfulness was happiness.

It was a lesson his dad had never learned, and it'd made him bitter and ungrateful. After that foul ball smacked him in the head, he could have moved into a different career like coaching or managing or just thrown himself into retirement, gone golfing with his buddies or collected and repaired classic cars, something he'd enjoyed doing before the accident. Instead, he'd thrown himself into an easy chair that he used as a pulpit to harass Mark and his mom.

I won't turn into him, he told himself. *I won't.*

Mark was thankful for ballet. He was thankful for Peri. When he looked around and took it all in—the people who had nothing and would kill for anything, the people who had everything yet thought they had nothing—he saw that he had it better than plenty of people. His goal was to keep it that way.

He gazed at Peri through the two girls onstage in grass-colored tutus who were whizzing through pique turns. Mark winced. The one downstage had just slipped in the same place he had earlier.

Peri placed the tip of her right pointe shoe on the floor. She pushed her arch over her toe before repeating the action with her left foot. She ran her tongue around her lips and then smoothed her hair. She did this every time before she danced.

His dad used to have a ritual, too, before he went to bat: touch his cap with his left hand, scuff his right cleat, and tap the bat three times. Sometimes, when the team was on a winning streak, he'd refuse to wash his uniform, no matter how badly it stunk.

Ballet dancers and baseball players. Superstitious to the last.

Peri and his dad, though, had nothing in common beyond their routine. Plus, Mark liked Peri, enjoyed seeing her every day. As for his dad, Mark didn't like him, hadn't missed seeing him.

That's why Peri had to come with him. Because every day he woke up to her was a good—make that a great—day. But she was going to need some convincing. Mark rubbed the back of his neck. But he was lining up his arguments and rehearsing them, so when the moment came, he'd be ready.

Mark turned his attention to the stage. Glenn was taking his place for his solo. Still plenty of time until Mark danced.

As the brisk, merry music started, Glenn glanced toward the wing where Mark was. Glenn wanted Mark to watch so he could psych him out.

Being the lead is cool, Mark wanted to tell Glenn, who was bent over in an exaggerated angle as he switched his legs in a string of *brisés*. *But the spotlight is lonely*.

Mark looked around backstage. Maybe, next year at this time, he'd be dancing on a bigger stage, doing a more interesting ballet. Mr. D's choreography, while flashy, wasn't exciting to him anymore. Mark was curious about James Prescott's choreography.

He spent weeks scrolling through the television channels in hopes of seeing the program again.

No luck.

When they checked out at the grocery store, he'd flipped through a TV Guide, fingers crossed, as he placed a bag of apples and a Styrofoam platter of chicken breasts on the conveyor belt.

No luck.

He'd dashed into a bookstore to see if they had any books on James Prescott and asked the librarian at the local branch.

No luck.

The only thing he'd found was a short article in an old magazine announcing James Prescott's appointment as artistic director of a company in a city Mark had never heard of. He memorized the two lines and then put the magazine back.

He sighed, not that it mattered. James Prescott was in West Germany, a place he wasn't visiting anytime soon. So Mark had to rely on his fuzzy memory. Peri had a good head for movement and was good with words, so she helped Mark say what he was trying to do.

"The angles are exaggerated, brutal even," she said. "It's geometry with an attitude."

Geometry with an attitude. Mark liked that.

The world was looking different to him. Inspiration was everywhere. When the twilight sunshine rebounded off his windshield, he thought of flickering jumps with the torso tilted backward. When a swaying palm tree casted a shadow, he thought of a man using his body to gently rock his female partner from foot to foot.

Sometimes, he grabbed Peri and pulled her into the studio, so he could try the things he'd thought up on a body other than his. She was a good sport, and she remembered his choreography, which he couldn't seem to do.

"I made it up. So how come I can't do it again?" Mark sighed and scribbled the phrase he'd created in the journal from Peri. He read through it: *grand battement, tombé* to fourth position with chin up, pirouette with spine tilted to left.

It didn't sound great: kick, lunge, turn, plus a few fancy touches.

Mark would have to keep trying.

Peri patted his knee. "Because you're not thinking of what's happened. You're thinking of what's going to happen."

He passed the notebook to Peri. "Did I get it all?"

She took the pen he offered her, made notes, and then passed it back. She'd corrected his spelling, added a step he'd forgotten and elaborated on the others, throwing in details about the placement of arms and head. Even if years passed, he'd be able to reconstruct it.

"What would I do without you?" Mark asked.

He wanted to kiss her, so he looked around to see if they were alone. A bob of movement by the door caught his eye. It was Mr. D, his white-suited back hunched over his cane, as he limped away. Mark's spine stiffened.

How long had he been there? What had he seen?

Mark relaxed. There'd been nothing to see, just him and Peri dancing around together in a studio. That wasn't illegal. Still, it was creepy since Mr. D was creepy.

Beside him, Peri had laughed lightly. "You'd be just fine without me."

But he wouldn't. She helped him, made him better.

And, he grinned to himself, he did that for her. He'd figured out some of Peri's anxiety.

After spending so much time together, he could read right through the pleasant expression she kept on her face. When they danced, a spray of wrinkles appeared between her eyebrows during the hard parts.

She was losing her technique. He didn't judge her for it. It happened to everybody, part of the bargain that dancers made with the devil. In their youth, they bought greatness on credit and paid for it later with bones and muscles that shriveled and rebelled. When he was around her age, he'd experience the same decline.

So Mark helped where he could. He held her hand longer before releasing it for a balance, he steadied her after a wobbly pirouette, and he let his hand linger on her back, so she'd know he was there for her. During her variation, he flashed her a thumbs up when she traveled in his direction.

At the studio, he made sure she always had a Tab an arm's length away, so the caffeine would power her through class and rehearsal. At home, he rubbed her shoulders, stroking her dove-like bones, and he brought her adhesive tape and wads of cotton so she could bandage the ragged, bloodied flaps of skin on her toes.

"That looks like a bullet wound," he said as Peri looped tape around a particularly gnarly blister. "Dudes have it so good in ballet."

"I've had worse." She pointed her feet, small but with high arches, like commas written in calligraphy.

Mark pulled himself out of his thoughts. He tugged at the neckline of his white tunic, trying to get some air on his chest. While his costume looked rich on the outside with its swoops of pearls and heavy gold embroidery, it was hot and itchy on the inside. He'd been standing for a long time by the lights, and he was sweating.

Across the stage, Peri placed a finger against her lips and then turned it toward Mark. He lifted his finger, pad turned outward, and then pressed it to his lips. They'd chanced upon it as a way to silently say . . .

What, exactly, were they saying? He knew what he was saying.

As for Peri, he didn't know although he'd put the words in her mouth plenty of times. Three small words that, when strung together, conveyed one big meaning.

He'd been feeling the words for a while. If he was honest, since he'd lifted her over his head during his audition. Maybe it went back to when she stepped onstage at his school although he'd been too young and dumb to understand why his heart had taken flight like a kite. Even if he had understood, it wouldn't have been real.

This was real because he knew Peri and she knew him.

Now, the words were always there, pushing up from his gut to land in his mouth, but he was too chicken to let them leave, so he kept swallowing them back down.

When the dust settled, he would tell her. He should tell her because he was pretty sure she felt the same way. It was in the way she looked at him in the morning when she thought he was still asleep, her heart in her eyes as she brushed the hair from his face.

But she would never tell him. Because of the age difference.

It was weird Peri being eleven years older than him.

I don't care, he thought. *And I don't care if other people care. We get along better and have more fun than plenty of couples who are the same age.*

If everything worked out, they and their new sofa would be stationed in a new city where Mark had a new job. Once they got settled, maybe they could get a pet. He'd always wanted one growing up, but his mom didn't want to deal. To be more exact, his mom didn't want to deal with his dad dealing with a pet. A dog would be fun, but they might not have time to take care of it, so a cat. A big, fat black one who would laze on their laps at the end of the day. They could call it Licorice. Or maybe Pepper.

And if everything went well, then in a few years, they could make their relationship permanent, nothing big or fancy. And a couple years after that they should start thinking about a kid because that was the one thing the age difference would—

Mark cut himself off. He was acting like a girl, planning their future after just a couple of months.

Don't you want to do the things that eighteen-year-old guys do? a voice in his head asked.

Like what? he snapped back. *Go to stupid parties and get drunk? Puke my guts out on a street corner somewhere? Sit through lame college classes I don't care about? Act like spring break is the most important thing in my life?*

No, thank you.

Maybe it makes me boring that all I want to do is dance during the day and then come home to make dinner with my girl, but so what? It's not illegal to be boring. Anyway, dancing is plenty exciting.

Don't you want to play the field, sleep with other girls? the voice in his head asked.

Okay, so this was tempting. It was crazy to want to spend his life with the first girl he'd slept with, but he was crazy about Peri. Besides, what if he dated around only to find himself with someone he didn't like half as much as Peri?

I hit a home run my first time at the plate, he told the voice in his head.

Mark shook himself to attention as the orchestra swelled into a crescendo. They were up next.

The big, grand music for their *pas de deux* was typical of classical ballet. Yet Mr. D had found an Armenian folk song that was sad and old-timey. The composer had woven it through the three big scenes between Peri and Mark, and it'd become his favorite part of the music.

"A leitmotif," Mr. D called it.

He extended his leg and stepped into a *renversé*, making sure his shoulders stayed down and his center pulled up. He unwound from the attitude into a couple of fancy walks before extending his right hand to Peri. She accepted and lifted her leg into an arabesque. He walked around her, keeping his arms from shaking even a little so she wouldn't be thrown off balance.

They danced through the adagio, and everything was going great, only the last few seconds of lifts and turns. Even onstage, under the lights, surrounded by the ring of ornate props and sets, they'd created their own world. Squeezes of hands, exchanges of glances, smiles thrown in the other's direction. They'd spent so much time together, onstage and off, that they could read and respond to each other in a fraction of a second.

He kept his eye on Peri as she drilled her toes in a *bourrée* forward, took fourth position, and then sprung up. As he paddled her through a pirouette, the stage door banged.

What a moron, Mark thought. *Don't they know a dress rehearsal is going on?*

Peri extended her leg to pull in for another set of turns. An argument broke out backstage.

"Let me see my faggot son," someone shouted. The sweat dotting Mark's upper lip froze.

OH. NO.

The slurred voice, the ugly words, the volume so loud that it sounded like a police siren. It was his dad. He'd finally figured out where Mark was, and he was here to do something about it.

The conductor halted the orchestra as Mark's dad pushed past one of the stagehands and ran onstage, his steps big and loopy.

"This is what you wanted?" His dad gestured at Mark's costume and laughed meanly. "To wear a sparkly shirt and pussyfoot around a stage?"

Mark stepped in front of Peri and faced his dad, who looked like crap. His pupils were huge, and his skin hung off his face like wet paper. The stink of beer and sweaty armpits coming off him was overpowering. Mark's stomach rolled.

His dad pointed at Mark. "I'm taking you home." "Mark!"

Mark looked to his right. His mom was dashing onstage, her eyes, blue like his, bulging with fright.

"Mrs. Watkins—she lives two houses down, you remember? Anyway, she brought over an article. From the paper. It was about how you have the lead in a new ballet by a famous choreographer, but you'd started as a base—"

His mom was almost hyperventilating, so she stopped talking to catch her breath as a few tears shot down her cheeks.

"Anyway, it was called *From First Base to First Position*. She thought we'd want to see it. I tried to hide it, but he found it and insisted on coming. I tried to stop him, told him you were an adult and free to make your own decisions, but he wouldn't listen." Her words were piling up like traffic.

The article he'd been interviewed for. Mark had forgotten about that.

"You have shamed me," his dad yelled. "Disrespected me. Gone behind my back, so you can dance like a sissy." He stepped toward Mark, still shouting, but Mark stopped listening since all the words were variations on the same theme. Mark was good at ballet, liked ballet, so he must be gay, a sin his father considered worse than murder.

His dad shook his fist. "It's time to beat sense into you."

Mark didn't think; he acted. He pulled his fist back and punched his dad in the face as hard as he could. Behind him, Peri gasped as bone cracked against bone. His dad's mouth slackened as he staggered back and forth. Then, he plunged to the floor, his mouth still moving, but with no sound coming out. Blood chugged from a nostril.

Good, Mark thought. *I finally shut you up.*

The wings, now filled with curious dancers, were rustling with whispers.

I'm ending this once and for all, he said to himself as he knelt beside his dad. Mark wanted to make sure his dad heard him, understood him.

"I don't care what you think," Mark said in the ugliest voice he could find to the crumpled, unmoving body. "Because I don't care about you."

"I'm sorry, Mark," his mom said, tears dripping.

"It's okay." He stood, hugged her, and then remembered Peri was there. He turned around. She had her hands clasped to her breastbone, and her eyes looked huge in her white face. "Mom, this is Peri, my dance partner and my girl . . . uh, she's my friend."

Peri shook his mom's hand.

"How's my son doing?" his mom asked.

"Fantastic." Peri's voice was pitched higher than normal. "You'd be proud, Mrs. Maroulis."

A couple of stagehands jogged out of the wings. "We're going to get him out of here," one said, swinging a hand toward his dad, who hadn't moved. "Unless you've got an objection?"

"I don't." He hugged his mom again. "I miss you."

Mr. D hobbled on stage. "What is the meaning of this?"

Mark took a deep breath and met Mr. D's gaze. "Nothing that will ever happen again."

Mr. D stared at him without saying a word, his eyebrows raised.

Then, he nodded. "The variation, Mark."

17

Contretemps

(BEATING AGAINST TIME)

PERI PACED around the living room, her gaze fixed on the door, hoping Mark would come bursting through it. They'd finished the dress rehearsal and then sat through Mr. D's interminable notes as Mark and she held hands under the tulle cover of her tutu. After, she'd rushed to her dressing room, thrown off her costume, tugged on her street clothes, and sped home.

She ran her fingers along the ruffled edges of her false eyelashes. She'd been too overwrought to dab her fingers in a pot of cold cream and rub off her stage makeup. She wanted to be with Mark as soon as possible. But it'd been an hour, and he still wasn't here.

Peri closed her eyes, remembering the sick thwack of Mark's fist connecting with his father's face, the finality of Mark's words, the anguish of Mark's mom as she watched her son rid himself of her husband.

Your son is a man, she wished she'd had the foresight to yell at Mark's dad. *One of the best. Ballet never emasculated him. Only you did.*

Tried to, she corrected herself. Mark's dad hadn't succeeded.

The door squeaked.

"Mark." She ran toward him. "I've been worried."

He hugged her. "I went for a drive. I needed to clear my head."

Peri placed her cheek against his kelly green T-shirt, breathing in its clean smell.

"So you met my parents today," he said.

She stepped back. "Is your mom going to be okay?"

"If you're asking if my dad is going to hit her, then no. He's never gone that far. But he's going to scream a lot and get drunk and generally make her life miserable."

Mark walked to the sofa and threw himself on it. "Ugh." He sat up and gingerly rearranged himself. "I can't wait until we buy that new couch."

Peri perched beside him and laid her head on his shoulder. "Can we do anything?"

He sighed. "I wish, but she won't leave him." "Does she love him?"

Mark grimaced. "I doubt it. He's a jerk."

She kissed his cheek. "I'm sorry. It was awful to watch."

"It felt good to shut him up." His tone was tight. "I'm never seeing him again."

"Maybe he'll change?"

He shook his head. "He likes being mean. It makes him feel like a big shot."

Peri stroked his cheek. She wasn't sure what to say. He, by his own choice, was fatherless at eighteen.

Mark turned to her. "Do you believe in God?" "I . . ." Peri trailed off.

Did she believe in God?

Her parents had been religious, not that it brought them much joy or comfort. They hustled Peri and her siblings to church every Sunday to listen to a man who looked like a Civil War general rant about God's deep discontent with His creation. When Peri was little, she spent the service twirling her hair ribbon around her fingers. After she started ballet, she tuned out the preacher and pretended she was in the studio. In her head, she went through the classroom exercises as she remembered the teacher's corrections. Once she moved to New York, she'd stopped going to church, using the time to catch up on sleep and do laundry. Then, in L.A., she had Mr. D on Sundays. That relationship had to disqualify her from entering any house of worship even if she'd wanted to.

For all the religion shoved down her throat when she was little, it hadn't left much of an imprint on her. She couldn't recite any Bible verses or remember any of the major players beyond Jesus, Joseph, Moses, and Mary. Now, her faith was rattled by all the times she'd asked God to explain his reasoning, only to hear a gaping silence on matters of life and death, health and sickness.

So did God exist?

Maybe . . . A disinterested presence watching them from afar seemed possible, but God hadn't revealed Himself to be more than that. At this point, she believed in God because not believing would take a strength she wasn't capable of.

"I think so," she said in a voice that suggested the opposite was true.

"I was thinking about it," Mark said. "When I went driving, I mean. Everyone says they know what God is, what he wants. Like my mom. She's stuck in this terrible marriage, and she can't do anything about it because she's Catholic." He lifted his shoulders. "There are so many awful things in the world that need God's attention. Why does he care so much about divorce?"

Peri threw her hands up helplessly. "Bob was the only person I knew who read the Bible."

"Bob?"

"He was a Christian."

"I didn't know you could be one if you were . . ."

"His father was a pastor, and Bob knew the Bible inside and out. He said Jesus never explicitly condemned homosexuality, but he did give pretty specific instructions about helping the poor. So that's what Bob did."

Peri hugged herself, missing Bob so much.

She looked at Mark, his eyebrows drawn together behind the hair that was flopping in his face.

Bob would have liked you, she thought. *He would have taken you under his wing, and he would have made everyone say hello when you walked into the dressing room.*

Her heart constricted.

Peri curbed her grief. "Bob worked with the homeless. Whenever he had free time, he'd go down to Tent City or under the freeways to hand out sandwiches and talk about Jesus' love." She was shaking. "He said he saw himself everywhere. That if he didn't have ballet, that would be him, living on the streets because he was gay."

"Where do you think he is now?"

"I hope somewhere good." She twisted her hands in her lap. "But I guess it depends on what God cares about more."

Mark tossed an arm around her and pulled her close. Together, they sat, holding on to each other, thinking about what they'd lost—a father, a friend—and taking comfort in what they'd found—each other.

∽

The run of *M+M* went well, surprisingly so. Although it'd been a while since Peri had been at her best, she was able to push through the choreography to achieve something approximating her old competency and sparkle.

Transcendence, though, was denied. That belonged to Mark, who was on fire. The reviews came in, and they were positive. Mr. D's choreography received acclaim—although one acid-tongued critic called it "a satisfying rehash of Dektember's greatest hits." Peri was referred to as "rejuvenated." They saved their exuberance for Mark.

"A talent so bright he glows," enthused one. "A one-man circus of turns, tricks, and torrid passion for dance," raved another.

Mark shrugged it off. "I'm more excited for it to be over. A new couch. Being in the open." He grinned. "I'm going to be a happy man."

She returned his smile, but her stomach was wobbling. Her dreams had become haunted by the Space Shuttle Challenger, cruising through blue skies before, without warning, exploding, innocence and hope going up in a funnel of flames. Sometimes, she woke Mark with her shaking. Half asleep, he'd tighten his arms around her and whisper something sweet and comforting.

Maybe she'd get lucky and Mr. D wouldn't care, see that this was the end of the era, let her go gracefully.

She shook her head, discarding that idea. Mr. D wasn't going to take it well. She shivered. If he took it at all.

She would pray, but she didn't know what to ask for.

A lump grew in her throat. That wasn't true. She knew what she wanted, but she couldn't ask for it. Mark was on loan, and she'd return him when it was time.

But please, she begged silently, too scared that admitting them out loud would just make God turn on her. *Let me hold on to him for a while longer. Until the end of the season. Let us sit on our new sofa and make dinner and kiss each other anywhere and everywhere.*

Then, she promised herself, *I'll answer the question: What's next?*

At the end of the last performance, Mark knocked on the door of her dressing room. Peri, clad in a silky robe, sat on a rickety chair in front of her vanity as she brushed the hair spray out of her locks.

With an embarrassed grin, he passed her a bouquet of white daisies, tied with a gold ribbon like the Act II bridal tutu she'd just taken off.

She tilted her head and inhaled their freshness, trying to hide her damp eyes. "Thank you."

Bob had always given her flowers after the last show. Mark must've gotten wind of that and wanted to do the same.

He kissed her. "Thank *you*."

Mark slouched against the wall next to Peri, who'd plugged in a curling iron and was twisting a handful of hair around the hot barrel. She glanced at him. He wore a dark gray suit with a red T-shirt. Mark had no formal clothes, so when they received the instructions from Trish to attend the donor party after the last performance, she'd offered to make him a suit.

Mark had groaned. "Suits are old-fashioned. And I hate ties. They're like nooses with a pattern."

"We'll pick a sharp style." She stepped back and took him in. "No ties and no dress shirts. Wear one of your bright T-shirts."

"You think?"

She kissed him. "You're young and exciting, and you just danced the lead in *The Maiden and the Mountain*. Let's give those rich old ladies something to talk about."

"Works for me."

And it had worked. There was plenty for those rich old ladies to talk about. Mark was never going to be handsome like Bob, but the suit clung to Mark's slim frame, his blue eyes were alert, and his skin glowed with health.

He felt her gaze. "Do I look okay?"

She smoothed a hank of hair away from his face. "About a hundred times better than okay."

"Are you ready?"

"I need to get dressed." She pointed to the strapless satin dress with a bubble skirt hanging next to her *M+M* costumes.

"I meant to be out in the open."

She ducked her head, so Mark wouldn't see the worry puckering her brow. "I think so."

This was their first official outing as a couple. While at the fabric store picking out a pattern for Mark's suit, his eyes had snagged on fabric as shiny and crimson as a new apple.

"Make a dress out of this," he said. "I'll wear a matching T-shirt. We'll go to the party as a couple. Nothing crazy. We'll walk in holding hands." He grinned at Peri. "That'll give those rich old ladies something to talk about."

She'd agreed, and now, here they were, about to announce themselves as a couple. She'd spent weeks trying to figure out how to tell Mr. D, even hinted furiously about it at their last couple of lunches. She'd mentioned cooking dinner with Mark, related a funny story Mark had told her, discussed Mark's relationship with his dad.

But she hadn't been able to summon the actual words. She wasn't even sure what words she should use. How did you break up with someone who'd never asked if you wanted to go together?

Mr. D had refused to acknowledge her gambits. Instead, he settled into his chair and gazed at her with eyes, black and glittering like a crow's.

"You seem overwrought, Peri-jan," he'd said. "Lightness and brightness. That is what I need from you." He'd raised his hand for the check. "Go home and rest."

So when Mark had suggested his plan, she'd agreed. Mr. D couldn't do anything—he wouldn't do anything—at a party with donors. As for afterward, Peri shivered. She would have to find the words to tell him.

She slipped out of her robe and into the dress. "Zip me up?" He did and then extended his arm. "Let's do this."

Please let it go okay, she prayed as she accepted his invitation.

She and Mark walked into the party, her small cool hand clasped in his big warm one. He was nervous, too. She squeezed his hand. He was sweet to want to be with her, to want everyone to know he was with her.

Mr. D's gaze swept to them immediately. His lips curled, and his skinny beige fingers pressed down on his cane as Mark tossed his head defiantly.

Mr. D knew. Everything.

If she'd made this entrance with Bob, Mr. D wouldn't have cared because Bob was gay and could never be anything beyond her friend. Mark, though, made Mr. D care. Because he was everything Mr. D was not, would never be again.

Mark and she performed the motions of being at a party. They ate canapés, drank a glass of wine, made polite chit-chat with the board members. From time to time, they stood awkwardly, feeling alone in the sea of expensive champagne and perfume.

Mark kept a hand on her at all times: against the small of her back, on the crook of her elbow, around the circumference of her waist.

So everyone would know she was his girl.

Her scalp prickled. She wished she'd found the courage to tell Mr. D beforehand. This had to be awful for him, a young, virile man sweeping his girl away. Even more awful, his girl wanting to be swept away.

I gave you half of my life, she told him in her head. *And I'm tired of it, tired of you. The heavy lunches, the feel of your hands on my body, the responsibility to inspire you. I want to have a normal relationship with a normal person.*

Her cheeks heated as her resentment picked up momentum.

You made all these ballets, and for what? What's going to happen to them? And what about me? You said you made them about me, for me, but after I danced them, then what? Even if they're performed in the future, someone else will dance them, and nobody will care that I danced them first. I'll just become a useless scrap of trivia, and right now, I don't know if the sacrifices were worth it.

She clenched her jaw. *Mark doesn't want anything from me beyond me,* she added in her head as an explanation. *And it is lovely to be wanted for the most ordinary version of myself.*

Her heartbeat slowed as she remembered the trauma Mr. D had experienced. *You lost your mother and your father and your sister, and you didn't want to lose me,* she told him silently. *But treating me like your possession just made that more possible.* She exhaled, spent by her internal tirade.

Finally, the party wound down, and Mark steered her toward the door.

"We did it," he whispered. Out in the hall, he pulled her toward the stairs to the stage. They ran up them, hand in hand, giggling as they entered the stage, which was dark and stripped bare of props and sets. Only a spotlight illuminated center stage.

Peri's muscles went limp with relief. The show was over, she'd been moderately proficient, and her body had held up, even with the strain.

Mark guided her to the spotlight. Once in its warm glow, he dipped his head, and they kissed, their bodies plastered together. If anyone was watching, the nature of their relationship was obvious. They were in love.

Eventually, they pulled away as Peri made a futile attempt to slow her frantic heartbeat.

Mark looked at her with flushed cheeks and glowing eyes. "I want to make it official. Will you be my girlfriend?"

She wanted to bang out a series of *fouettés*, run a victory lap around the stage, do something that would match her elation. Instead, she said, "Yes!"

Mark grabbed her waist and lifted her overhead, just like he had in his audition. Her soft blonde hair fell around them as they acknowledged what that moment had really meant. He set her down until her head was pressed against his chest. He went in for another kiss. Their lips had barely touched when they both started.

Tap, tap, tap, each one getting progressively quieter.

Together, they turned toward the wing where the noise was coming from. Mr. D was hobbling away from them.

Peri gasped.

Mr. D stopped, pivoted his head over his shoulder, and met her gaze as Mark stiffened beside her. Mr. D's face was broken with sadness. The skin, now white like his suit, hung in limp folds around two empty eyes and drooping lips. He looked like a ghost, the spirit and blood sucked clean from him.

"I . . ." Peri tried to find words, but none were needed because Mr.

D was limping off, his back sagging over his cane.

18

Croisé

(CROSSED)

THE CALL CAME EARLY. Mark fought his way out of the black bliss of sleep and into the white sun of reality as Peri handed him the phone.

He sat up, rubbing the crusty bits from his eyes, as he forced his brain into high gear.

"It's Trish," Peri said, her voice high and thin.

Mark pressed the receiver to his ear. "Mr. D needs to see you," Trish said. "Immediately." He could practically see her mascara wobbling in apology.

His stomach slammed to the floor. Time to face the literal music.

Peri was rubbing her hands as she paced back and forth. "He's going to take it out on you."

Mark kissed her, trying to keep his cool. *I'm not leaving you,* he wanted to tell her. *I don't care what Mr. D does to me.*

What Mr. D was going to do was fire him.

"Your service is no longer needed," Mr. D said as soon as Mark sat down. "I am releasing you from your contract effective immediately."

"What? I mean, you can't do that." Mark tripped over the words, his tongue refusing to perform under pressure the way his body could.

"I am the artistic director. I can do what I wish." Mr. D stared at Mark with eyes like black ice, an envelope clutched in his skinny beige fingers. "You did read the contract you signed?"

Mark groaned internally, remembering how quick he'd signed his name, how thankful he'd been for a job, which apparently he was out of now. "I . . . uh."

Mr. D sneered. "To ensure you leave with minimal fuss, I have had Trish cut a check for the balance of the month."

"You're paying me not to dance?" "I want you gone."

"But my reviews were incredible. I was called a talent so bright he glows." The heat was rising, and Mark fought to keep his head above the red mist.

"I would suggest you cash this check and get on a plane to a company that might care about that."

"Is this because of Peri?" he asked, desperate to have it out in the open.

Mr. D pushed the envelope toward Mark. "I do not know what you're talking about."

"You do know," Mark shouted. "You do." Mr. D gazed at him blankly.

"Me and Peri. You saw us kissing last night." Mr. D pressed his lips together.

"I love her," Mark said. "I'm asking her to come with me."

Mr. D stood and shuffled to where Mark was sitting, his hand heavy on his cane. He bent down until they were nose to nose. Mark wanted to barf. Mr. D smelled sour, like death and regret. Instead, Mark kept his face emotionless.

"You are eighteen years old. What could you possibly offer Peridot Jones?"

"My love," Mark said. "I'll figure out the rest."

Mr. D shook his head. "I let you play with her for a while, used your little romance to build *The Maiden and the Mountain*, but it is time for you to run along."

Mark blinked. "You used me?"

Mr. D stood and hobbled back to his chair. He settled himself before meeting Mark's eyes. "Like an artist uses paint. You were the right color at the right time. But it was a color I would only use once."

"Are you firing Peri?"

"She is the color I return to again and again." Mr. D stroked the gem on top of his cane "Peridot Jones is the color of Levon Dektember."

Mark tried to get his head around what Mr. D was saying. Mr. D knew the whole time, had, in fact, used their relationship to make *M+M*.

"How did you know?" Mark asked helplessly.

"I may not see well anymore, but I hear everything." Mr. D tapped his ears. "During your audition, I listened. Your heart was loud and clear." He chuckled like he was pleased with himself. "It was simple from there. Hire you, put you close to my jewel, let your youth revitalize her, so she could inspire me to make my masterpiece with her lightness and brightness. She was tormented by Bob's illness. No man can resist a beautiful woman in anguish." Mr. D twisted his lips at him. "You gave a good performance, Mark. Almost flawless."

Mark widened his eyes at Mr. D, confused.

"The exit. Take your check and run along to the next adventure."

"I'm not running along without Peri."

Mr. D sighed. "You are very young, Mark. Once, it was your biggest asset. Now, it is a liability." He paused. "You can never give Peridot what I've given her. Nor will you. To immortalize her beauty, talent, spirit." He narrowed his eyes at Mark. "What life will give her? The opportunity to molder in a small, ugly apartment while you dance every day? To follow you around the country as you bounce from job to job? To feel your attention slip as you tire of her? To be tossed out like a piece of litter when you move on to someone your own age?"

It's not like that, Mark wanted to yell. *I may be eighteen, but I would never toss Peri out like a piece of litter.*

Mr. D cocked his head, as if reading Mark's thoughts. "Or maybe she will tire of you, your immaturity, your inability to provide a meaningful life for her."

Mark crossed his arms, mad that Mr. D had guessed Mark's big worry.

"Do not be naive," Mr. D said. Mark opened his mouth to protest.

Mr. D held up a hand. "I know, I know. You think your love can withstand anything." He laughed like a movie villain. "But it cannot. It will not."

Mark's fist itched. He wanted to punch Mr. D in his ratty little face, and if he did it hard enough, maybe he could break a few bones in return for the way Mr. D was breaking his hope.

Mr. D waved his hand. "You are dismissed." Then he looked deep into Mark's eyes. "Today, you think I am cruel. Tomorrow, you will thank me."

Mark stood. "I'm going to prove you wrong." He turned to leave.

"The check, Mark."

The tips of his ears burning, Mark grabbed the check and ran out the door, refusing to look at Mr. D.

As he drove home, he replayed the conversation with Mr. D in his head.

So Mr. D had been choreographing onstage and off, and Mark had just followed directions, meeting all expectations with his performance.

My love for Peri is real, he told himself. *You can't make someone fall in love with someone else.*

As for the rest, they'd work it out. He'd find a job with another company. He was a male dancer, a good one coming off a success. There'd be an injury or an opening somewhere, and someone would hire him for the rest of the season even if it was just a regional company in the Midwest. Over the summer, he could audition for a better job in a better city. It would take a few months, but by September, they'd be settled, maybe in New York or San Francisco. They meaning him and Peri. In every scenario he came up with, she was there.

Because he could do anything if she was there at the top and bottom of every day. As for the stuff Mr. D said about Mark's youth, he was wrong. Mark wasn't going to get tired of Peri. And he was going to do everything in his power to make her happy.

If you saw us together, you'd see that the eleven years aren't a big deal, he told Mr. D in his head. *We get along great. Better than she gets along with you*, he couldn't resist adding.

After he told Peri and convinced her to come with him, he'd hit the library. It had dance magazines with listings in the back. He'd make a list of all the professional companies and call until someone said yes. Maybe they'd have something for Peri to do.

It'd be tight, moving to another city, maybe even two cities, finding places to live, staying on top of their bills, but they could do it.

We'll have a good life, he would tell Peri. *As long as we have each other, we will.*

Peri was sitting white-faced on the couch when he walked in and kicked off his sneakers. She jumped up at the sound of his footsteps. She was holding today's newspaper. The front-page article was about how the crew cabin for the Space Shuttle Challenger had been found. *Dead are Aboard*, the headline blared.

His blood slowed to a crawl. *Those poor people*, he thought. *One minute on top of the world, the next, falling to their death in a ball of fire.*

Mark shoved down his pity. He had to focus on getting Peri to come with him.

"He fired me," Mark said, getting the worst over. "But it's okay. I got paid through the end of the month. That'll buy me time to look for a job in another city."

Peri's eyes bulged with tears as the newspaper slipped through her fingers.

"Come with me." He extended his hand to Peri, who was trembling. "Please."

She shook her head.

"Is this about the age difference? Because I don't care. I never have."

"I do care." Peri drew her body up to her full height. "I can't run away with an eighteen-year-old. What am I going to do in this pretend city where you get this pretend job?"

Mark took a deep breath and opened with the first of his arguments.

"You could find a company to guest with."

"Guest?" she asked. "Who's going to hire me? I've danced Mr. D's choreography for the last fourteen years. I can't switch styles on a dime. Not at my age."

"Then teach. You'd be good at it."

"Teach?" She laughed. "I'm supposed to go from dancing leads to demonstrating first position for preschoolers?"

"You would start higher than that."

Her face collapsed. "I've never taught a class in my life. I'm not starting higher. Not for any decent paycheck."

Mark rubbed his damp brow. All the arguments he'd rehearsed in his head sounded dumb when he said them aloud.

"Then stay home and sew. I'll take care of us," he said. "Just come."

A couple of tears squirted out of her eyes. "You want me to stay home and sew while you support two people on a dancer's paycheck?"

"We'll figure it out."

"We're not figuring anything out."

Please help, Mark prayed. *Tell me what to say.*

He rocked back and forth on his feet, waiting for the words that would help him persuade Peri to trust him, to believe in him, to stay with him. She stood, one hand in a fist by her side, the other wrapped around the pearl necklace he'd given her for Christmas. The skin around her eyes was bunched up.

He was losing her. He grabbed his hair, gazed at the ceiling, and then back at her.

"I love you," Mark said. He went for broke, hoping this would cut through her resistance. Because, really, this was all he had to offer her —his love.

She didn't say anything, just looked at him with wet eyes and a mouth curled down at the ends.

"I love you." Like a pinch hitter, he swung with all his might, hoping the words would connect.

Peri stayed silent, her tiny frame shaking. "Do you love me?" he asked.

Don't say no, don't say no, he telegraphed to her. She shook her head.

"Say it," he shouted, desperate to prove her lie.

The tears were coursing down Peri's cheeks. "No," she whispered. "Tell me you don't."

"I don't."

"Say the whole thing."

Peri pressed her hands together. Through big, quaking gasps, she said, "I . . . don't . . ." She was crying so hard that she couldn't get out the next word for a few seconds. "love . . ." She took a couple of raspy breaths before muttering something Mark couldn't hear.

Then, trembling so much he could barely make her out, she said, "I'm leaving for an hour, so you can get your things. Please be gone when I get back." She grabbed her purse and ran out the door.

"Peri!" he yelled as the door slammed.

He threw himself on the sofa, not caring when it refused to yield to his shock. In less than an hour, he'd lost his job and his girlfriend. Minutes ticked by as he tried to figure out what to do. Mark stared at the dish of butterscotch candies on the coffee table, remembering all the times he watched Peri, cheek puffed out, sucking on one.

His body sagged. He would never see her do that again.

Mark pushed his feet into the floor to ground himself to the present problem. Something sharp dug into his left pinky toe. He reached down, pressed the pad of his finger over his toe, and lifted the object to his eyes. He blinked. It was a sliver from the water glass he'd kicked off the table on Christmas Day. Mark sat up straight, not breathing. An idea had stopped up all the air in his throat.

He didn't think; he acted. He jumped up and grabbed his dance bag. He pushed in as many tights, T-shirts, and jeans as he could. On top, he threw his ballet slippers and the suit Peri had made him, his eyes hot and scratchy as he remembered her sitting at her sewing machine, her hands confidently cutting through yards of fabric. Panting a little, he zipped it closed.

As for the rest of his clothes, he tossed them into a trash bag, which he threw into the garbage bin. The thud it made when it crashed against the metal bottom was the horrible downbeat to the rest of his life.

Mark went through the rest of the motions as fast as he could. He drove to the bank to cash Mr. D's check and remove the few dollars he had in his account. He placed some of the bills in his wallet, some in his dance bag, and hid the rest in his shoes. It felt weird and wrong to walk on money, but he had to have cash if this was going to work.

He drove to his craphole room. There was almost nothing left in it since he'd been living at Peri's for the last few months. He took his passport and a picture of himself and his mom at a dinner for his sixteenth birthday. He had a thought that it might be cold where he was going, so he grabbed a leather jacket in his closet that he'd worn maybe twice in his life. He left a few bucks for the guys plus a note saying they should rent out his room.

He stopped at the first used car lot he drove by.

Mark got out and tapped the hood of his car. "How much?"

The dealer gave him a number. Mark asked for a couple hundred more. His eyebrows shot up when the dealer nodded and counted bills into Mark's hands. He called for a taxi.

"LAX," he told the driver.

At the airport, Mark went from counter to counter until he saw the place he wanted to go. He waited in line, fingering the money in his pocket, hoping it would be enough. When he got to the representative, he swallowed hard and pointed toward the last flight listed. "I want to go there," he said, not sure how to pronounce the name of the city in West Germany.

The agent followed his finger. "You're in luck. I've got a seat." Mark was already pushing cash across the counter to her.

19

Brisé

(BROKEN, BREAKING)

"YOU ARE NOT EATING," Mr. D said. He adjusted his white suit jacket, which hung off his bony frame.

Peri looked up from the piece of chicken she was pushing around her plate. "I'm not hungry."

"Is this about Mark?"

"I'm just tired," she said faintly.

Of course it was about Mark. Mr. D had fired him, so Peri did what she said she would do.

It'd been almost a week since she asked Mark to leave, and she'd been unable to summon the energy to do anything. Mark's absence had sliced a line from her heart to her guts, and all she could do was lie in bed and stare at the ceiling, her viscera spilling metaphorically around her.

How big and cold her bed felt without him to curl her body around. How quiet and depressing her apartment was without him by her side in the kitchen, on the sofa. How fearful and empty her thoughts were without him to fill them up with his jokes and opinions.

I broke your heart, so I wouldn't break your spirit, she telegraphed to Mark, wherever he was now. *I said I didn't love you because I did love you, and loving you meant letting you go.*

Mr. D sipped wine as he eyed her thoughtfully. "Where is Mark?"

"I don't know."

"I paid him through the end of the month. I am not cruel, you know."

She twirled her fork in the potatoes, lifted it to her mouth, and then put the fork on her plate, the potatoes untouched.

Peri wanted Mr. D to stop talking about Mark. While she'd done the right thing, how she'd done it was awful. She couldn't erase the image of Mark, his blue eyes filled with hope and love, as he begged her to come with him. She'd left because if he asked her one more time, she would've gone. So she'd slammed the door in his face.

I didn't even say goodbye, she thought for the hundredth time.

Mr. D curled his hand around her wrist and pulled it toward a cluster of candles. He pried open her fingers and held them over the open flame. "What were you thinking?"

The heat from the candle made her flinch, but she refused to answer.

He squeezed her wrist, his frail fingers surprisingly strong. The flame danced near her palm. "How could you?" he asked, his voice a low hiss. "I have given you everything. And you risked it? For a boy?" Peri gazed at her plate, her lips pressed into a hard, angry line. *But you didn't give me everything. Not laughter. Not fun. And definitely not love,* she thought furiously. *You kept me locked up in an invisible cage, so you could use me. You never let me have anything for myself: girlfriends, a boyfriend, a life outside of ballet, anything that might take me away from you.*

And now, I'm almost thirty, and I have nothing because I threw away the best thing I ever had.

"Mark fancied himself in love with you." He narrowed his eyes at Peri. "Were you in love with him?"

"No." The lie slipped easily down the tear-soaked path she'd forged earlier.

Mr. D removed her hand from the candle. He dipped his hand into his water glass, fished out an ice cube, and then pressed it to her hot palm. "You need to retire."

She closed her hand around the cold sliver, the heat from her hand issuing a stream of water that dribbled to the table. "I know." The drops pooled into a still life of tears.

"What are your plans?"

"I don't know." The exhaustion was rising like water. A few more inches, and she would give in to it, let it carry her somewhere blissful in its blankness.

"I am closing the company at the end of the season. We will retire together."

"Okay." As if she cared. Losing her job was nothing compared to what she'd already lost.

"I have choreography in mind for my last act." He pulled up the corners of his lips. "My best ballets have ended with it."

Peri mumbled something. "A wedding."

She gazed at him dumbly.

"I want to marry you, Peri-jan."

Her head jerked back in surprise. "Excuse me?"

"I want to marry you. Nothing will change except what happened with Mark . . ." He gazed at her with cold black eyes. "That must not happen again."

Marry Mr. D? Although empty, her stomach heaved.

He leaned back in his chair and smiled at her. "If you agree, I will give you my ballets as a wedding present. You can set them on companies. It would be a good second career for you."

Mr. D reached into his jacket pocket, removed a black velvet box, and slid it across the table to her. "Open it."

With numb fingers, she threw wide the box. Inside rested a gold ring topped with an enormous oval peridot contoured with diamonds.

"Peridot is my favorite," he said. "It has been for a long time."

MALE VARIATION

A solo, usually filled with impressive leaps and turns, for the danseur.

20

Écarté
(SEPARATED, THROWN WIDE APART)

MARK GAZED at the date he'd scribbled on the piece of airmail stationery. Had it really been three years since he'd left Los Angeles?

He licked the tip of his pencil.

Dear Peri, he wrote.

He pulled back and studied his words. His handwriting was big and amateurish, like a third grader's. *Dear Peri* also seemed kind of formal. He stroked his eraser through the words. *Hello Peri,* he wrote, slowly, carefully, so the letters would look casual and confident.

He groaned. *Hello Peri* sounded like a joke. As for his handwriting, it looked the same even with his effort. He shrugged it off. It wasn't like Peri didn't know his handwriting was bad. He rubbed out the *ello* from *hello* and traced an *i*: *Hi Peri.*

That sounded wrong in every way. Mark sighed, erased it, and wrote *Dear Peri* again.

How could he write this letter if he couldn't figure out how to greet her?

He told his inner critic to shut up and got down to the business of writing a letter.

I hope you're doing well. I'm in West Germany, dancing for James Prescott. After . . .

Mark stopped. What should he say here? Broke up? Could you break

157

up with someone you'd only had a secret relationship with? He scratched it out. And technically, Peri had kicked him out, so there was that. He thought for a moment.

After I left, I bought a plane ticket to West Germany. I showed up at Jim's studio with my M+M reviews and begged for an audition. Jim's a good guy, and he could see I'd been through some stuff. So he gave me a chance. It was hard in the beginning. I had so much to learn. Jim's choreography is fast and complicated and athletic like you can't imagine. Plus he uses all these improvisational techniques to make his dances. It took forever before I could get my head around it.

Thank you for suggesting that I write down choreography. I bought a new notebook . . .

Mark stopped writing. He'd bought a new notebook because he couldn't bear to use the one Peri had given him. Instead, he'd shoved it deep in his dance bag. He drew a line through *I bought a new notebook.*

Anyway, it was a lot of busy months trying to learn choreography and German. Speaking German is like eating rocks. Lots of long, crunchy words. Fortunately . . .

Mark frowned. Was that how fortunately was spelled? He added an *e* after the *n*, but that looked weird. He erased it and left it the way it was. Peri knew he couldn't spell.

Fortunately, I got better at both. The kids in the company nicknamed me nerd because I was writing things down all the time, but I didn't care.

Mark rubbed the pencil between his fingers. That was a lie. He'd cared. A lot. The early months in West Germany had been so bad that if he'd had the money for a return ticket, he would have bought one.

• • •

Jim's choreography and the German language had been the least of his problems.

He'd been crushed by naivety and loneliness and the biggest problem of all, heartbreak. Going from spending all his time with Peri to none of his time with her had almost crippled him.

Mark hadn't realized all the ways she'd wedged herself into him. He opened his eyes in the morning expecting to see her only to blink back his disappointment when she wasn't there. At night, his body swam miserably in the empty bed, his arms light and lonely without her in them. When something funny or awful happened to him, he planned how he would tell it to Peri only to remember he wasn't going to be telling Peri anything again.

That thought was so terrible he couldn't even think it. Instead, he pretended Peri was coming at some date in the near future. It was the only way he could get out of bed every morning.

Jim's company was a hodgepodge of dancers from Europe and a few Americans. Lucky for him, classes and rehearsals were in English. He was the youngest by far with not even a full season of professional experience, which was the problem. He didn't know enough to know that he knew nothing. These dancers had been places, done things. After a couple of failed tries at making friends, Mark gave up, embarrassed by their obvious disinterest.

Then, there was West Germany, a country with so many unspoken rules that Mark still was offending its citizens even though he'd been there for a while. On one of his first days, his headphones jammed against his ears as he rocked out to some metal to keep the homesickness from coming for him, he'd walked through a red light, thinking it wasn't a big deal since the coast was clear. An old lady had yelled at him in German—a terrifying experience. He made the same mistake twice more before he figured out he wasn't supposed to walk when the light was red, even though the streets were empty.

Plus, there was the grocery store, which wasn't open all the time like in America. On his first Sunday there, Mark had gone to the nearest one, hoping to stock up. Instead, it was closed. As was every grocery store he visited after that. He was stuck buying a pretzel and soda from the train station.

Even once he figured out the store's hours, everything was in German, which meant for months, he bought weird things that he had no idea what to do with. One time, he bought a can of tuna fish only to pry off the lid to find himself staring at cat food as his stomach growled.

There were a thousand other rules and a bureaucracy that liked things done just right. Mark wanted to pull his hair out trying to get his residency straightened out. After almost collapsing in frustration, one of the women in office who had an American sister-in-law took pity on him and helped him.

But that was the exception, definitely not the rule. There was no service with a smile here. Cashiers rarely spoke, and waiters wore sour expressions. People cut in line all the time. It fed his isolation to the point where Mark would have paid someone to talk to him.

It will get better, he told himself all the time. *It will.*

It didn't. It, in fact, got so much worse that Mark tried never to think about that time. He'd been in West Germany for three months, and things were looking up. His language skills were improving. He'd gone to the grocery store, bought what he wanted, and managed to check out offering the correct number of Deutsche Marks.

Jim cast him in his new piece, which blew Mark's mind. Jim's process was collaborative, and although Mark didn't have friends at the company, people had to talk to him in rehearsal. A couple of times a week, he stopped by a beer hall that was popular with American college kids doing semesters abroad. He felt a decade older than most of them, but he found enough common ground to stretch a conversation over a beer or two. They didn't understand his job, but he was used to that.

Then, Gabrielle waltzed into his life and did her best to wreck it. She was a senior dancer with Jim's company, and she looked like a movie star with long dark hair and full lips. She had a husky voice that made Mark think of smoky nightclubs, and she wore designer clothes in all black. He'd steered clear of her because she was too pretty and established to care about a kid like himself.

Mistake number one.

If Mark had spent any time around her, he would have picked up on how crazy she was. Instead, he'd been thrilled when she paid attention to him although she was six years older and should have had her pick of boyfriends. Maybe because he was so lonely, maybe because Gabrielle was American and it was nice to be around someone who sounded like himself, maybe because Peri had been as pretty and even older than Gabrielle, or maybe because he was just that young and dumb, but Mark didn't consider Gabrielle might have a motive for seeking him out that had nothing to do with him.

They went out a few times, and when Mark brought her back to his place—a tiny, ratty, barely furnished apartment—he'd been bouncing with excitement.

The next day, she moved her stuff in.

"Now we can be together all the time, Marky," she said by way of explanation as she sauntered through his door with a couple of suitcases.

"Uh . . ."

His apartment was barely big enough for him, much less two people, but before he could say anything that made sense, she'd opened her suitcases and was lifting out her clothes. Mark ignored the bad feeling in his stomach and decided to enjoy his good luck. After all, he'd pretty much moved in with Peri when they started sleeping together. That felt way different from this although he couldn't explain why.

Mistake number two.

If Mark had kicked her out then and there, he could have saved himself a lot of money and a really bad time.

Gabrielle tossed all his clothing out of the wardrobe—Germans didn't seem to like closets—and into a corner.

"My things are expensive," she said by way of explanation. She picked up the suit that Peri had made, rubbed it between her fingers, and then let it drop to the floor. "This doesn't even have a label."

"Hey," he said. "Be nice." Gabrielle rolled her eyes.

Because "be nice" were not words Gabrielle was familiar with. She was mean, and she got her kicks from riling him up. She called him Marky even though he hated it.

"You look like a Marky. So young and dorky," she said by way of explanation.

"I don't call you Gabby," he said. "So don't call me Marky." Gabrielle ignored him.

The day after she moved in, trying to be romantic, Mark made dinner for them. He splurged on some pork chops and pan-fried them before throwing in a handful of mushrooms afterward to roast in the juices. When he passed her the plate, he prepared himself for a compliment or two.

Instead, Gabrielle scowled. She dragged bits of the pork chop around her plate and speared mushrooms on the prongs of her fork that she'd lift to her lips and then put back down, untouched, on her plate. Finally, he asked her what was wrong.

"I don't eat beige food. It's the color that has the most calories," she said by way of explanation. "But it was a nice effort, Marky."

"You watched me make it," he said. "You couldn't have told me before?"

She yawned as she reached for a banana.

Gabrielle loved to pick on Mark. About everything: his hair (too long), his clothes (too casual), his voice (too loud), even the way he smiled (too many teeth). She made fun of him when he wrote down the steps to Jim's new choreography. She grabbed the journal from him and doubled over in hysterics as she read through his notes.

"You're so dumb, Marky," she said by way of explanation. "You didn't spell one step right."

"It doesn't matter," he said. "It's to jog my memory, not yours." She was laughing too hard to respond.

Mark might have been six years younger than Gabrielle, but he was the adult in the relationship. She had no concept of money and was constantly asking him for some even though she, a senior company member, made more than he did. She didn't cook, do laundry, or clean. Instead, she picked at food from his plate (he refused to make dinner for her after the beige food incident), shoved her dirty clothes at him when he headed to wash his, and left messes everywhere for him to clean up: hills of powder on the bathroom sink, clumps of hair in the bathtub drain, shoes strewn around the apartment that he tripped over.

After a month, the beauty that he'd found so incredible had disappeared, and all he saw was her ugly heart. He tried to break up with her, but she waved him off.

"Don't be silly, Marky. No one else wants you," she said by way of explanation.

"Wrong," he said under his breath. "No one else wants you." She tossed her hair and glared at him, daring him to say it again.

But no one did want Gabrielle. She'd been through all the straight men in the company, even one of the women, and Mark was her last stop.

Finally, he had enough. One night, they were at a loud disco that reeked of beer and loneliness, which Mark hated but Gabrielle insisted on, and she kissed another guy in front of him. When he said something, she snickered.

"He was better looking than you," she said by way of explanation.

"I'm leaving," he said. "Kiss whoever you want."

He headed back to his apartment, threw her stuff into her suitcases, and placed them in the hall. He made sure the front door was locked tight and waited in grim silence for the show that was sure to begin.

Gabrielle tried everything. She screamed, she threatened, she laughed, she teased. But he stayed firm.

Then she cried. "I'm sorry, Mark."

He waited for the punch line, but it never came. Just a lot of tears and "I'm sorry, Mark."

Not Marky. Mark.

He opened the door. Mistake number three.

If he'd just stayed put on the sofa, she would have left and found some other sucker she could dazzle with her good looks.

It took another two months of grinding misery before he got her out of his life. Gabrielle, who was usually well behaved at the studio, got into a huge argument with Jim about casting. Jim was a nice guy, but he didn't tolerate prima donnas, so he didn't renew her contract. When she came home crying to Mark, he could barely contain his relief.

"I'll help you find another job," he told her.

One far away from here, he said to himself.

Mark went with her to auditions all over West Germany until she landed another job three hours away. He helped her move her stuff into a small apartment and gave her some money, knowing he was never getting it back but seeing it as the price to get her gone for good. He didn't say goodbye. Instead, he'd walked out of her life and to the train station feeling like he was forty although his nineteenth

birthday was around the corner.

Good riddance, he thought. *Both then and now.*

Mark looked down at the letter he'd been trying to write to Peri.

He read the last line:

Fortunately, I got better at both.

Where to go from here?

He certainly wasn't going to tell her about Gabrielle. Just remembering her made him hate himself. After he got rid of her, things did get better.

Glenn came to audition. Mark's heart had dropped when Glenn walked into the studio. Mark expected taunting, but Glenn was happy to see him.

"You punched out your dad, and you stole Mr. D's girl." Glenn's eyes were wide with awe. "That was boss, man," he said, dropping the fancy words he'd used back in L.A.

Mark grinned. "Thanks." It was dumb and he shouldn't care, but Glenn's praise had hit him straight in his ego's soft spot.

Glenn got the job, and they went out for beers to celebrate. He apologized to Mark.

"Sorry for being an asshole. I'd been waiting in the wings for a while, and then you came in and got the lead in the first ballet Mr. D had made in ages."

Although it'd only been a year, the tiff with Glenn felt so far in the past that Mark didn't care anymore. So he said, "No hard feelings, man." He meant it, too.

Glenn told him the gossip. To be more exact, Glenn told him that Peri had married Mr. D. Not knowing how to take that bullet, Mark got black-out drunk for the first time. He woke up the next day with a crushing headache that didn't come close to how bad his heart hurt.

With Glenn in the company, Mark wasn't the new guy anymore. He and Glenn became friends now that jealousy wasn't an issue— Jim's work was too collaborative and democratic for stuff like that. Mark had been right all those months before. Glenn was nice, and they had fun together, going to beer halls and chatting up girls. They even tried to have the conversation they couldn't have outside the jewelry store.

"I'm glad to be out of the United States." Glenn pushed down his cowlick. "I was going to go ballistic if another person assumed I was gay because I was a ballet dancer."

Mark nodded. "It's stupid, man. We spend all our time with girls in skintight clothing while football players run around in shiny pants and wrestlers roll on top of other dudes and baseball players pat each other on the butt. Yet we're the ones who are gay."

Neither of them said anything for a while. Just to do something, Mark flagged down the dirndl-wearing server and ordered another round.

"You know what's weird?" Glenn traced a circle with his index finger through the condensation on his boot-shaped glass. "Plenty of gay guys I know are more manly than some straight guys. And I'm not talking about shooting guns or playing basketball or driving fast cars. I'm talking about stuff like taking care of your friends who are sick and staying true to who you are."

Mark took a sip of his beer before speaking. "Everyone thinks my dad is a man because he played baseball and made a bunch of money, but he's a spoiled princess. He throws fits if other people don't do what he wants, when he wants it, and he's never stood up for anybody other than himself."

Glenn thumped him on the shoulder awkwardly. "That's rough, man."

"Do you still have the motorcycle?" Mark asked, wanting to change the subject.

"I sold it to get money for a plane ticket here, but I'm buying a new one as soon I get the funds together."

"You must really like riding."

"I do now." Glenn's face flushed. "My dad likes bikes. He's the one who got me started." He drained his beer. "It was something we could do together."

Feeling weird, Mark elbowed Glenn and jerked his head toward a group of college girls wearing T-shirts emblazoned with Greek letters. The girls were giggling as they pulled out chairs at the end of the long table Mark and Glenn were sitting at.

"Sorority girls," Glenn said as they scooted down a couple of seats. Mark dated around (the mess with Gabrielle had put him off relationships for a long time) and danced as much and as well as he could. Jim was using him more and more, and Mark was learning more and more.

Jim's not a choreographer. He's a philosopher, he wrote.

He's one of the smartest guys I've ever met. He sees the body as this arrangement of points that can be connected or disconnected. For each piece, he gives us parameters, and then we make up the movements. It's totally different from Mr. D. Remember how Mr. D used to say, "Dance, children. Do not think." Jim says his job is to help us become better thinkers because then we'll be better dancers.

Jim even lets us critique his pieces. We sit in a circle at the end of rehearsal and talk about what we worked on that day and what we would need to work on the next. In the beginning, I just sat there, like I was on the bench for the team. But once I gained some confidence, I started speaking up. It makes me feel connected to the work, like I'm more than just a body executing tasks.

The company toured America last year with Jim's new piece. We even went to Los Angeles. Did you know I danced one of the leads? I was hoping you were in the audience and would come backstage to say hello.

. . .

Mark's hand stopped moving.

Because I was still thinking about you, he thought. *You left this hole in my heart that nothing has been able to fill, not moving to a new country, not dancing, and definitely not other girls.*

He'd reached for the phone a hundred times once he found out he'd be in L.A., but his fingers would push a few buttons and then stop.

Because what if Peri didn't want to see him?

Although they'd had no contact since he left L.A., Mark still believed he'd see Peri again, for no other reason than his heart told him that he would. When he had a rough day, he leaned on this. Even when everything was fine, sometimes great, a piece was missing. Because Peri was missing.

It's just temporary, he told himself all the time, even when temporary had stretched to a couple of years. *We got ourselves into a mess, and it's going to take us time to get out of it.*

And that's how he found himself not able to call her. Because what if she didn't want to see him? Then, he'd have to admit to himself that it was over. For real. So he was a coward and didn't call. Instead, he silently begged her to come to the show.

From the wings, he'd stared into the black mouth of the audience, hoping to catch a glimpse of Peri. After the show ended, he parked himself by the stage door, his hope leaving him like air from a balloon when it became clear she wasn't coming, not that he had any reason to expect her to come beyond that he wanted her to come more than anything.

Disaster hit after they returned to West Germany. He ruptured his Achilles tendon landing from a *tour jeté* in class, mindlessly confident in his ability to land on one leg, the other extended behind him like a banner. Instead, a pop sang through the air as he fell to the floor in mute disbelief, which soon became full-bodied horror, as he understood exactly what had happened and how bad it would be.

I ruptured my Achilles tendon, which started out as a big blow but ended up as a lucky break. Jim was swamped with commissions for his choreography, plus he had to run the company. He'd seen how I wrote everything down and he was still paying me, so he drafted me into becoming his assistant.

I was limited in what I could do physically, so Jim set me up in his office and taught me how to run a company. He started me with the easy stuff, just sitting in on meetings and taking notes about things he needed to do later. Fortunately,

There was that word again. To add the *e* after the *n* or not? He shrugged and left it the way it was.

Jim didn't care that I wasn't a good speller. He bumped me up to doing things like assisting with casting and organizing the rehearsal schedule. After I got good at that, he taught me about finances and dealing with the bureaucracy. That was harder than dancing. The Herr Doktor who oversees all the performing arts companies is a total tool. He has a doctorate in logic, which means he can argue anybody down although Jim tries his best.

Mark had spent more time at the studio than he'd ever before, punching long strings of numbers into a calculator, trying to make what was not enough be enough, figuring out what holes needed to be plugged and what could stay unplugged for a while longer.

When I got better physically, Jim had me help out in rehearsal. I'd always been on the dancing side of things, so it was cool to see how everything worked from the creative side.

Do you remember how we used to get into the studio and try things?

He walked over to his dance bag and pawed through the jumble of tights and T-shirts until his hand closed around the journal Peri had given him. He opened it to the back where he'd scribbled in his ideas. His heart clenched at the way Peri's neat handwriting intersected with his sloppy scribbles.

We made each other better, he thought, remembering the two of them passing the journal back and forth.

Mark walked through his early attempts at choreography. They were pretty bad: repetitive, unoriginal, the product of an over-excited imagination with no understanding of space, time, or dynamics. He'd learned a lot working for Jim.

He traced his finger over the words she'd written: *Geometry with an attitude.*

Geometry with an attitude. Mark still liked that.

Because he still liked her. More than anyone he'd ever met. It was true then, and it was true now, even though he'd met hundreds of people since meeting her.

His eyes had grown hot and scratchy. He pushed the book deep into his dance bag.

Anyway, I'm about to begin choreographing my first piece with Glenn (Remember him? He came after Mr. D closed the company. We're friends now! Can you believe it?) and my girlfriend Bea

Mark stopped. He didn't want to mention Bea. She was his girlfriend, but it wasn't serious, not for him and not for her. They'd started going together last year, mostly out of the mutual desire not to be alone.

He liked Bea. She was four years older than him—he couldn't seem to date anyone his age—and from London. She had curly auburn hair and a wicked sense of humor. She was nice and treated Mark with respect. But besides dancing, they had nothing in common. Bea hated staying at home, so she was always dragging Mark to this or that disco.

This is awful, Mark wanted to say as he looked around whatever packed place Bea had picked. The music made his head pound and the press of bodies made him sweat and his drink made him want to barf. Why did anyone think this was fun?

He'd rather be at home, relaxing on the sofa, dishes soaking in the sink from a nice home-cooked meal. Once he and Bea became official, he begged off more and more. Bea didn't care. She had more fun with her friends anyway.

"My tender ears," Bea called him.

He scratched out the part about Bea. It wasn't if it would end, it was when. A few months ago, they'd had a fun, romantic night. They went out to dinner and ordered a nice bottle of wine. Then, they met up with a couple of her friends for drinks and dancing before walking back, hand in hand, to their apartment, which Bea had moved into a few weeks ago. They came together in a tangle of passion, and when it was over, the moment was there, just waiting for Mark to fill it with some big words. Instead, he retreated into himself to think about Peri. Again.

Because having fun with Peri was easy. It wasn't easy with Bea.

It felt like a show where he had to perform the part of Mark Maroulis, Jr., perfect boyfriend. It involved an outlay of cash for dinner and entertainment because Bea wanted to go out. It involved him trying to be continually funny, interesting, and charming because Bea expected him to amuse her. It involved winning over her friends, again and again, because Bea had so many friends that he couldn't keep track of who he'd met and who he hadn't.

His heart shrunk and hardened. He'd had a great night with a great girl, and he'd rather have gone shopping for light bulbs with Peri.

"Who is she?" Bea asked, yanking him from his thoughts of Peri.

"A girl I danced with in L.A.," he said, forgetting to lie.

Mark glanced at Bea, preparing himself for her sad eyes, the hurt frown. Instead, she was staring out the window, her face creased with longing for someone who was not Mark.

"Who is he?"

"A bloke from uni." She sighed and turned toward Mark. "So it's like that?"

"It's like that," he said.

"Brilliant." Her accent emphasized the sarcasm.

That night, they'd slept in each other's arms as their hearts beat out of time.

Mark sighed and put his pencil to the paper.

Some kids from the company agreed to be in it, and I'm going to enter it in a choreography competition. Finding my voice has been difficult. Mr. D had such a strong voice, and I've spent so much time absorbing Jim's philosophy that I have to fight my way out of their influences. I think I've found something, though, that combines the emotions of Mr. D with the crazy angles of Jim's choreography. Plus, I took my early years as a baseball player and added the pathways of a baseball game, which . . .

He read through what'd written. He was blabbing about nothing. Peri would think he was an idiot.

She never thought you were an idiot, a voice in his gut told him. *Not then. Not now.*

He sighed and crumpled up the paper. The letter was a failure, just a rambling mess of him telling her everything except what he wanted to tell her, which was . . .

What did he want to tell her?

Mark pinched the bridge of his nose. He wanted to tell her that what he'd thought then was what he thought now. That he loved her. That fate tripped up and made her eleven years older than him, but he didn't care. That he'd tried to move on but couldn't because loving Peri was the same to him as having blue eyes or being good at ballet.

He had tried to move on, searched everywhere for another Peri. He'd dated petite blondes with pale skin, none of whom he'd asked out a second time. He'd dated women for stupid reasons: because they cooked or sewed, because they drove a beige car, because they had the quick, precise motions that Peri used when she stitched ribbons to her pointe shoes. He'd asked one girl out because she had a pink leotard like the one Peri wore when he auditioned for Mr. D.

Not one of them had worked out, and that's how he found himself with Bea, who was his roommate he slept with.

"I have to see her," Mark said out loud. "So I can ask."

He wanted to ask if she'd lied about not loving him. Because he was pretty sure she had. This idea had only grown stronger over the years, maybe because he'd grown up enough to understand why. She'd told Mark she didn't love him because she did love him. She'd been scared that she would hold Mark back, that Mark would resent her and dump her. And Mark had done a terrible job of reassuring her about the future. So Peri had let him go.

A memory jolted through him. *Outlast him*, Bob had told Mark from his deathbed all those years earlier. Mark hadn't understood what it meant, just assumed it was the babbling of someone in the last inning of his life. But now he understood that Bob had understood, had seen what Mark and Peri hadn't yet admitted to themselves. Bob was telling Mark that Mr. D wouldn't live forever, that Mark just needed to stay true to Peri.

Mark straightened his spine, an idea flickering in his brain. He was coming back as soon that miserable bastard—

He stopped himself. As soon as Mr. D died. And he was coming back with something better to offer her than sitting around sewing clothes all day.

FEMALE VARIATION

A solo for the danseuse, usually with quick spins and pretty poses.

21

Retiré

(WITHDRAWN)

DEAR MARK, Peri wrote in her best cursive handwriting.

She pulled back and examined the words. They looked innocent enough, but the hand gripping the pen that had written them was pulsing with emotion. This was at least the twentieth time she'd tried to write to Mark. Even if she finished the letter, something she'd not managed to do before, she didn't know where to send it.

That was a lie. True, she didn't know his home address, but she did know where he worked.

After Mark left, she'd been consumed with concern for him and recrimination for herself. She argued with herself constantly.

What were you thinking? her heart asked her head. *Mark had nowhere to go, nobody to go to. And you sent him out into the world with nothing. You should have helped him. Researched companies. Booked airline tickets. Made sure he had enough money. But you didn't.*

I had to make it a clean break, her head said to her heart. *If I didn't, then I was going to go with him. I couldn't do that. Have him worry about my happiness when managing his own was going to be hard enough.*

Then, one miserable year after he'd left, she was flipping through a ballet magazine, and her eye caught on a small picture of a man with his legs split in the obtuse angle of a *sissonne.* Peri gasped. It was Mark. He was in West Germany, dancing for James Prescott.

She held the magazine to her chest, bursting with pride. "You did it!" she whispered.

She reached for her stationary to write him a letter of

congratulations. She made it through a few sentences before she was shaking too much to continue.

Knowing Mark was well and dancing should have filled her with joy, with validation. Instead, she felt lonelier than ever. She'd always thought absence was a hollowed-out feeling, the lack of presence, but Mark's absence was a cold, heavy stone she carried around wedged between her stomach and heart.

Peri sighed and turned her attention back to the letter. Maybe this would be the one she finished, sent to Mark in care of James Prescott's company.

Congratulations on all your success. I saw your picture in a magazine two years prior, and I was delighted to see that you were in West Germany, dancing for James Prescott.

Peri read back through what she'd written. It sounded stilted and formal, like something a grandfather would write to a grandchild he barely knew. She crossed it out. She would rewrite it later. Make it perfect. She tried a new opening.

I've been meaning to write you. I saw you when James Prescott's company came through L.A. You were fantastic. I couldn't believe how beautifully you danced, how I couldn't watch anyone but you.

This was worse. She sounded like a lovesick fan, which in a way she was, but she didn't want Mark to know that.

The piece in which he'd performed had taken the dance world by storm the year before in Paris. To a score that sounded like electronic bullets, three men and six women in slick jade-green costumes strode on and off stage. They thwacked and whacked with a hostility that revealed ballet as competition for the scarce, sacred resource of center stage.

Mark mesmerized her. His rangy frame had filled out and his technique had become more sophisticated, more voluminous, but he was still Mark in every other way: sweet, alert, and striving for the moon. She perched rigidly in her seat, her back ruler straight, her arms wrapped around herself, as she tried to imprint his every movement onto her memory.

In the middle of the ballet, he performed a solo. Tripping walks segued into violent cabrioles, his legs slapping each other as he sailed through the air. As other dancers entered, Mark slung his body into lashing *battements*, his hips tilted forward.

Fabulous, she telegraphed to him.

After the show, she'd taken a few hesitant steps toward backstage but stopped. She couldn't figure out what would be worse—Mark refusing to see her or Mark agreeing to see her so he could show her exactly how easily he'd moved on. Instead, she sat in her car and had a hurricane of a cry for Mark, who was doing everything she wanted him to do, and for herself, who was not doing much of anything she wanted to do.

She traced a line through her words. Maybe she should start with herself? But there was so little to tell and most of it was unpleasant. She'd accepted Mr. D's proposal, not because she wanted to but because she didn't know what else to do.

The wedding was one of the saddest days of her life.

It took place in Mr. D's church—a white building with a swooped roof. The interior was plainer than the exotic decadence she'd been expecting. There were honey-colored pews, exposed beams on the ceiling, and, the only point of beauty, three stained-glass windows above the altar. She wore a fussy ivory satin dress that Mr. D had picked out, the giant peridot sticking up from her fourth finger like an ugly bug.

During the ceremony, the priest intoned some gibberish that Peri ignored before she exchanged simple gold rings with Mr. D. Unlike an American ceremony, where the kiss acted as the pinnacle, in the Armenian one, ornate crowns were positioned on their heads, symbolizing their home as their kingdom.

When she felt the weight of the crown, Peri's heart constricted, and for a moment, she indulged herself. She closed her eyes and pretended she was onstage for *M+M*, Mark placing the pearl crown on her head as her heart thudded with unfaked fervor for him.

Their witnesses to the ceremony were the reedy board president who'd arranged for Mr. D's *M+M* appeal to the Armenian community and his wife. Peri didn't pay them much attention, but supposedly, they were a cross between bridal party attendants and godparents.

After the crowning, Peri and Mr. D placed their foreheads together as a golden cross was held over them. The four of them drank sour wine from a common cup, and then they received the blessing from the priest, who asked God to protect them under the shadow of the holy and honorable cross in peace.

If she cared, then she might find this beautiful, meaningful. Instead, being a bride was just another role in an elaborate ballet she was playing.

The celebration continued with an interminable dinner attended by his Armenian acquaintances at Mr. D's favorite French restaurant. Course after course came out as Peri's mood slipped lower and lower. Maybe if she had someone there for her, she would feel better. But she didn't have anyone to invite.

When they cut the cake, she attempted a smile for the camera, but inside, the contours of her heart had collapsed into those of a teardrop.

Because this was a transaction. Nothing more, nothing less.

The wedding night dragged on as she fought back her revulsion at Mr. D's wizened body, his dry fingers stroking her, the little yelps he made in her ear as his cross necklace bounced against her chest. She closed her eyes and imagined herself shuttling through the dark void of space, all the jabs and pokes being administered to her by Mr. D the sharp edges of stars.

You can choreograph my life, she told him in her head. *But you can't choreograph my feelings*.

Mr. D kept his word. Nothing changed. She had lunch with him every Sunday and continued to live in her apartment. At the end of the season, she retired to much fanfare, not that she cared, and Mr. D closed the company. He gifted her with his ballets, and she studied his notes, the choreographic scores, the videos.

Word got out that companies could acquire a Mr. D piece, and her schedule filled up with flying around the United States to set his works. Having spent years at his side, she knew his flamboyant, dramatic style inside and out.

In the beginning, she floundered. She was used to being told what to do. Now, she was the person who was doing the telling, and it took her time to figure out how to do that telling. She didn't want to be like Mr. D with his manipulation and infantilization. So she taught herself to be pleasant but precise, kind but not a pushover.

Although there was no way to get around telling people what to do, she made it a dialogue wherever she could. She asked the dancers questions and responded to their answers. She couldn't change the choreography, but she could help each performer find personal meaning in the steps.

"What do you think?" she asked all the time.

Her efforts weren't always successful—teachers trained dancers from a young age to never question authority—but when they were, it breathed life into phrases that could have been calcified by repetition.

Peri never acknowledged it outwardly, but she hoped that by engaging their brains, she might save one or two from the blind obedience she'd practiced for so many years.

To her surprise, once she got going, she enjoyed the work, found it fulfilling to pass on everything she'd learned. The dancers looked at her with awe, and the directors treated her with deference and professionalism.

Retirement. When you become a sum of your successes.

The days passed in a quick, agreeable fashion, and when she was working, she wasn't thinking about Mark. Out of work, though, that was when she struggled. She'd stopped listening to the radio after hearing the band Mark had taken her to see the day Bob had died. She'd been right about their talent, and she couldn't go anywhere without hearing them sing about paradise city.

Peri was assaulted by memories of her first kiss with Mark, her first time sleeping with Mark, her first time waking up in his arms, his face so sweet and serene in the flood of morning sunshine.

To keep thoughts of Mark at bay, she doubled down on sewing brightly colored and whimsically patterned robes for AIDS patients. She dropped them off at hospitals and hospice centers and all the organizations that had sprung up to fight the disease. One day, a man being wheeled down the hall caught her eye. He reminded her of Bob, his good looks stretched and his spirit shrunken by the disease.

Peri leaned her head toward the nurse on duty. "Would any of the patients like company?" She flushed at her boldness. "Just for a few minutes."

The nurse's jaw dropped. "My goodness, yes." She pointed toward the hall. "Take your pick."

So Peri made a few timid knocks on a door and tiptoed in after a young man issued an imperious welcome. She offered him a robin's egg blue caftan and haltingly asked if he wanted company. He'd snatched the caftan from her hands and examined it.

"My color is royal blue." He sighed, a big, put-upon one. "But I guess this will do."

Peri turned toward the door, but he called her back.

"What do you think of this outfit?" He shoved a fashion magazine in her face.

Peri studied the image of a woman dressed in blousy, head-to-toe leopard print. Even her short hair had been dyed to resemble a leopard. "It's hideous," she said honestly.

The man laughed. "I'm Tim." "Peri."

"Like Perry Ellis?"

The famed sportswear designer had died a few months earlier from AIDS complications, yet another talented man the world had lost to the scourge.

She nodded. "But spelled differently."

Tim patted the seat next to him. "Let's dish."

They spent the good part of an hour flipping through magazines and giggling at the loud, outrageous outfits that passed for fashion these days.

When he dozed off, she moved to the next room, which held a black man in his forties. He was close to the end, but he arranged his lips in the approximation of a smile when she came in. On his nightstand was a hefty astronomy textbook.

"Would you like me to read aloud?" she asked. He nodded.

She opened the cover. At the top of the title page was a sticker that read Melvin C. Washington, Doctor of Aerospace Engineering.

Wow, she thought. *A real-life rocket scientist.*

Peri did her best, tripping over the dense prose and unfamiliar terms, although it didn't matter since he fell asleep after a few paragraphs.

She kissed his cheek. "I hope the stars are bigger and more beautiful than you thought."

After seeing the need, she came back. Although, at this point, AIDS had left no group untouched, gay men were still disproportionately affected. So Peri sought them out. She stopped learning names, after returning to find both Tim and Dr. Washington dead. Instead, she treated it like a one-off cocktail party where the guests were in hospital beds and nightgowns. She made brisk, polite conversation; she squeezed hands; and she listened to their gossip, amazed that people so close to death could be riled up about who said what to whom. Sometimes, she told them about Bob, and she was pleasantly surprised to find how many of the men had seen them dance.

She also called mothers. Many were nicer than Bob's mother, but plenty refused to visit. "God's punishment," she heard more than once. Her heart would clench as she remembered Bob dying alone, unreconciled with his mother.

After one harrowing day, when a man all of eighteen died as she rang frantically for the nurse with one hand while holding his hand with her other, she looked at the sky, blue and benign with fat, lazy clouds scooting across it.

"Why?" she asked God. "Why now? Why them? It's not like they're the first to walk across your great green earth."

She shook her fist at the sky, like she was a heroine in a melodramatic film. "You made them that way. So why do hate them so much? Why do you hurt them so much?"

God didn't respond.

Not that she'd expected Him to.

It'd been enough to keep her busy, and then came Mr. D's diagnosis of stomach cancer. She wasn't surprised. He'd been fading for almost a year.

Mr. D knew.

Not the diagnosis, but that he was sick. He put off going to the doctor for months until he couldn't. When the doctor told them, Mr. D only nodded with dull eyes.

Like a roller coaster, he'd get better for a while and then take a turn for the worse. She cut back on visiting AIDS patients to play nursemaid, driving him to his doctor's appointments and chemotherapy treatments, spooning runny potatoes and mashed bananas into his mouth, making sure he stayed clean.

This is why he married me, she thought as he spit up into the bucket she held under his chin. *Because he knew I'd take care of him until the end.* She looked at the long slender fingers gripping hers. *And so he didn't have to die alone.*

His doctors couldn't believe how long Mr. D held on.

"He should have died a long time ago, Mrs. Dektember," they said. "It's a miracle."

It wasn't a miracle; it was sheer determination on Mr. D's part. Death terrified him. He'd outrun it all those years before, and he considered it a credit with a mighty interest rate that he'd have to remit in full once death came knocking.

"It won't hurt," she told him. "It will be dark and warm and comfortable, like pulling a blanket over yourself after a long day."

He shook his head. "Death is a monster that will swallow me whole."

She held his hand and wiped his brow, startled that, in less than a year, their roles had been reversed. Mr. D had been in her life for over half of it. Often, he'd been the most important person in her life—the artist who molded her body and spirit like clay.

But now, as she looked at his frail, beige body, she couldn't arouse any feeling for him. Not love, not hate, not pity, not even compassion. He'd withered in her eyes until he was virtually invisible. He wasn't a person; he was a body whose needs she oversaw.

Even at his sickest, she refused to move in—finally, too late, asserting herself. Instead, she hired him around-the-clock nurses. She came when she could, which was every day when she was in town, but she left him at night to face his demons alone.

Peri scanned over what she had written to Mark. There was nothing, save the greeting, which made sense because it'd been three years. Why was she even trying? He'd done what she'd wanted him to do—move on.

She was writing the letter for herself because she was the one who hadn't moved on. Peri scrunched up the paper and lobbed it into the trash where it hit squarely. A memory buzzed of Mark and her in their early days, him impressed by her ability to sink a soda can.

She reached into her drawer for the little notebook in which she'd written down the small, inconsequential details of her days with Mark.

January 7, 1986

Mark and I were almost late to class because we started kissing during breakfast, and one thing led to another, and we ended up back in bed. It was a nice way to start the day although I was off my leg because I didn't warm up. Oh well. I'm off my leg plenty these days even when I do warm up. At least today I had an excuse—a wonderful one.

January 10, 1986

For the first time, we ran the M+M pas de deux all the way through. Although we had some rough patches—Mark forgot the choreography in two places, and I was wobbly on a big balance—it went well otherwise. Mr. D was impressed. He had notes—he always has notes—but he seemed more concerned that we continue to dance with emotion.

Mr. D knows. He has to. I can't believe he hasn't confronted me yet. I'm not looking forward to that conversation, but I am looking forward to officially being Mark's girlfriend so we can—

• • •

Peri stopped reading. Her heart felt so heavy that she was surprised it hadn't plunged down and out of her body. She turned the page.

January 20, 1986

Yesterday, I needed to sew ribbons on my pointe shoes and Mark had T-shirts with holes that needed to be closed, so I pulled out the sewing basket and he grabbed the paper. He read an article about how this song about friendship—it's been playing everywhere—hit number one. All its proceeds are going to an AIDS foundation, which is wonderful. Finally, people are starting to realize how bad AIDS is. How bad it could get.

I couldn't stop thinking about Bob when Mark was reading. I still miss him every day, but hearing about the song made me wonder if there was something I could do to help beyond moping. So I'm thinking about making hospital gowns for AIDS patients. The ones Bob had to wear were so ugly and threadbare. Even at home, he was stuck in baggy T-shirts and pajama bottoms that swam on him. Before AIDS, I never saw him with a shirt that hadn't been perfectly pressed or shoes that hadn't been shined. The disease took so much away from him. It didn't have to take that from him. Even skinny, sick people should be able to wear clothing that's not hideous and worn out.

Peri flipped forward. She couldn't bear to continue reading about days this ordinary that, in retrospect, seemed extraordinary in their happiness and purpose.

February 14, 1986

Mark wore a red T-shirt because, yay, it's Valentine's Day. Although we had a full day of dancing ahead of us, he got up early. Yes, Mark got up early, before me, and I didn't notice. He made me breakfast in bed. There was an omelet with tomatoes and green peppers and fresh-squeezed orange juice, even a red rose. After I ate, I showed him the steaks I bought for tonight, which got him excited.

It's the first time I've celebrated Valentine's Day since I was a kid, and I like it. Maybe it is a silly, made-up holiday, but still, it's nice to acknowledge the person I—

• • •

She hadn't written the word love. Instead, she'd drawn a little heart, like a besotted teenybopper. Peri slammed the notebook closed with shaking hands and stuffed it in the back of the drawer.

"I miss you," she said out loud, and then cringed at her honest admission. Not that anyone was around to hear her, especially Mark, who, even if he were here, wouldn't care.

She massaged her temples. She had to move forward. Because this would be mortifying if it weren't so sad, writing a letter to her twenty-one-year-old ex-boyfriend whom she'd never see again, reading journal entries about things that had happened long ago.

Peri selected another piece of stationary, white with a swirl of purple flowers around the border. At the top, she inscribed *Peridot Jones, Act 2.*

A New Place, she wrote.

When Mr. D died, she was leaving L.A. She was tired of California where the sun only cast shadows. Nothing was keeping her here, beyond the real and figurative tombstones that commemorated what she'd had and what she'd lost. The only grave she'd miss was Bob's. She visited a few times a year to sweep it clean and scatter a handful of bright flowers over it. Sometimes, she'd walk around the cemetery afterward, spotting the names of Bob's friends on tombstones. Every time, it seemed like there was a new one.

Peri could move wherever she wanted as long as it was close to a major airport, so she could get to whatever company hired her to set one of Mr. D's pieces.

Seattle, she thought with a smile. *Good coffee, misty weather, green things, smart people.*

She'd been there last year to set *M+M* on a company. She'd loved the coffee shops and bookstores, their cozy mellow light contrasting with the soft gray dampness outside.

And if she didn't like it, she could go somewhere else. Nothing and nobody were stopping her from moving from city to city every year if that's what she wanted.

A New Person

. . .

She'd had two romantic relationships, both with men of inappropriate ages. Mr. D was fifty-plus years her senior and Mark had been eleven years her junior. She should date someone her age, which meant, as she groaned resignedly, her options would be limited and unappealing: newly divorced men who needed help with their children, men who acted like they were still in a college fraternity, men who were too broken or too volatile to attract a spouse.

She sighed. It wasn't like she was a great catch. She was going to be a widow with her worldly experience limited to the stage and the studio. The parade of dates that lay in front of her with their tongue-tied conversations and awkward first kisses and their inevitable disappointment made her yawn with exhaustion.

But she had to try. There was a whole world of men out there. The probability was that one of them would like her and she would like him.

Peri squared her shoulders. *I will try*, she thought.

A New Passion, she wrote with special emphasis.

This was the most important thing. Dancing had defined her since she was eight, and that would be true until she died. But she felt emaciated by feeding on one thing for so long. She was going to find another role that would expand her capacities, get her in touch with the parts of herself she'd long since buried so she could pursue ballet fully focused.

Maybe she could do something with her sewing. Peri enjoyed making pretty clothes, wearing them, receiving compliments for her efforts. She liked making hospital gowns for AIDS patients, knowing the difference they made was incremental, but still. It was something positive in a situation of mostly negatives.

She shook her head, discarding that idea. She had no desire to expand sewing into something beyond what it had been for years—a hobby.

Maybe she could go back to school. She lingered over this idea for a minute before tossing it in the trash heap of bad ideas. She didn't even have a high school diploma. It'd been the '70s when she moved to L.A. to dance for Mr. D, and nobody had thought it important that she graduate, herself included. Even if she wanted to go back to school, she couldn't imagine how that would play out, sitting in classrooms with kids a decade and a half younger than she, trying to reacquaint herself with algebra equations and sentence diagramming, skills that she knew for a fact had no practical use in the real world.

Maybe she could . . . She can't even write down what she wanted. Because it wasn't an idea based in reality. She was never going to have a baby and be someone's mother. By the time Mr. D died and she'd moved and she'd gotten her life in order and she'd met someone—if she even got lucky enough to meet someone who wanted children—she'd be too old. Her heart, though, paid no attention to this cold logic.

Sometime over the last year, she, who'd previously been indifferent to children, started cooing at babies, throwing exaggerated smiles at toddlers, chatting with elementary school kids while she checked out at the grocery store. A small but burning light had flicked on of its own accord, and it refused to turn off.

"Stop it," she said out loud to herself in a useless bid to prevent herself from dreaming a dream that wasn't going to come true.

She sighed. She wasn't sure what else she wanted to do, but she'd keep brainstorming. Something was bound to appeal to her.

Peri looked through her list. Three items. Not many and none holding the promise of happiness and fulfillment, but they did offer a lifeline to the future that, if nothing else, would be different from the present and the past.

CODA

The final dance of the classic *grand pas de deux*.

22

Échappé

(ESCAPING OR SLIPPING MOVEMENT)

MARK STEPPED into the airport terminal, scanning the crowd. He found Peri immediately. She was wearing a blousy black dress with a thick black belt and high-heeled ankle boots. Her silky blonde hair floated to her waist. She was weaving the gold chain from her purse around her fingers.

His heart seized. He wanted to point to her and shout, *That's my girl*, so the knots of travelers passing him would know that he'd scored someone like that.

Going to be my girl, he corrected himself.

Peri turned toward him as her face lit up. He slung his knapsack over his shoulder, ran to her, placed his hands on her waist, and hoisted her over his head. Her hair fell around them in a shiny curtain as they locked eyes.

It was like the first time they'd done it.

Gently, he placed her down and then threw his arms around her in a gigantic bear hug.

"Mark," she said in a tiny voice, her head pressed against his chest. "I didn't think I'd ever see you again."

You were always going to see me again, he thought.

They stayed like that for a long time until Peri pulled away. She was shaking.

"Are you okay?" he asked.

Peri nodded. "Just happy to see you."

Mark unzipped his knapsack and pawed through it until his hand closed over a bag. He yanked it out and handed it to her.

"Butterbonbon. The German version of butterscotch candies." He paused. "If you still like them, that is."

Peri pressed the bag to her chest. "I do." She fiddled with a corner. "Thank you."

Mark grinned. *Still my girl*, he thought.

She pointed at his bag. "Do you have any more luggage?"

He shook his head and reached for her purse where she kept her keys. "Why don't you let me drive?"

He drove them to Peri's apartment as they talked about minor things like Mark's flight and the weather. They had major things to say to each other, but those could wait until they could do it face-to-face.

Peri's apartment looked the same except for one thing. "You got a new couch," Mark said.

She giggled. "Take a seat."

He flung himself on the pale blue sofa and then groaned with delight when he sank into its soft, cozy cushions. "I want to sit here forever."

He looked up. Peri was standing in front of him, holding neatly folded sheets and a pillow.

"I didn't know where you wanted to stay," she said. "I can book you a hotel room, or you can sleep here on the sofa."

I'm not staying at a hotel, and I'm not sleeping on the sofa, he wanted to say. *I know that, and you know that.*

Instead, he said, "I'll stay with you."

She placed the bed linens on the sofa's arm and then perched next to him. "It was nice of you to come. Mr. D would have appreciated it."

Mark doubted that.

"I wanted to come. He gave me my first job." He paused. "I also wanted to see you."

When he saw the announcement of Mr. D's death in the newspaper, he didn't think; he acted. He stopped at the first travel agency he found and booked a ticket to L.A. for the next morning. Then, he called Peri—he still knew her number by heart—and left a message on her answering machine with his arrival information. She called him back while he was in the stupor of sleep to let him know she'd be waiting. Then, the endless flight to New York followed by another one to L.A., his excitement growing as each minute ticked by.

The timing couldn't have been better, he thought. *At least the miserable bastard—*

Mark stopped himself from finishing the thought. While it was true that Mr. D had died conveniently, it was also rude considering Mr. D wasn't in the grave yet.

"I'm glad you're here," Peri said, her cheeks pink. "I've tried to write you a few times, but I didn't know if you'd want to hear from me."

"I tried to write you too. Let you know I was okay. I figured you'd be worried."

Peri's face collapsed. "I've never forgiven myself for that. I'm sorry, Mark."

"It's okay."

"You did about a hundred times better than okay," she said.

"Thanks." His heart was pounding. "Peri, uh, I came to L.A. because I needed to ask you a question." He paused. "It's a question I've had for a long time."

"Okay?"

Mark scuffed a foot against the floor, unexpectedly nervous, wishing he'd cooled his heels instead of jumping right in. "Did you lie when you told me you didn't love me?"

She nodded as she squeezed her eyes shut. "I couldn't do that to you—burden you with me. You were eighteen. You had your whole life in front of you."

He breathed out and sank back into the couch. "It took me six months before I calmed down enough to realize that. By then, it was too late. I had a contract in Europe, and you were married to Mr. D."

"How did you find out?"

"Glenn," he said. "He saw the same show we did on Christmas, and when Mr. D closed the company, he came to audition." Mark shook his head in amazement. "He was happy to see me. Apparently, I'd become a legend, punching out my dad and stealing Mr. D's girl." Mark laughed. "Anyway, he got the job, and we went out for a beer to celebrate. That's when he told me." He rubbed his temples. "I had my first hangover the next morning."

Peri leaned over and patted his knee. Mark breathed her in. She still smelled like the color pink. He shifted uncomfortably.

"Did you want to marry him?" he asked.

"Not really. But he promised to give me his ballets if I did." She shrugged. "It was a transaction. Although the cancer diagnosis didn't come until later, I think he knew he was sick. He'd seen how I'd cared for Bob. He knew I'd do the same for him."

"Are you okay?"

She lifted her gaze heavenward. "I'm fine. It was a long time coming. I just hope he's somewhere peaceful."

They sat in silence for a few minutes, remembering Mr. D and all the ways he'd brought them together and then torn them apart.

Mark faced her. "I did it, Peri. I did everything you wanted me to do. I dated girls my own age." He paused. "Well, closer. I had a couple of girlfriends. I danced. I traveled. I went out, I had fun, and I learned a lot. But I kept running into the same problem."

Peri tugged her left earlobe. "What's that?"

"You. None of the girls were you. None of the places I went were with you, and none of the things I did were with you." Mark looped an arm around her shoulder and pulled her close. "I was sure then. I'm sure now."

She didn't say anything for a long time, and Mark's stomach tied itself in knots at his directness. Maybe her feelings had changed. "Say something," he said. "Please."

"But I'm eleven—"

Mark rolled his eyes. "I know and I know what it means and I don't care. If our ages were reversed, then this would be the most boring story in the world." He winked at her. "Anyway, with all the stuff I've been through, I have to be at least forty on the inside."

Peri closed her eyes as if debating something. Then, she opened them, the brown determined, the gold soft. "If you don't care, then I won't care." She leaned forward and kissed him. It was even better than he'd remembered.

Yes, he silently cheered as they dashed to the bedroom.

23

En Croix

(IN THE SHAPE OF A CROSS)

IT SHOULD BE illegal to be this happy at a funeral, Peri thought, as she shook hands, kissed cheeks, and accepted condolences.

Tonight was the first of the three-part Armenian funeral ritual. That morning, she'd attended the washing of the body with the priest and helped dress Mr. D in one of his white suits. She placed his cane in his cold hand, the peridot flat in the pale blank light that poured from fixtures above.

At Mr. D's home, a black-draped platform held the open casket. Various people mingled around it, occasionally peeking in. A few older women sat in chairs and wept, their wails so shrieking it sounded as if they were actors rather than grievers. Tomorrow, the casket would be moved for the church service and gravesite burial. The day after, she had a meeting with Mr. D's lawyer, and then the whole thing would be done.

Not technically.

There was supposed to be something on the seventh day, the fortieth day, the one-year anniversary of the death, and thereafter, every January 7 on Cemetery Day, according to Armenian customs, but Peri was skipping those. She wasn't Armenian; knew little about the culture or the country that had formed the broken, brilliant Mr. D; and executing rites she didn't understand or care about felt like the worst kind of performance.

As Peri headed to the casket, she gagged at the sweet smell from the countless wheels of roses and gigantic cones of lilies that lined the casket.

Why did people honor the dead with the almost dead?

The turnout for his last performance would've pleased Mr. D. Former dancers, longtime board members, and a huge portion of the Armenian community had come to pay their respects and honor his accomplishments.

She peered in. Mr. D lay there, looking the same as he had since she'd known him. Peri tried to read her feelings since, after all, she was burying her husband, but she felt nothing beyond hope that the wrinkles of Mr. D's soul had been ironed out in the afterlife.

"I wish you peace, Levon," she whispered.

The wobble in her stomach slowed and then stopped. All the nervous responsibility she'd felt since Mr. D singled her out to feed his inspiration had dissipated. Her muscles slackened.

She was free. Finally.

Mutely, she backed away to let another person take her place. Mark slipped beside her and discreetly placed his hand on her back. Her body, gooey with relaxation, spread into the warm crevice created by his palm. He squeezed her and then backed away.

Peri pulled her features down, striving for a somber expression, but a goofy smile kept threatening to break through. Because Mark!

He'd fallen asleep right after they'd made love as she, her adrenaline sky high, smoothed his hair back from his brow, letting her fingers linger on his warm skin.

You need a haircut, she thought affectionately. She would have stayed watching him sleep until he woke, but she wanted to run out and stock the fridge, which was yawning with empty shelves. She would bet her big toe that Mark would wake up hungry. Maybe they could cook dinner or maybe they could go out or maybe they could just hang around in bed. She didn't care as long as it was with him, but she wanted to be prepared.

She left a note, but there'd been no need. Mark was still out cold when she returned. After she put away the groceries, she undressed and fit her body into his familiar nooks and crannies. With a growl, he pulled her on top of him in a frenzied rush of raw emotion as they gazed at each with starry eyes.

Later, they migrated to the kitchen, falling into old habits easily, Peri chopping mushrooms as Mark pounded chicken breasts. After they put the chicken marsala in the oven, she poured them glasses of wine to commemorate Mr. D and to celebrate their reunion. They leaned against the counters and caught each other up on their lives.

Any awkwardness from spending three years apart had dissipated, and they bantered easily, happily.

She told a story about setting *M+M* on a tiny company in Texas. "They didn't have enough guys, so the six brothers were played by girls and—"

"This," Mark said, sweeping an arm around the kitchen to end pointing at her. "I've missed it so much. I looked for it everywhere."

Peri pressed a finger to her smiling lips. "Making and breaking bread. Who'd think that would be so hard to find?"

He groaned. "You can't imagine how many loud clubs and bars I've been to in search of it. Seriously, Peri. I compromised my hearing."

"Can you hear this?" she asked as she opened the oven door. The chicken marsala was bubbling, and the aroma—meatiness touched with sweetness—wafted around the kitchen.

Mark beamed. "Dinner. A good one."

And it had been a good dinner, perfect in its ordinariness.

Peri blinked away her memory of last night as she pressed her hand to her heart, sure everyone could hear its happy throb. She glanced at Mark through the black-clad bodies. He was wearing dark pants and a dark shirt, hanging out by the door where the coffin lid had been placed—supposedly, that let neighbors know there'd been a death in the family. Mark took his index finger, placed it on his lips, and turned it outward.

It was their old signal, the one they'd used to silently say *I love you*, even though, at the time, they'd pretended otherwise. When she could, she returned it and then refocused her attention to the business of getting Mr. D buried.

Among the mourners, no one save a few former company members noticed Mark. Although they made casual conversation with him while shooting her curious glances, nobody said anything. When the last person she knew left—one of the many people she hoped never to see again after the funeral—she turned to Mark.

"It's over," she said. "Until tomorrow." She half-smiled. "Armenians really like funerals."

"You did great." Mark pushed his hair out of his face. "That was so many people to talk to."

"Mr. D didn't have many friends, but he knew a lot of people. It's how he kept the company going for so long."

They gazed around Mr. D's home. A few old women from the

church were tossing half-eaten pastries and empty coffee cups into the garbage.

"Can we get out of here?" Mark asked.

"Let's." She placed her hand in his, not caring if anyone saw and, if they did, what they thought.

The next morning, they went to Mr. D's church where people packed the pews. She let her mind wander during the service, sneaking glances at Mark, who'd positioned himself in such a place that, if she cocked her head leftward, she could see him. Finally, it was over, and she followed the casket out of the church where the pallbearers spun it a couple of times before placing it in the car. At the gravesite, she said a brief prayer for Mr. D. Not that she thought God would listen to her.

The day after held one order of business—the reading of the will. Mr. D's lawyer, a portly Armenian sporting a gold tie bar with a chain dangling off it, met her at the door to his office.

"Mrs. Dektember," he said. "I'm sorry for your loss."

"Thank you," she murmured as he escorted her to a conference room where a dark wood table was circled with gray leather chairs with short backs. They looked like toadstools.

He pointed at the toadstool closest to him. "Please take a seat."

Peri settled herself, fingers crossed this wouldn't take too long. She wanted to go home to Mark, who was napping on the couch.

"Best thing ever," he'd said, flinging himself face first on the sofa and then stroking a cushion. She laughed, one mellifluous in its joy. In just a couple of days, Mark had banished the shadows of her soul to the sidelines.

Peri gazed at the papers fanned in front of the lawyer. Mr. D had probably left her his house and some of his art collections with instructions to divvy up the rest among his associates and a few charities. If this were the case, then she'd have the lawyer take care of everything. He could take his cut and give her the rest. She didn't really care.

How could she care when Mark was here?

The lawyer waited until she lifted her eyes to him. Then, he shuffled his papers and cleared his throat. "Minus a few small artworks for former employees and loyal board members, Mr. Dektember has left you everything." He looked down at the papers spread in front of him and folded the corner of one. "The list is substantial: the house and everything in it plus his investments."

"Okay," she said, frowning. The lawyer was acting squirrelly, as if he were about to tell her something unpleasant. Had Mr. D been in debt, left her nothing save the opportunity to pay off creditors?

"No matter what you choose to do with the assets, you'll be a wealthy woman. The art collection alone is worth a fortune. Mr. Dektember had an eye for emerging talent."

Peri nodded. *Get on with it*, she wanted to say.

"There's a caveat," he said, making a big deal of reaching in his suit pocket, pulling out a pair of glasses, and putting them on. He went silent as he pretended to read something. "For you to take possession of Mr. Dektember's assets, you must sign an affidavit stating that you will never remarry."

"An affidavit that I'll never remarry?" Peri echoed. "That's the condition."

"What happens if I sign and then remarry, say, a decade later?"

"The courts will take whatever's left and levy a serious fine."

Goddamn you, Levon, she thought as her pulse stomped in an angry march. *Choreographing my life from the grave? The years I gave you weren't enough?*

The lawyer leaned forward, his eyebrows knitted in faux concern. "You could fight it in court. You were his wife after all, and although your marriage was . . . unconventional, many witnesses can attest to the immaculate care you provided to Mr. Dektember during his lengthy illness."

"How long would that take? How much money?"

"Probably some time. As for the money, I would do it for a small retainer with a promise for a cut of the final ruling, which, I believe, would be at least partially in your favor."

"What happens to the house, the money if I say no?"

The lawyer flipped through a few papers. "It goes to an AIDS charity."

So that's how Mr. D set it up? Between the memory of Bob and her actual life? Between Mark who was alive and Mr. D who was dead?

Mr. D couldn't hear her but, wherever he was, must have anticipated her thoughts.

Because Mr. D knew. Everything that had happened and everything that was going to happen.

And she was going to perform the steps he'd choreographed from the grave for her. He was sending her to the next stage, but he was going to exact one last sacrifice from her because the sweat, tears, and virgin blood she'd given him hadn't been enough.

Peri took a deep breath to neutralize her frenzied thoughts. She was being ridiculous. How could Mr. D know everything? She didn't know everything. Mark might leave, and these few days with their big words and bigger emotions would be nothing more than the coda of their *pas de deux*.

Maybe Mr. D thought Mark wouldn't come or would come too late.

Maybe Mr. D thought she'd choose the money, desperate for the security it'd provide.

Maybe Mr. D thought she'd loved him.

It didn't matter what Mr. D thought because Peri was done with Mr. D.

Heat flushed through her body. She pushed herself up from the toadstool and grabbed her purse, its gold chain sliding through her slippery hand. "No," she said, issuing the word as if it were profanity. "I don't want any of it."

The lawyer blanched. "You should at least think about it, Mrs. Dektember. The art alone is enough to keep you comfortable for years. You can date again, have a boyfriend, even a live-in one. You just can't marry." He shrugged. "It's 1989. Marriage isn't a big deal these days."

She was at the door, still shaking her head.

The lawyer lifted his portly body up to reason with her. "No," Peri said. "I don't want it. Not now and not later."

24

Ouvert

THE SUNSHINE STREAMING through the door roused Mark from his stupor. He'd been lounging on Peri's couch, rehearsing in his head the song and dance he'd come to Los Angeles to perform.

Peri stomped through the door, her fists clenched, her forehead creased in angry folds.

"What happened?"

"I said no to Mr. D." Her eyes were glassy with wonder. "Tell me."

They sat on the couch, and Peri told him about Mr. D's will. At first, he was bewildered by the lengths Mr. D would go to keep Peri his. Then, Mark got angry.

Mr. D knew. That Mark would come back for her, and now, even in death, he was trying to manage them.

His breath stalled. Because Mr. D was jealous that Peri loved Mark, and she only . . . he searched for the word . . . tolerated Mr. D.

"I turned it down: the house, the art, the investments." Peri's spine curved. "The lawyer thinks I'm an idiot. Who turns down that type of money? Who doesn't at least try to fight it in court? But I'm not. Absolutely, I'm not. I'm tired of being Mr. D's puppet."

That's my girl, Mark wanted to say. Instead, he held her tight. "What are you going to do?"

"I have his ballets. That'll buy me time." Mark tilted his head at her.

"They'll be a hot commodity since he died. But how many companies are going to want more than one or two in their repertory?" She pressed her lips together. "Not many. Then, the work will dry up." She sighed. "It's something for now."

He pulled her to the sofa. "I have news." Peri looked at him expectantly.

"I got a new job." "Congratulations?"

He kissed her. "Are in order. I resigned from Jim's company last month."

"Why?"

"Because I was bored of just dancing. I wanted to choreograph, stretch my brain and not just my body. So I made a piece, a good one. It was good enough to win a big competition in Europe."

She gave him a quick hug. "That's great."

"It is because I got a job that's going to allow me to do both. I got approached about taking over a small company. They liked that I'd danced for Mr. D and Jim, two totally different choreographers. And I'd won this big competition, so I had name recognition. They offered me the job immediately." He paused. "They'd also been trying to hire someone for a year, and they were desperate."

Peri stared at him with big eyes. "Wow," she said. "Where?"

He told her and then groaned. "It's the ugliest city. All the buildings look like parking garages."

"Still," she said. "That's impressive."

"My first order of business is to ask if you'd set the M+M *pas de deux* for the upcoming rep program." He raked a hand through his hair. "Also, I need help. Someone to assist me in rehearsal, teach classes, do administrative stuff." He winked at her. "Plus, I need someone to remember my choreography."

She was staring at him, her mouth a big *o*. "Are you offering me a job?"

He nodded. "I can't pay you much, but I'm hoping the bonus will make up for it."

"What bonus?"

He placed his hands on her cheeks and steered her face to meet his. "Me."

25

Entrelacé

(INTERLACED)

"I THINK THAT'S EVERYTHING," Peri said, handing the journal back to Mark, so he could check her notes. She was lying with her head in his lap as the afternoon sunshine glazed everything with gold.

Mark scrunched up his brow as he read. "Looks good to me," he said and passed it back. "What do you want to do for dinner?"

She sat up, reached for her bag, and pulled out a women's magazine. She was trying to teach herself German, and women's magazines with their emphasis on food and fashion—two things she knew a lot about—seemed a good place to start. "At lunch, I found this recipe . . ."

Peri stopped. Mark was gazing at her, his face unreadable.

She pointed to a shadowy place in the studio by the barre. "Do you want to go to where there's no sun?"

Mark's blue eyes had narrowed with purpose. "Are you having a good day?"

"I'm having a great day," she said, confused by the question but honest in her answer. She was having a great day. Mark had passed teaching company class to Stick, who'd moved to West Germany at Mark's request.

"She helped make me the dancer I am today," he'd said before picking up the phone to call her. "And she knows I hate mornings."

To get Mark going, she rolled on top of him, and they made love quickly, urgently.

"That's the way to start the day," he said with a grin.

They went to the studio where Peri rehearsed *M+M*. After it was over, Mark had been waiting for her outside the studio, and they walked to the open-air market for lunch. They purchased a bag of cherries and a loaf of bread, and Mark had gotten himself a sausage and a beer. They ate by the fountain, enjoying the June breeze. Mark listened to a tape of music he might use for a ballet as she flipped through a magazine. In the afternoon, she assisted Mark in his rehearsal, excited he'd come to the same conclusion she had—the hive mentality of ballet hurt more than it helped. While it fed the director's ego to have dancers mindlessly follow commands, in the end, it bred reflexive obedience and blind trust in traditions that may not have earned it.

To move forward, art needed people to challenge it.

Instead of Mr. D's kingdom where he cast his dancers as fawning courtiers and himself as its king, able to make and break dreams indiscriminately, Mark ran a benevolent democracy with himself as president. Although he was the same age as or younger than his company members, he had confidence, charisma, and plenty of technical chops to back up his directorship. Yet he kept a constant dialogue going with his dancers. At the end of rehearsal, everyone sat in a circle on the floor, including Mark with Peri beside him, and they talked about what they'd done that day and what they needed to do the next.

Mark believed that hearing things he didn't agree with made him stronger and, more importantly, the work stronger. Because then he had to defend himself and his choices. If his defense was weak, based solely on ego, he pivoted, responded to the feedback and incorporated it into the next iteration, which got him closer to the end result—a good piece.

"I learned it from Jim," he said when she'd asked him about it after the first day. "He says art needs friction and dissension. That making a dance should be the most perfect form of democracy."

He opened and closed his mouth. "I don't always like it. It would be easier and faster to be like Mr. D. Tell everybody what to do and enjoy being the boss. But Jim says director is an archaic term. He calls himself a unifier, someone who weaves a bunch of different strands together into something meaningful, which takes more creativity. So that's why I ask for their opinion. Then, I go from there."

It wasn't all a kumbaya, let's-sit-in-a-circle-and-talk-about-our-feelings vibe. Mark expected technical virtuosity from his dancers. Stick taught most of the company classes. Moving to West Germany hadn't changed her work ethic, and she gave murderously difficult combinations that even the strongest dancers occasionally stumbled through. After Mark set choreography, he sent Stick in to refine the movement until it was sleek, tensile, clear.

Peri pulled herself from her thoughts and looked at Mark, who was still gazing at her with strange, bright eyes. She rubbed the corner of the magazine, her stomach tightening with worry that Mark hadn't responded to her.

"I'm having a great day," she said again, bolding the words with conviction. "Is everything okay?" She hoped it was. She wanted them to go home, make dinner, and watch German television, finish the day like they had yesterday and hopefully would tomorrow.

Mark continued to stare at her as if he was trying to decide something. He stood. "I'll be right back."

He jogged out of the studio and then returned a minute later carrying something, his upper lip beading with sweat.

He sat down and slid a tiny box toward her. "I'm having a great day, too. Every day since you've been here has been great." He popped the lid open. "I want to keep having great days with you."

Mark pulled the ring out and placed it on her fourth finger, left hand. He traced the outline of the small diamond that sat atop a thin band of gold.

"It looks like a drop of water, which seemed perfect because of the all the salt water in our relationship: sweat, tears, the big ocean we had to leave behind and the other big one we had to cross, so we could be together," he said. "Then, the salesperson told me the shape was called pear." He laughed. "Pear for Peri. I was sold."

She stared at the tiny, perfect diamond on her finger, her stomach fluttering.

"I was going to wait a few more weeks and do it right at a nice restaurant, so you could wear a pretty dress." He swept a hand around the studio. "But this is us." He kissed her—a gentle one full of promise. "Will you keep having great days with me?"

CURTAIN CALL

The appearance of dancers onstage at the end of a performance to acknowledge the audience's applause.

26

Assemblé

(ASSEMBLED OR JOINED TOGETHER)

ROBBIE CHEERED.

Mark looked up from the computer where he'd been plugging in notes from today's rehearsal. Seven-year-old Robbie was sitting on the sofa, leaning forward, not blinking, as he followed the soccer game on the television. Germany was playing the United States in the 1998 World Cup, and Germany had just scored its first point.

Mark glanced at the clock. It was only eight minutes into the game, but it was time for Robbie to go to bed.

Mark should probably care about the game, feel torn about who to root for—his home country or his adopted one—but soccer was boring, just a bunch of guys with big calves running back and forth. It was like recess for grown-ups.

Robbie, though, was crazy about it.

Mark shrugged. Although Robbie had two American parents and was a carbon copy of Mark, he was German through and through. He even liked rules, had no problem waiting patiently for the red light to turn as Mark stood next to him, antsy to go, go, go. Because the street was empty.

When Robbie was younger, he and Peri had talked about moving back to the United States to give Robbie an American childhood, so he could play in a big yard with a swing set, join a Little League team, and make construction-paper turkeys for Thanksgiving. But, if they returned, they would lose more than they'd gain.

The arts had little state support in America, so Mark would spend half his time at cocktail parties or fancy lunches trying to use his words to convince rich people and corporations that dance was worth funding. And, once he raised the money, he'd be stuck making straightforward, easy-to-enjoy pieces like Mr. D's because a lot of Americans were either too religious or conservative for the type of ballets he made.

So they stayed in Germany although neither Peri nor he felt especially German. But they had a nice life here, better than they would in the United States, with good health care, good schools for Robbie, and good vacations that included beaches in Spain and pasta in Italy.

Glenn had become the ballet master for Jim's company, which was only a short train ride away. He'd married Gabrielle of all people.

A while back, Glenn had invited Mark and Peri to meet his new girlfriend—"the one," Glenn said sheepishly without mentioning "the one" was Gabrielle. When Glenn strolled in with Gabrielle on his arm, Mark stood to leave. Fortunately, Glenn reached Mark first, and as he thumped Mark on the back, he whispered in Mark's ear, "They got her meds straightened out."

That may be true, but Gabrielle was still a handful. She picked on Glenn and bossed him around and acted put upon if he slighted her.

"Hold this," Gabrielle would say as she shoved her enormous designer handbag overflowing with makeup and receipts toward Glenn.

He knelt and extended his arm. "Anything for the beauteous lady," he said as Gabrielle rolled her eyes.

"Watch it," Gabrielle snapped because Glenn wasn't holding the bag tightly to his chest. "That purse is expensive."

"I know. I bought it for you." Glenn's cheeks glowed as red as his hair. "Because you deserve only the best."

Mark watched this exchange, trying not to barf. Finally, after Gabrielle made Glenn change his dinner order in a restaurant from a steak to a salad because, according to her, "Between the red hair and the big white belly, Glenn looks like a beach ball," Mark asked Glenn about it.

"Being a straight guy in ballet meant I always had my pick of the ladies. It was too easy. Gabrielle made me work for it." He shot a sappy look at Gabrielle, who was exchanging recipes with Peri, as Robbie kicked a soccer ball around with Glenn's daughter. "She still makes me work for it." He pointed to his belly. "She makes me better."

Peri makes me better, Mark thought. *But without making it about her.*

Glenn yanked at his cowlick. "Plus, she's so hot." He dropped his voice. "When my dad met her, he almost had a heart attack. He couldn't believe I scored someone like Gabrielle." Glenn grinned triumphantly. "I told him, 'That's ballet.'"

Over the years, Glenn and Mark had become best friends, joking and commiserating over beers, just a couple of dudes who did ballet, with beautiful wives they'd met doing ballet, and cute kids they supported thanks to ballet. They called each other "man" in every conversation, and when things got deep, the silences got long. It wasn't like the friendships girls had, where they told each other everything, but for American guys, they were doing okay.

Mark shook himself out of his thoughts and looked again at the clock. It was way past time for Robbie to go to bed.

Should he make a big deal out of it?

In his head, he heard Peri tell him not to bother.

He turned his attention back to the computer where his notes cascaded down the screen. There were a lot of squiggly red lines under the words. Even after all the years, Mark still couldn't spell. At least his handwriting wasn't a problem anymore thanks to computers. The new all-male piece was going pretty good although Mark kept second-guessing himself, mostly because the material was so close to his heart. After rolling the idea back and forth in his head for a couple of years, he'd decided he was ready to use his dad as artistic inspiration.

His dad had died five years earlier from cirrhosis of the liver, never once reaching out, even when Robbie was born. Mark had thought about flying to Los Angeles when the end was close so they could patch things up. But his dad didn't ask, didn't seem to care, so Mark didn't go. It left him with some messy feelings, which he was trying to work through in the new piece.

It wouldn't be autobiographical or narrative, but Mark was going deep, finding memories of his dad to inspire the movement motifs: him standing at home plate with his bat raised, him shaking a fist at Mark because Mark had knocked into his easy chair, the look in his dad's eyes when he popped the top off the first beer of the day.

He got back in touch with the metal bands he'd loved as a teenager. The composer was taking leitmotifs from Mark's favorite songs and rewriting them for a string quartet.

Sometimes, it got so heavy that he had to step away, but Peri was there to jump in. When his confidence drooped, which happened a lot because of how much he wanted to get every single thing right, she told him it was shaping up to be his best piece yet. She believed it too.

"You're making the personal, universal, and the literal, abstract. That's what dance does best."

Mark twisted his lips. Only the critics and the audience could decide if what he made was any good, but he was glad for Peri's support.

His gaze flicked to the wedding picture he kept by the computer next to a bowl of Peri's favorite butterscotch candies. He counted backward.

Nine years to the day that he'd proposed, the wedding following hot on the heels of their engagement.

Mark reached for the photo.

He was wearing a black suit and white crewneck sweater, his arm thrown around Peri, who had on a short flouncy dress, her blonde hair arranged in a big, complicated updo.

Fashion had changed a lot, and Peri found the picture embarrassing. She wanted him to switch it out for a family photo, but he refused because he liked the picture. He looked young and, to be more exact, not fat. He quit performing four years ago when it got to be too much, running the company, choreographing, taking care of Robbie, *and* trying to maintain his technique. His appetite, though, didn't get the memo after he quit, and he'd put on weight every year since.

Good thing I talked you into marrying me then, Mark said to Peri in the picture.

As Mark put the photo back, he caught sight of himself in the glare of the monitor and groaned. Not only was he chubby, he was also going gray, had permanent wrinkles above his eyebrows from concentrating so hard, and wore glasses that made him look nerdy although Peri said they gave him gravitas.

He sighed, but it was a small one. He had everything else to be grateful for. He had a great wife who adored him. He had a good job with the company, which, after years of hard work by Peri and him, was finally getting some international attention. Next year, they had a tour planned to the United States. It would be short—New York and a few other cities on the East Coast—but it was a big deal for them. Plus, he had Robbie, an awesome kid who was happy and healthy.

Thinking of his son, Mark gazed at Robbie for the third time. Felix had jumped into Robbie's lap and was purring as Robbie dragged his fingers through the cat's ginger fur. Robbie's eyes hadn't budged from the game.

Mark tossed his hair out of his eyes and accepted the inevitable. "Robbie."

Robbie turned, tossing his hair out of his eyes, just like Mark had done a second earlier.

Mark blinked at the weirdness of parenthood, watching a miniature version of himself do and say the things Mark had thought were unique to him.

Robbie's face was screwed up like he was ready to argue. "After the game," Mark said. "Straight to bed."

Robbie pumped his fist in the air. "Danke, Papa."

Mark headed toward the bedroom. He pushed the door open and then stopped. His heart was slapping against his chest, like a fly ball crashing into an outstretched mitt. Peri was sitting at her vanity, braiding her hair. The glow from the lamp had placed her in a circle of yellow light, and she looked like a star that had dropped in from outer space.

He wished someone were around, so he could point to Peri. *That's my girl*, he'd say.

27

Révérence

(CURTSEY)

PERI SLIPPED INTO HER NIGHTGOWN, a lacy number in ivory, and then dabbed her fingers in a pot of expensive wrinkle cream, her sole splurge. She added a few more drops to the already large globule on her index finger. She rubbed it into her skin, using the gentle, circular strokes she'd been perfecting for years. She had turned forty almost two years ago, and she was waging a resolute battle against the signs of aging.

The sounds of a soccer game drifted through the closed door. It was Germany versus . . . She couldn't remember. She'd made a valiant effort to appreciate soccer, but it'd been fruitless. Even Mark who liked sports couldn't get into it.

Mark said something in English to Robbie, who responded in German.

He's not going to bed until the game is over, she telegraphed to Mark. *No use in even trying.*

With quick fingers, she braided her hair. Feeling eyes on her, she looked up. Mark was standing at the door, staring at her.

"Everything okay?" she asked.

Mark grinned. "Great," he said, walking into the bedroom. "I told Robbie he had to go to bed as soon as the game is over."

"He wasn't going before then."

He stood behind her and kissed the top of her head as she smiled. Mark lifted his arms out of his T-shirt and then examined himself in the mirror over her head. He grabbed a handful of flesh while groaning. "I need to go on a diet."

She bit back her laugh. Mark had gained weight over the years. Every once in a while, he'd make a stab at losing a few pounds, but he always gave up after a few days.

Peri herself stayed thin through rigorous self-discipline. Unless it was fruit or vegetables, she allowed herself only a few bites before passing her dish to Mark or Robbie, both of whom would wolf it gratefully.

Peri stood, walked around her chair to end behind Mark, and latched her arms around his midsection. "More of you to love." She kissed a vertebra. He would always be Mark to her with his alert blue eyes, warm hands, and good humor.

"How do you still look the same?" he asked as he went through a pile of mail that rested on the windowsill.

She smiled into Mark's back. She didn't look the same, but Mark was sweet to say it. She'd stayed thin, true, but her blonde hair came from a bottle these days and her pricey wrinkle cream had done little to halt the imprint of time on her face.

Peri shrugged. Time was merciless, but she was lucky to have Mark hold her hand as they marched to its incessant beat.

Mark slipped his finger under the flap of an envelope. From the handwriting, Peri guessed it was a letter from his mom, who wrote every week religiously. "Do you know what day it is?" he asked as he pulled out the letter to read.

"Nine years."

It seemed impossible that it'd been almost a decade since Mark proposed. Both everything and nothing had happened since then. They'd gotten married soon after at the *standesbeamte*, Germany's version of a justice of the peace, before going back to the studio for a party filled with *sekt* (sparkling wine), *baumkuchen* (cake with almonds and honey), and lots of laughter and love. Less than a year later, she gave birth to Robbie.

Mark had declined to name his son after himself. "It's my dad's name. I don't want to do that to him." His lips had drooped before they curved into a big smile. "Let's name him after Bob. He's a big part of the reason why we're here."

In the beginning, she'd been worried. Mark was twenty-two with a wife, a son, and a company. But he didn't flinch. She did whatever she could. She taught company class so he could sleep in, memorized his choreography so he wouldn't have to, took over administrative tasks so he would have more time in the studio. A few times a year, she left to set Mr. D's pieces on companies around the world.

Mr. D had been right about *The Maiden and the Mountain*. It was his most-requested piece. While it would never be celebrated as a work that moved ballet forward, it'd proved to be a crowd-pleaser that audiences loved for all the reasons people loved ballet—a fairy tale come to life.

She rarely thought about Mr. D these days, never regretted not taking the money, even when things were tight. Only when the curtain closed at the end of one of his pieces, would she look around at the happy, rapt faces in the audience and remember his resolve to fight ugliness with the silkiest, most insubstantial weapon of all.

"You're still giving the world beauty," she would whisper to Mr. D, who, wherever he was, would know his legacy was safe for a little while longer.

The early years of her marriage to Mark hadn't always been easy. There was never enough money. There was never enough time, except when there was too much, like when they took two-year-old Robbie with them to Australia where Mark had received a choreographic commission for a piece about the Berlin Wall coming down. They both left the plane feeling ten years older. Or, like three years ago, when her calf acted up, the nerves in her back on strike from overwork. Mark's mom, finally free of the millstone of Mark's dad, stayed with them until Peri was back on her feet.

The men continued to die from AIDS—one awful year in the early '90s they'd lost two company members and a neighbor almost back to back—until, finally, the drugs got better and they started staying alive, a few heartbeats at a time.

Even with the challenges, it'd almost always been pleasant, days that passed by in a golden fuzz of dancing, cooking, making love, and watching Robbie grow up. When they had a rough day where it felt like everything was conspiring against them, Mark lifted her over his head, just like he did the day they'd met. Their eyes would meet, and all the minor things that had seemed so major just a moment ago receded to leave the truth standing tall in the spotlight. They loved each other, and they made each other better, and even the worst day with each other was better than the best day without the other.

Mark had tried over the years to add her as co-artistic director, to give her a choreographic credit, but she always refused, which was probably bad for feminism but she didn't care.

"I'm happy in the wings," she told him.

And it was true. Mark had given her the best roles of her life, all of which took place offstage: adored wife, doting mother, his right-hand woman at the company.

And now, here they were, thirteen years after they'd fallen in love. Like all happily-ever-after couples, they were boring in their gratitude for each other and the small, precious life they'd built.

Peri's relationship with God remained fraught, but every once in a while, she'd look up to the heavens, pick the brightest star, and pray to God to keep Mark and Robbie safe.

She doubted God cared or would heed her wishes. She'd watched too many sick men pray to Him only to have their pleas (to not die, to not die alone, to die without pain or embarrassment, to die after reconciling with estranged mothers) thwarted to ever believe God cared about his creation.

Why else would He make hate—against them, the other whose religion or sexuality or gender or race threatened those in power—so easy, so satisfying to feel? Hate filled a person with fervency, superiority, the heated purpose of certainty.

Who would quit that druggy fanaticism for the fuzzy resignation of empathy where a person shrugged and admitted he or she didn't know everything, and, as such, wouldn't, couldn't, shouldn't judge anyone?

Hate enabled a person to believe they had all the answers, that morality was a bright line, slicing actions into right and wrong with no regard to nuance, sensitivity, or context.

Compassion—where the heated pink of passion had been grayed by common sense—was hard. Maybe even impossible because it required people to retreat from the hot, stale air of a moral vacuum, to admit that, just maybe, they didn't have a direct line to God, that God's understanding of life superseded their own. Because why else would those who claimed to know God best insist that God hated huge swaths of the people He'd created?

Living in Germany had only reinforced this belief. The country had enacted one of the worst tragedies in the history of the world with the methodical extermination of six million Jews along with the slaughter of anyone else deemed the other (homosexuals, dissidents, atheists). It was an unfathomable event that had altered the collective DNA of its people.

Germans knew, without intense vigilance, hate could once again parade into public conscience and seduce everyone with blasts of bombastic rhetoric. But they also knew not to depend on God to prevent another atrocity. They depended on themselves.

Two years ago, a German artist began placing concrete cubes topped with brass plaques over cobblestones, first in Cologne and Berlin, now in other locales. The first time she stubbed her toe against a *stolperstein,* she'd backed up in horror after she read the inscription. There was a name, and then there were the dates: birth, deportation to a concentration camp, death at that concentration camp. These *stolpersteine* were raised a little above the regular cobblestones, and they'd been designed to catch people when they were walking fast, not paying attention, forcing them to trip on the past. So people would remember, feel the shameful weight of hate, say to themselves, NEVER AGAIN.

And it wouldn't happen again in Germany. The people had learned, and they passed the lesson on, in grim, obvious ways. But it would happen again somewhere in the world, probably was happening again, because hate was like a weed. Without acute mindfulness, its dandelion-gold temptation of us versus them would easily overtake the bloomy, thorny rosebush of a multi-cultural society.

Peri roused herself from her thoughts that had little to do with her quotidian existence. She pressed her cheek into Mark's warm back. "How's your mom?" she asked.

"She wants to know if she should book her ticket for Thanksgiving."

"Tell her yes. Robbie misses her."

Although they'd been in Germany for years, she and Mark still celebrated Thanksgiving, mostly because they loved to cook. They gave the dancers the day off, and everyone piled into their apartment for turkey, mashed potatoes, and pumpkin pie. The company members were from far-flung places, so for many of them, it was their first introduction to the American tradition of eating oneself silly.

"I'll write her back tomorrow," Mark said as she smiled into his back.

I love him, she told God. *I don't love easily, but Mark is easy to love. And he is wonderful in all his roles, as husband, father, director, choreographer, a man of the first order. Whatever vengeance you enact next, let Mark escape it.*

She tightened her fingers around Mark's abdomen, underneath the furry hole of his belly button, and mouthed another prayer: *Please let Robbie be the apple of your eye as he is ours.*

Even with her bleak view of God and humanity, Peri prayed. She was too overwhelmed by the fragility of life, too acquainted with how everything could be snatched away with no explanation or warning, not to do everything possible to keep the people she cared about protected.

In all the years she'd been with Mark, their tragedies had been slight, banal even. They were still standing, creating things and offering them to the world as payment for the privilege to be within it: their upside-down romance that showed love didn't care about following scripts; their sweet son; their ballets that celebrated the athletic prowess of mankind; their company that was a moving multi-hued mosaic where everyone participated in the artistic process because harmony comprised of many pitches resounded more than the shrill keen of one.

So with all the grace in her life, maybe, just maybe, one of her prayers had landed and God was keeping them safe.

Mark turned to face her. "Still having great days?"

"The best." She hugged him, taking comfort in his warmth and good humor. Unlike Peri, who fretted about what if, Mark found thankfulness in what was.

In the living room, Robbie cheered. Germany had scored. Mark stepped back and held out his hand. She placed hers in his and then he brushed a kiss against the top of her hand.

"So am I," he said.

Outside the window, a cloud drifted over the half moon, white and bright, like a spotlight in profile. With her free hand, she shut off the lamp and then pulled the curtain closed, casting them into darkness.

THE END

Author's Notes
OR WHY I WROTE IT LIKE THIS

AIDS: Then and Now

While the specter of AIDS has receded in public consciousness, the hysteria surrounding the disease in the '80s was intense—for good reason. When the novel opens, over 10,000 Americans had died from it, and many, many more were HIV-positive.

President Ronald Reagan first mentioned AIDS in 1985, four years after the original CDC report. His first speech solely addressing AIDS didn't occur until 1987 in which he called for increased testing; at that point, over 20,000 people had died from the disease.

Famously, pastor Jerry Falwell said, "AIDS is not just God's punishment for homosexuals, it is God's punishment for the society that tolerates homosexuals." In 1992, 36% of Americans believed this to be true. In 2014, that figure was 14%.

Since the original report through 2016, over 675,000 Americans have died of AIDS or AIDS-related causes. 22 million people have died worldwide, and 36 million are currently living with AIDS/HIV.

The Structure of *The Pas de Deux*

The novel follows the classical structure of a *grand pas de deux* as formalized by Marius Petipa in 19th-century Russia: entrée, adagio, male variation, female variation, and coda. While not technically part of it, I included the curtain call, which can occur either at the conclusion of the *pas de deux* or at the end of an act.

The *grand pas de deux* is the climactic moment of a ballet where the danseur and the danseuse articulate their love for each other in a show of motion forged by emotion, hence, my decision to employ the structure for a romance novel.

Those who are fluent or native French speakers may question an English article with the title, but that is, in fact, how dancers refer to it in the United States.

Fact versus Fiction in *The Pas de Deux*

~Mark's audition with Peri would be an unlikely occurrence. If a formal audition isn't on the schedule, then prospects are usually invited to take company class and perform a short solo. I utilized the *pas de deux* audition to get the plot moving and to introduce the novel's structure.

~I based *The Maiden on the Mountain* on an Armenian folktale known as *Zoulvisia*, which appears in Andrew Lang's *Olive Fairy Book*.

~The Guns N' Roses show took place November 22, 1985, at The Troubadour in Hollywood. This was the band's first sold-out gig. I used the set list, pictures, and a short recording to create the most accurate description possible.

~The Armenian Genocide was the Ottoman government's systematic extermination of 1.5 million Armenians from 1914 to 1923. I crafted Mr. D's story using first-person accounts, historical records, and my imagination. At the time of writing, the United States has not officially recognized the Armenian Genocide nor has Turkey.

~Balletomanes will already have guessed that James Prescott is inspired by William Forsythe. One of the preeminent choreographers of the late 20th and early 21st century, Forsythe has been called both the heir to Balanchine and the antichrist of ballet. The two pieces I evoke are the second act of *Artifact* (1984) and *In the Middle, Somewhat Elevated* (1987), the latter of which is one of ballet's most important works. The television program Mark and Peri watch is fictional.

~Those unfamiliar with concert dance may wonder if Germany is a fanciful choice for Mark and then Peri to relocate to. However, it has been, and continues to be, one of the world's great artistic hubs. Many dancers and choreographers have moved there for both short- and long-term opportunities. The funding structure is less fraught than the United States, and audiences are open to more avant-garde work.

~Mark's appointment as artistic director at the age of twenty-two may raise eyebrows. Dance, however, is a meritocracy where talent is more important than paying one's dues.

~All choreography (save that attributed to James Prescott) described is mine although it's fairly typical of the classical ballets choreographed in 19th-century Russia and 20th-century contemporary works.

~Most spellings and definitions of steps align with Gail Grant's *Technical Manual and Dictionary of Classical Ballet*.

~The Stolpersteine project was initiated by German artist Gunter Demnig in 1992. It commemorates individuals by placing a plaque at their last place of residency or work—in other words, the last place chosen freely by the individual before he or she was sent to the concentration camps. The project is ongoing with over 50,000 stones placed in twenty-two countries.

~You might not remember the quote by George Balanchine at the beginning, so allow me to jog your memory: "Put a man and a girl onstage and there is already a story." The content isn't that interesting, just Balanchine declining to explain his plotless ballets. The verbiage, however, is. Here's the quote with the words bolded on which I hung the novel: "Put a **man** and a **girl** on stage and there is already a story." Not a man and a woman. Not a boy and a girl. A **man** and a **girl**.

While I strove to keep everything respectful, consensual, and legal (Mark is 18 when their relationship turns romantic—a societal bright line I wouldn't cross) between Mark and Peri, their backward May/December courtship is unusual in the world of romance where the man is often older, sometimes decades older, than the woman. Perhaps, though, the connection of Mark and Peri makes perfect sense in the ballet world. One of my goals with *The Pas de Deux* was to point out the differences between the men and the women who pursue ballet.

Even well into the 21st century, the gender ratio remains lopsided. To participate in ballet, boys and men must demonstrate great personal resolve and discipline in the face of homophobic stereotypes and teasing. Women, due to the intense competition, will turn themselves body and soul over to ballet, doing anything and everything requested of them by those in charge—often men, some of whom, like Mr. D., wield their power inappropriately. When you're always a girl, no matter your real age, growing up can be hard.

Thanks!

Thank you, thank you, thank you for reading *The Pas de Deux: A*

Classical Ballet Romance. Words only quicken to life when read, and I am so grateful to you for reading. If you found the book to be a four- or five-star reading experience, then I would be delighted by and deeply appreciative of a review and/or rating. A recommendation to a reader whom you think would enjoy the book would also be welcomed. If you have a critique or would like to offer suggestions for improvement, I hope you'll contact me at erin@erinbomboy.com with them; I'm constantly trying to improve my craft and create a meaningful, enjoyable experience for readers.

If you would like to read more of my writing, my bright, emotive story told through dual narrators, *The Winner: A Ballroom Dance Novel* ("one of the best books I've read this year": Library of Clean Reads), and my darkly provocative domestic thriller, *The Piece: A Contemporary Ballet Novel* ("a compellingly vivid story": Midwest Book Review), are available for purchase. Please visit me at erinbomboy.com to learn more and to check out my blog, which includes links to my professional criticism for *The Dance Enthusiast* as well as posts on writing and life.

Also by Erin Bomboy

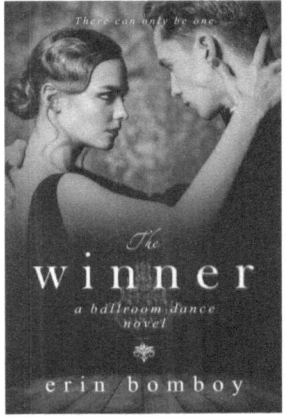

The Winner: A Ballroom Dance Novel

The most prestigious ballroom dance competition in the United States.

Two dancers need to win.

Only one can.

Nina Fortunova wasn't supposed to end up almost thirty, divorced, with her dreams of winning shattered. She teams up with Jorge Gonzalez, a hunky and hard-working Latin dancer, to reinvent the flashy Smooth style. When the Chairman of the Judges offers to throw the competition in their favor, Nina must decide how far she will go to win, even if it means losing Jorge.

Carly Martindale is doing everything she's been taught not to do—placing her happiness first by dancing with Trey Devereux, the former champion who's returned to competition for mysterious reasons. Carly falls deeply in love with Trey, but beneath his good looks and Southern manners lay a tortured soul. To heal Trey, Carly must push herself beyond her limits—even if she loses herself in the process.

Co-workers, then friends, and now arch competitors, Nina and Carly face off to determine who will be the winner—in love and in dancing.

Bright, emotive, and told through dual narrators, *The Winner* examines the costs associated with winning, the internalization of parental ambition, and the effect of gendered roles on and off the dance floor.

The Winner is a literary romance that's perfect for readers who love *Dancing with the Stars, Strictly Come Dancing, So You Think You Can Dance,* and the classic elegance of Fred Astaire and Ginger Rogers.

"one of the best books I've read this year."

The Library of Clean Reads

⁓

The Piece: A Contemporary Ballet Novel

Their eyes met through the heat and glare as their hearts crisscrossed from stage to pit. Only good things could happen. Right?

Against the pitched backdrop of pointe shoes and bloody blisters, Elinor Roth confronts her decaying dream. She is unlikely to become a leading ballerina. Longing for affection, she leaps into the arms of Jon Hansen, a seemingly nice music conductor. When the fling ends, Elinor abandons her stalling ballet career and moves to New York.

The city's contemporary dance scene stirs her imagination, and she enters into a showcase that will launch her as a visionary choreographer. Unable to forget Elinor, Jon joins her and struggles to become a composer. Soon, he grows dependent on Elinor for inspiration and alarmed by her dwindling affection.

Determined to keep Elinor as his muse, Jon devises a plan to take her far away from dance. When she uncovers his deceit, Elinor must decide how far she will blur the line between life and art.

Acutely dark, brutal, and provocative, *The Piece* explores the manipulation of honesty, the perpetuation of trauma, and artistic obsession. Designed for readers who appreciate moral complexity, it combines the dance setting of *Black Swan* with the domestic noir of *The Girl on the Train* and *Gone Girl*.

"a compellingly vivid story"

Midwest Book Review

About the Author

A native of Richmond, Virginia, Erin Bomboy trained as a classical ballet dancer before spending a decade as a professional competitive ballroom dancer. She holds an MFA in Dance Performance and Choreography from New York University Tisch School of the Arts. She lives in New York City with her husband and daughter where she works as a writer, editor, and teacher in the dance field. In her free time, Erin enjoys bacon, books, cats, and wine.

She is the author of *The Pas de Deux: A Classical Ballet Romance* ("a powerful saga": Midwest Book Review), *The Piece: A Contemporary Ballet Novel* ("a compellingly vivid story": Midwest Book Review), and *The Winner: A Ballroom Dance Novel* ("one of the best books I've read this year": Library of Clean Reads).

www.erinbomboy.com/
erin@erinbomboy.com